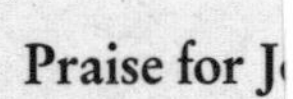

## Praise for J

'A magician of genre fiction'

'Lindqvist is Sweden's answer to Stephen King' *Daily Mirror*

'A terrifying supernatural story yet also a moving account of friendship and salvation' *Guardian*

'Lindqvist has reinvented the vampire novel and made it all the more chilling . . . An immensely readable and highly disturbing book in which grim levels of gore and violence are tempered by an unexpected tenderness' *Daily Express*

'Reminiscent of Stephen King at his best, there are some truly scary bits in the book that will haunt your dreams. Best read by sunlight' *Independent on Sunday*

'Some books are just too good. A masterpiece' *SFX*

'A Scandi chiller with elements of fable and even social satire, but told with great energy and flair that confirms Lindqvist's reputation as Sweden's answer to Stephen King' *Daily Mail*

'A very scary tale indeed from a writer who is master of his genre' *Financial Times*

'Combines an atmospheric coming-of-age story set in Stockholm with a shocking (and very gory) thriller. His vampire is an original, both heart-breakingly pathetic and terrifying. This was a bestseller in Sweden and could be equally big here. Don't miss it' *The Times*

'A surprising and sometimes delightful reading experience . . . Lindqvist manages to maintain a light touch in an otherwise bleak landscape' *Sunday Times*

'A compelling horror story, but it's also a finely calibrated tale about the pain of growing up' *Sunday Telegraph*

'So strange, so mad, so weirdly inspirational' *Guardian*

'Both an eerie, enigmatic mystery and a compendium of fascinating vignettes, this is a third consecutive masterpiece for an author who deserves to be as much a household name as Stephen King' *SFX*

Also by John Ajvide Lindqvist

*Let the Right One In*
*Handling the Undead*
*Harbour*
*Little Star*
*Let the Old Dreams Die*
*I Am Behind You*

John Ajvide Lindqvist lives in Sweden and has worked as a conjurer and stand-up comedian. His first novel, the international bestseller *Let the Right One In*, was published in more than thirty countries and adapted into two feature films: one by Swedish director Tomas Alfredson, and an English-language version, *Let Me In*. *I Am Behind You* is the first book in a planned trilogy; John is currently working on the second.

Marlaine Delargy is based in the UK. She has translated novels by Swedish writers including Åsa Larsson, Ninni Holmqvist and Johan Theorin – with whom she won the CWA International Dagger 2010 for *The Darkest Room*.

# I Always Find You

JOHN AJVIDE LINDQVIST

*Translated from Swedish by*
*Marlaine Delargy*

riverrun

First published in Sweden in 2015 under the title *Rörelsen: Den andra platsen*
by Ordfronts Förlag.
This English translation first published in Australia in 2018 by The Text Publishing Company
First published in Great Britain in 2018 by riverrun
This paperback edition published in 2019 by

riverrun

An imprint of
Quercus Editions Limited
Carmelite House
50 Victoria Embankment
London EC4Y 0DZ

An Hachette UK company



Book design by Text
Cover images by Arcangel, iStock and Shutterstock
Typeset by J & M Typesetting


A CIP catalogue record for this book is available
from the British Library.

Paperback 978 1 78747 452 9
Ebook 978 1 78747 449 9



10 9 8 7 6 5 4 3 2 1

Printed and bound in Great Britain by Clays Ltd, Elcograf S.p.A.

To Magnus Bodin
and Carl-Einar Häckner
In reality you existed
In imagination

Listen to the movement.

Tage Erlander's advice to his successor, Olof Palme, in 1969

# CONTENTS

# 1. Outside

There is a house in a courtyard at Luntmakargatan 14 in Stockholm. I was nineteen years old when I moved there in September 1985. After growing up with my mother on Ibsengatan in Blackeberg, this was the first time I'd had a place of my own. I had resigned from my job at the after-school centre where I had worked since leaving high school, and I had also ended my first and so far only relationship, with a girl I had met a few months earlier.

I moved into the city in order to take my first real steps into the adult world. The plan was to make my living as a magician. Over the summer I had amassed start-up capital of twelve thousand kronor by performing on the street in the Old Town and Kungsträdgården, which covered four months' rent.

Three thousand kronor a month for a centrally located house might sound like a bargain, but we're not talking about a charming little place that might appear in an Astrid Lindgren story, but rather a pile of bricks measuring twelve square metres, where hardly any daylight found its way in. It wasn't even meant for residential use, and there was something very shady about the arrangements. I didn't even sign a lease.

When I went to check it out for the first time, an enormous desk made of dark wood with a grubby telephone on top of it occupied a fifth of the floor space. Papers and betting slips lay scattered across a dirty grey fitted carpet. I never found out what the previous tenants had actually done, but there was an atmosphere of petty criminality about the cramped room, impregnated with cigarette smoke. Men in shabby suits, overflowing ashtrays, brief, muttered conversations down the sticky telephone receiver.

It had a sink and two electric hotplates, but no shower. A cubicle measuring some two square metres housed a toilet with no seat, plus a brown-stained washbasin. There was a shower in the laundry block, I was informed. A shower and a bath. In spite of the gloomy look of the place, something clicked and I moved in as soon as I could.

Thirty years later I really do wonder how I survived that autumn and winter, but things are different when we're young. Our gaze is fixed on a vague but glowing future, and the dirt and darkness of the present are no more than a temporary inconvenience. After all, plenty of people are worse off.

I was going to be a magician. I had achieved some impressive placements in Swedish and Nordic championship competitions; I had business cards and a flyer advertising my skills; I had the necessary equipment. What I didn't have was enough bookings to live on. The move to the city centre was part of a determined effort to change that situation.

What happened during the six months—or just over—while I was living at Luntmakargatan 14 hurled my life in a different direction, and in the long term led to my starting to write horror stories. We'll come to that in due course.

*

The all-encompassing memory of that period is darkness. Spending my waking hours in darkness. This was partly due to the location of the house, and partly due to my sleeping habits.

The building was in the middle of a narrow courtyard, which was virtually never reached by direct sunlight. Because the four-storey buildings all around were built on the slope of the Brunkeberg Ridge, there was a difference in the level of the main doors, and two of them were reached by a staircase running along the side of the house. Anyone using those stairs could see straight into my poky hovel. These days I would put up some thin curtains to have some privacy, while still making the most of the small amount of daylight, but at the age of nineteen I opted to keep the blinds closed.

On top of this, I was and am a night owl. It would often be three or four in the morning before I laid out my mattress on the floor and made up my bed. I would sleep until midday, and after having coffee and breakfast at my desk, it might be two o'clock before I ventured out. During the winter months, it had already begun to get dark by that time.

The light in my life came from street lamps and shop windows, and—when I was at home—from a fluorescent tube on the ceiling that suffused the twelve square metres with a cold, white glare. I usually made do with my desk lamp, and spent my days in semi-darkness.

I also recall the local area as a place in permanent shadow. When I left the house I went through a door into a stairwell with brown walls and dark grey marble, which I crossed to reach the main door and Luntmakargatan. To the left lay Sveavägen with its bright lights and traffic, to the right the entrance to the Brunkeberg Tunnel.

There will be more to say about the Brunkeberg Tunnel during the course of this narrative, but for now I will simply state that the tunnel, which had been excavated through the esker, ran alongside the building of which my house was a part. That's enough for the moment.

My usual route took me in the opposite direction, down the narrow passageway of Tunnelgatan between windowless facades. It was always damp, with the water trickling along the cracks between the paving stones. After around fifty paces I reached Dekorima's brightly lit shop window.

It would be six months before photographs of this spot were sent all around the world and I myself became a wanted man, but I already felt there was something special about this place, where a bronze plaque now commemorates the murder of Sweden's prime minister Olof Palme.

I often stopped there, partly because I had finally reached the lights of the city after a walk through dark passageways, and partly because that unprepossessing crossroads seemed like the quintessence of *Stockholm*.

If a tourist, after ticking off the city sights and photographing the reflection of the City Hall in Lake Mälaren, the view from the Western Bridge and a Djurgården ferry with the hills of Söder rising up in the background, had come up to me and asked, 'Where should I go to find the real Stockholm, beyond the Vasa Museum and the Old Town?', I might well have answered, 'Go and stand at the junction of

Tunnelgatan and Sveavägen. Stop. Look around you. Listen. Stay a while. Then you can go home and say that you've been in Stockholm.'

Everything is close at hand there, even though the place itself is nothing. The steps leading down to the Hötorget subway station are a short distance away; you can see the blue facade of the Concert Hall, and the glass obelisk in Sergels torg. Behind you is the Brunkeberg Tunnel, linking Norrmalm and Östermalm, and right beside you is the meeting point of Stockholm's two main arteries, Kungsgatan and Sveavägen. Nothing happens at the exact point where you are standing, but you only need to take a few steps in any direction for that to change. You are at the hub.

*

I moved into the house a week before the election, and the city was plastered with images of people who had something to say. I had received my first polling card before I left Blackeberg, and I intended to use it to vote for the Social Democrats. I had probably inherited a vague commitment to the left from home, and the alternative seemed repellent. There was something sly about those right-wing faces, while Palme was always Palme.

That business about the darkness didn't apply to the early days. It was September and we were enjoying an Indian summer, a honeymoon period when I always emerged into a bright, airy city. I spent my days wandering around and feeling at home. I belonged to Stockholm.

I sat in the Konditori Kungstornet drinking café au lait, reading Stig Dagerman and trying to look interesting. I might spend an hour or so in front of the TV screens in Åhlén's record department, watching videos of Madonna, Wham! and A-ha. I stole records from that same department by tucking them under my arm and walking out. My evenings and nights were devoted to magic.

The Nordic Championships were due to be held in Copenhagen at the end of September, and my ambition was to win in the close-up magic category. It would look good on my CV when I was trying to get work as an entertainer in restaurants. Close-up magic requires a high level of technical skill, because the audience is only a metre or so away. The sleight of hand must be invisible.

When I was thirteen I spent a week walking around with a five-kronor coin in my right hand, training my fingers to act naturally and to give no indication that anything was concealed in my palm. When I was fifteen I scraped at the skin on the same palm until it bled, with the aim of creating a callus that would make it possible to perform a coin trick known as Han Ping Chien. Magic was my passion, my direction in life.

I had come second in the junior Nordic Championships twice. In Copenhagen I would be competing as a senior for the first time, and to be honest I didn't think much of my chances. I was determined to try, though. My double lifts and side steals were second to none, and street magic had taught me the importance of arousing the interest of the public and maintaining that contact.

On the third or fourth night when I was sitting at my desk in front of a mirror studying my hand movements—passing the coin and not passing the coin must look *exactly* the same—the phone rang. It was just after one o'clock in the morning, and I couldn't imagine who would be calling me at that hour, but I put down the coin and picked up the receiver.

'Hello?'

There was a brief silence, then a subdued male voice asked, 'Is Sigge there?'

'I think you've got the wrong number,' I said. 'There's no Sigge here.'

Another pause. Then: 'Has he been there?'

'No. And he's not going to turn up either.'

'How can you be so sure?'

'Because I don't know anyone called Sigge.'

'Of course you do. Everyone knows Sigge.'

'I don't.'

The person on the other end sighed, as if my refusal to accept an obvious fact made him weary. I was about to hang up when he asked, 'What are you doing?'

'I'm sorry?'

'What are you doing? Right now?'

My eyes took in the objects in front of me. The close-up mat, the coins, the decks of cards. At this point I must remind you that I was nineteen years old. These days I would probably say something dismissive and put down the phone. I have a family, a home, a well-defined life. At nineteen my boundaries were different, so I replied, 'I'm practising.'

'Practising what?'

'Magic,' I said, not without a certain amount of pride.

The man on the other end summed up the situation: 'You're sitting there in the middle of the night practising magic.'

'Correct.'

'And what are you hoping to achieve by that?'

I could detect nothing unpleasant in the way the question was asked, merely a tone of genuine interest. There was a simple answer: 'It's the Nordic Championships in a couple of weeks and—'

The man interrupted me. 'No, no. What are you hoping to achieve?'

'I don't understand what you mean.'

'No. Well, maybe you should think about it.'

The call ended, and I remained sitting there with the receiver in my hand. I was using the same phone that had been in the house the first time I came to see it. I had cleaned it up and changed the number. Now I was struck by the tricky thought that the old number was somehow still within the phone itself.

*What are you hoping to achieve?*

It could have been a prank call. An existential joker, ringing random strangers and questioning their motivation in life. I went back to the coins, because there was still a certain jerkiness in my technique.

I had practised the false throwing movement a dozen times before I realised that I wasn't paying attention to what I was doing, that my mind was elsewhere.

*What are you hoping to achieve?*

I was trying to make it look as though I was throwing the coin from my right hand, when in fact I was holding on to it, dropping a coin from my left hand at the same moment so that it appeared to be the coin from my right hand when it landed. I wanted to do it so that not even someone who knew the technique would suspect it was being used. It was virtually impossible, but that was what I was hoping to achieve. It had taken me fifty or sixty hours of repeating the movement to master it as well as I had at that time, and it still wasn't perfect. I hadn't yet reached the final level, the one at which it became second nature.

Development in magic occurs in leaps and bounds. You practise a movement until you're sick and tired of it, and then one day, all of a sudden, a distinct change takes place. Every single muscle in the hands, fingers and arms works together, and the movement is as natural as holding a fork.

That was where I wanted to be before the championships, but now I was distracted. My hands were moving mechanically, without grace. I decided that was enough for the night; I would go and take a shower before I went to bed. I grabbed some clean underwear and a towel, and headed for the laundry block.

*

The laundry block was a place full of contradictions. On the one hand it was set into the rock face next to the Brunkeberg Tunnel, and I sometimes felt the weight of that mass of stone as a pressure inside my head, my body. On the other hand it was light and clean, with a fresh smell. There were two washing machines, two tumble dryers and an airing cupboard, plus a table on which to fold the laundry, and a surprisingly comfortable chair where you could sit and wait for the machines to finish. Right at the back was a door leading to a combined toilet and shower room.

This area hadn't been afforded the same care and attention as the rest of the block. The bathtub was an old-fashioned model; the enamel surface was worn, with dirt ingrained in the scratches. The shower-head was rusty, and half the holes in it were blocked. The floor tiles were worn too, and a deep crack ran along the plaster in the ceiling above the bath. As if to conceal the miserable state of the place, the room was illuminated by a single dim bulb.

The appearance and location of the shower room could create a feeling of claustrophobia as I stood in the bath with water trickling over my body. I think it was because of the rock. Even though I couldn't see it, I could *perceive* it all around me—its age, its weight.

I usually showered quickly so that I could get back into the brighter environment of the laundry room, and that was what I did on this particular night. I left the dingy room with my towel over my shoulder and sat down in the chair, because the same old feeling was beginning to grow within me.

At this time of the night the laundry room could be regarded as an extension of my house, because nobody used it after ten. I placed my arms on the rests, closed my eyes and took a deep breath. I hesitate to call my nightmares 'angst' out of respect for those who really are caught in the vice-like grip of that condition, but they were certainly a kind of milder version. A growing sense of unease, a dark sea crashing against a distant shore in my breast.

The laundry room helped. The light caressing me through my eyelids, the fresh smell of clean clothes. Though I had it to myself just now, at the same time it was a collective space that eased my loneliness. I breathed through my nose as calmly as I could, inhaling microscopic particles of my neighbours' lives.

As so often during my sleepless nights, the memory of the child in the forest came back to me. There was a locked door inside me, something that prevented me from really connecting with other people and condemned me to isolation. The key to that lock lay in the events surrounding the child in the forest, but I couldn't find it.

I had been sitting there clutching the arms of the chair for perhaps fifteen minutes when I made up my mind. If I was going to succeed in becoming an adult, I had to tackle the demons of my childhood—or at least name them.

I left the laundry room and went back to my house and my desk. I pushed my magic paraphernalia aside and set out a notepad and pen. I had never tried to write anything in this way, so to get going I began to tell the story of the child in the forest as if it were a fairytale.

*

*Once upon a time many years ago, in a place called Blackeberg, there was a boy who was happiest in the forest. The other children used to tease him and call him Piggy, saying that he was ugly and disgusting. Eventually the boy started to believe they were right, and withdrew to the forest.*

*Which was really only a wooded area between Ibsengatan and Råcksta Lake. The boy had built a cabin out of planks and branches, way up high in a tree. Every afternoon when school was over the boy sat in his tree house fantasising about worlds that were similar to ours, yet completely different. Worlds where he was popular and had an important role. He dreamed of superpowers and vampire friends, played out scenes where he fought back and tore the heads off those who tormented him, or sent fire to consume them.*

*One afternoon at the beginning of September, the boy went along to his tree house as usual. He had with him a Dime bar and a Mars bar which he had stolen from the corner shop. He was planning on eating them as he dreamed of future triumphs.*

*As he stood at the bottom of the tree looking up, he could already tell that something was different. Through the gaps in the floor he saw something red that hadn't been there the day before. He also glimpsed a fleeting movement, but when he called out, there was no response.*

*He wasn't a courageous boy, except in his imagination, and he almost turned and ran off home in the hope that the problem would sort itself out, that whoever was in the tree house would be gone by the following day. But there was something about the movement he had seen, something furtive, that made him clamber up after all.*

*Inside the tree house, pressed into the furthest corner, sat a child aged five or six. He was wearing a thin, faded, ragged padded jacket and stained tracksuit bottoms. His face was dirty and covered in sores, his eyes filled with terror. He looked like a refugee, maybe from the Iran–Iraq war. But he also looked Swedish.*

*'Hi,' the boy said to the child. 'What are you doing here?'*

*The child simply stared. When the boy heaved himself up into the tree house, the child pressed himself still further into the corner, as if he thought he might be able to push his way through the wall and disappear. The boy sat down in the opposite corner and scratched his head. He glanced out through the opening. Such a small child shouldn't be alone in the forest.*

*'Where are your parents?'*

*Something changed in the child's face, as if the shadow of a cloud passed across it. The boy leaned forward and asked, 'Shall we go and look for your parents?'*

*The child's eyes widened even more and he shook his head—such a tiny movement that it was little more than a tremble.*

*'Okay,' the boy said. 'So what shall we do then?'*

*The child had no answer, and the boy took out his stash of chocolate. The child's expression brightened a fraction, and the boy held out the Mars bar. 'Would you like it?'*

*Cautiously, as if the chocolate were a cobra that might strike at any second, the child reached out and took it. There was something strange about his fingers: they stuck out in different directions. As soon as the child had the chocolate at a safe distance, he ripped open the wrapper and bit into the bar with such ferocity that fragments of the paper ended up in his mouth too. The child chomped away, breathing hard through his nose.*

*'Wow,' the boy said. 'I guess you were hungry?' He looked down*

*at the Dime bar, weighing up the pros and cons. He wasn't exactly starving, but he did want something sweet. However, when the child had gobbled up the Mars bar, the boy held out the second bar of chocolate.*

*'Here. You can have this one too.'*

*This time the child grabbed the gift more readily. The boy sat in his corner, watching as the child's jaws loudly demolished the crunchy centre. It was quite good fun. Like having a pet.*

*

Dawn had come creeping along while I was writing, and a faint glow was seeping in through the slats of the venetian blind. My eyelids had begun to feel heavy as I wrote the last few sentences, and I put down my pen. I wasn't sure if this was a good project, but at least I'd made a start.

I laid out the mattress, made up my bed and got in, but then I lay awake for a long time, wondering how to continue the narrative. That was the first time I encountered the torment and joy of writing, and I decided that it was mostly a positive experience. The story lost its menacing, formless quality in the telling and became something I could twist and turn, looking at it from different angles as if it were something manageable.

*

The following day was something of a shock for me, as I spoke to no less than two of my neighbours.

Though I spent quite a lot of time in the laundry block, I still hadn't used it for its designated purpose. However, the IKEA bags I shoved my dirty washing in were getting as full as my wardrobe was empty, so I had booked a slot to do my laundry.

It took me a while to figure out how the machines worked, and I used up almost all of my allocated time. Only five minutes remained as I piled the clean, dry clothes into the bags, and at that moment a smartly dressed man walked in.

'Nearly done,' I said.

He waved a dismissive hand and asked, 'Are you the person who lives in the house across the courtyard?'

I wasn't sure about the legality of my situation, so I mumbled and jerked my head in a way that could mean just about anything. He must have taken it as a yes, because he went on.

'Good. It feels more homely when there's a light on in there in the evenings.'

Reassured by his positive response, I took the opportunity to ask a question: 'Do you happen to know who lived there before me?'

'No. People came and went. It didn't feel quite…right, if you understand what I mean.'

I gathered up the rest of my laundry from the tumble dryer and cleaned the filter. On my way out I passed the basket containing the man's dirty clothes—shirts, trousers, underwear. The odd thing was that every item was meticulously folded. *Before* it was washed. I said goodbye and went back to my place.

After putting away my clean laundry I decided to go and have lunch at Kungstornet. I took my notepad and pen in case I wanted to carry on writing. On the way out I bumped into an elderly woman I had noticed earlier. She was somewhere between sixty and seventy. Her apartment was on the floor above my house, and I had learned to recognise her footsteps on the staircase outside my window.

She was often accompanied by small children of different ages, and I had drawn the conclusion that she was a very involved grandmother. When I met her at the main door it turned out I was right. A boy of about seven was holding her left hand.

'Aha,' the woman said, looking at me with interest. 'I believe you're our new watchdog?'

She used the word *gårdvar*. At the time I didn't know what it meant, but I realised it had something to do with my house—or *gårdshus*. Encouraged by the friendliness of the meticulous man I had met in the laundry room, I bravely said, 'Yes, that's right.'

The woman held out her hand. 'Elsa Karlgren,' she said, bending down towards the boy. 'And this is Dennis, my grandson.'

The boy glanced up at me shyly, then reverted to studying his shoelaces as he tugged at Elsa's hand. I took out a five-kronor coin and showed it to Dennis, then I made it disappear before producing it from his ear. I wasn't sure whether it was appropriate, but in a moment of inspiration I offered him the coin and said, 'It's yours. If you want it.'

Dennis shook his head, his eyes firmly fixed on his feet. Elsa smiled at me and said, 'Wasn't that clever?' She and Dennis carried on towards the staircase. I stayed where I was for a moment before leaving the courtyard, feeling like a child who doesn't understand how things work.

After I'd worked my way through a tuna salad and collected the coffee that was included in the price, I opened my notepad and read through what I had written during the night. It was astonishing how the unpleasant course of events lost its sting when it was written as a story. Was that why authors wrote?

Everything had happened exactly as I had described it, but it was impossible to convey all the details and perceptions linked in my memory to what had gone on, making it come alive. The smell of rust from the child's jacket, the streaks of dirt on his neck, and his distorted fingers, like a broken machine. I couldn't describe it then and I can't describe it now. Then, as now, all I can do is write: first this happened and then that happened, while the real sense of the event eludes me.

I didn't care whether I looked interesting or not as I bent over the pad and carried on with my narrative.

*

*'What's your name?'*

*No answer. The dirt on the child's face was now mixed with melted chocolate. He opened his mouth as if he were about to say something, but instead his tongue emerged and licked his lips.*

*The boy sighed. 'Do you understand what I'm saying?'*

*A nod, as minimal as the previous shake of the head. All of the child's movements were so slow and tiny that it was difficult to work out how he had climbed up to the tree house.*

*'My name's John,' the boy said. 'I'm twelve. How old are you?'*

*The child held up one hand, its fingers pointing in different directions as if they had been broken and then healed badly. Five. The gesture was accompanied by a vague head movement, as if he wasn't sure. Encouraged, the boy asked, 'Do you live here? In Blackeberg?'*

*The child simply stared at him, and the boy was at a loss. What did you do in a situation like this? Ring the police, probably. The boy had had some dealings with the police due to his petty thieving, but no doubt that was what he ought to do. Ring the police.*

*'Listen,' the boy said, 'whatever your name is. I think I need to call someone, someone who…'*

*There was no indication that the child understood, so the boy nodded to himself as if to confirm the wisdom of what he had just said. As he was clambering down through the opening to run home and call the police, the child spoke.*

*'What? What did you say?' the boy asked.*

*'Fuckin,' the child said. 'Fuckinlittlebastard.'*

*The child uttered the words without a trace of emotion, his eyes fixed on the floor.*

*'What are you talking about?' the boy said. 'I haven't done anything to you!'*

*'Gonnakillyou youfuckinlittleshit.'*

*The boy wasn't stupid. Ugly and repulsive perhaps, but not stupid. He realised that the child's garbled threat wasn't aimed at him, but was simply a repetition of something he had heard. If the boy called the police, if he…*

dropped the child in it

*what would happen then? They would track down the child's parents, or he would end up in the clutches of* social services. *The boy himself might get into trouble, because the police had already described him as a 'cowardly little thief'. As a general rule, his experiences of turning to adults for help weren't great.*

*'Wait,' the boy said. 'I'm just going to collect a few things.'*

*He climbed down from the tree house and ran home.*

*Having a pet was good fun. Working out what the pet needed. His knowledge of small children was limited, as he had grown up without siblings, but he had kept a rabbit for a couple of years, and now he tried to use the knowledge he had gained.*

*Something to eat, something to drink, somewhere to sleep. The trickiest part was the toilet issue. It would be best if the child could do what was necessary in the forest, but the boy had the impression he was reluctant to leave the tree house.*

*Down in the cellar he found an old sleeping-bag that smelled a bit mouldy, plus a bucket with a lid. He stuffed the sleeping-bag into the bucket, then went back upstairs and put some crispbread, fish paste and several apples in a carrier bag, along with a roll of toilet paper and a bottle of water.*

*

The lunchtime rush had subsided while I was writing. I tapped my pen on the pad as if I was seeking entry to my own story.

Why do we become what we become? The simple answer is that we are the sum of the choices we have made, the actions we have carried out. But why did we make those particular choices, carry out those particular actions? We have to go further and further back—like a child who keeps repeating 'But why?'—until we reach the maternity ward and what took place there.

But even if we were given a minute-by-minute account of our first days of life, we still wouldn't be able to explain all our decisions. There are incidences of uncertainty, there are leaps, and perhaps it is those very leaps that shape us, when we step outside ourselves and act without any regard for our previous experience.

The incident with the child in the forest was just such a leap for me.

I tapped my pen on the paper and realised what I was doing only when the sound began to echo around the room.

I stopped tapping and looked up. There was a man sitting at the corner table right at the back; he was wearing shabby, greyish-brown clothes that made him blend in with the wood-panelled wall. His hair was thin and greasy, and he was staring at me with his bulging eyes as he tapped his finger on the table next to his coffee cup. When our eyes met he gave me a conspiratorial grin.

I smiled back and shuddered inside as it occurred to me that I was looking at a possible version of myself in thirty years' time. Perhaps I would still be sitting alone in the Kungstornet cafe, but by then I would have withdrawn from the light. If I made the wrong decisions, took the wrong roads. I picked up my notepad and pen and walked out.

I needed to succeed as a magician so that I wouldn't end up sitting in that corner. I should have gone home to practise, right then, but anxiety had me in its grip, so instead I wandered along to Stureplan, where I sat down on a bench in the square and read through what I'd written.

In my highly strung state it seemed to me that everything depended on my success in writing the story, in continuing to write down what had happened. I stood up and hurried along Birger Jarlsgatan so that I could cut through the Brunkeberg Tunnel and get home more quickly.

The tunnel looked different back then. What is now a futuristic corridor that wouldn't be out of place in an *Alien* film had a rawness about it in those days, and the ceiling was nothing more than bare rock. As I walked in through the doors I could hear music. A busker with a guitar was playing Towa Carson's Eurovision song 'Everyone Has Forgotten'. Drawing closer I dug out the five-kronor coin that Dennis had rejected. We street artists have to stick together.

During the summer in the Old Town and Kungsträdgården I had

grown heartily sick of 'House of the Rising Sun', 'Hotel California' and 'Stairway to Heaven', so the busker's unconventional choice of song made him worth the five kronor, which I dropped into his hat as I passed by.

'Thanks, brother. By the way...' he said, and stopped playing. I turned around. The man didn't look like a typical busker. He was wearing khaki trousers with a sharp crease, a short-sleeved white shirt and a pair of deck shoes. He could have been an accountant who had suddenly decided to give music a go.

'Yes?' I said, looking into a pair of blue eyes surrounded by crow's feet. The man gazed up at the ceiling and said, 'It's getting stronger, isn't it?'

I took a step closer, unsure if I'd heard him correctly. 'I'm sorry?'

'It's getting stronger. Don't you think so? The pressure. It's getting stronger.'

So that was the explanation. The man was a little bit crazy, he had strayed outside the norms of society, and maybe his clothes were an attempt to compensate.

'Sure,' I said, not committing myself to anything in particular. 'Good luck.'

I waved to him as if he were a child, then turned and went on my way. Behind me the man began to sing yet another Eurovision entry, 'It's Beginning to Seem Like Love', and the sound followed me out into Tunnelgatan.

*

*As he approached the tree house, it had changed. It was no longer merely a rickety construction made of old planks and branches; no, it was also a container, and its contents emitted a pull that made the boy quicken his pace as he drew closer.*

*'Are you still here?'*

*The question was unnecessary. He knew that the child was still there, just as we know when we are not alone in a pitch-dark room. He wanted to warn the child of his arrival, though, to avoid frightening him. He left the bucket at the bottom of the tree so that he could climb up.*

*The child was sitting in exactly the same spot, pressed up against the wall in the corner. He stared as the boy heaved himself over the edge and put down the carrier bag in the middle of the floor.*

*'There you go,' said the boy, taking out a piece of crispbread. Before he could do anything else, the child had grabbed the food and stuffed it in his mouth. In ten seconds it was gone, and when the child reached out for the bag, the boy moved it away and said, 'Just hang on a minute.'*

*The child, who had leaned forward to eat, hurled himself backwards into the corner with such force that the tree swayed. The boy dug out the tube of fish paste and showed it to him. 'Look. I was just going to—'*

*He fell silent. A lump of something was working its way out of the child's nose. It didn't look like blood, because it was black. At the same time, it was too dense to be snot. However revolting the thought might be, it resembled some kind of diseased faecal matter. The boy gestured towards his own nose and said, 'You need to wipe your nose.'*

*One of the child's crooked fingers shot up in a spastic imitation of the boy's gesture, and the black thing disappeared, back where it had come from. The boy unscrewed the lid of the tube and squeezed a string of red paste, which suddenly disgusted him, onto a piece of crispbread and handed it to the child. 'Here. It tastes better this way.'*

*As the child ate, slightly less greedily this time, the boy looked at those bent fingers. They were barely human, more like claws in fact, and some of the nails were missing.*

*'So what happened to your fingers?' he asked.*

*'Fuckoff,' the child said. 'Fuckoffyoulittlebastard.'*

*The boy understood. Someone had done this to the child, and that was probably why he had run away. He also understood that this was way too heavy for a kid in sixth grade to handle.*

*'Listen, don't you think I ought to call the police?' he said.*

*'Police,' the child repeated. 'Dadda police.'*

*'What are you saying? Are you telling me your dad's a cop?'*

*'Dadda,' the child said again. The word was followed by an unpleasant grin. Several of his teeth were missing. Then he turned his face to the wall and made himself as small as possible.*

*The boy clambered down to fetch the bucket. Back in the tree house, he shook out the sleeping-bag on the floor, and explained how the child should use the bucket and the toilet paper. He had no idea if the child knew what he was talking about.*

*'I'll be back tomorrow,' he said.*

*Then he went home.*

*

When I had finished writing and run through my magic act a few times, I made dinner. My culinary skills were limited to pasta and a couple of combinations using Uncle Ben's stir-fry sauces. On this particular day I diced a Falun sausage and mixed it with the sweet-and-sour variety. Plus rice. I ate sitting at the desk, staring at the wall where smoke and age had stained the plaster the colour of a hard-bitten nicotine addict's fingers.

*The pressure. It's getting stronger.*

The busker's words left me no peace, because I could feel the pressure too. A rushing sound in my ears, a faint whistling deep inside my skull that I had dismissed as a consequence of thick walls and isolation. The sound of loneliness, if you like.

*The pressure is getting stronger.*

I washed my plate, knife and fork and left them to dry on a tea towel. Then I stood with my arms dangling by my side and glared at the wall with its sick pigmentation. The evening lay before me, plump and empty. I considered going out and buying a pack of cigarettes to see if smoking had anything going for it. A pause, an escape. I decided not to bother. I stood completely still, feeling the pressure. Feeling it grow stronger. As if I were in a tank filled with water, sinking slowly, so slowly. The whistling inside my head, the pressure on my eardrums. I couldn't move, daren't even breathe for fear of actually feeling the water pouring into my lungs.

The sound of the telephone ringing caused a rupture. A sledgehammer struck, relieving the pressure. My hand was free to lift the receiver to my ear so that I could hear the familiar voice.

'Can I speak to Sigge?'

'We've already been through this. Sigge isn't here.'

'Hasn't he arrived yet?'

'He's never been here.'

I was about to add that he wasn't going to be here either, when the voice on the other end interrupted me. 'How do you know?'

'Sorry?'

'How do you know he's never been there?'

'Because I'm the only one who lives here.'

'Mmm. But we're not talking about you at the moment. We're talking about Sigge.'

Had the pressure really eased, or had the phone merely distracted me so that I no longer felt it? I cautiously took a breath, just to check if anything would prevent my lungs from expanding.

'Aren't we?'

I must have tuned out; I couldn't work out what he meant, so I said, 'What?'

'It's Sigge we're talking about now.'

'Yes. We are. But he isn't here.'

'Are you absolutely sure about that?'

I lowered the receiver and looked over at the toilet door. As I stood there listening, I got the idea that there was someone in there. The man on the other end of the line said something, and I put the receiver to my ear once more. 'What?'

'I said you don't seem absolutely sure. Maybe Sigge's there after all?'

I was about to hang up so that I could go and investigate the toilet, but then I pulled myself together and came out with the question

I should have asked in the first place: 'This Sigge you keep talking about—who is he?'

The man guffawed, and I could picture him shaking his head as he replied, 'Oh my goodness—that's something you'd really like to know, isn't it?'

'Yes, please.'

'I'm afraid that's not possible. If you don't know, you'll find out. But I think you do know. Just don't get too caught up in that Sigge business. I mean, what's a name? Anyway, I've got to go.'

Before I had time to say another word he ended the call, leaving me listening to the atmospheric hissing of the phone lines. I could hear distant voices without being able to make out what they were saying. When I had sat there for a while, I hung up and opened the toilet door. It was empty, and the only sound was the movement of the water in the pipes. Rising, falling.

I survived that night too, as one does. Minute follows minute, and time passes. The election was the following day, and I intended to go and vote. Which I did. I probably listened to 'Shake the Disease' by Depeche Mode several times that night; I had stolen it a few years earlier. Martin Gore's lonely voice as he sang the desolate intro was like a companion, somehow familiar, as if he was describing something I knew.

*

*The boy found it difficult to sleep that night. He lay there with his head buried in the pillow, thinking that he had forgotten to take a pillow for the child. From there his mind wandered to the image of the child curled up on the floor of the tree house. In the forest, in the darkness.*

*He might have been able to sleep if his thoughts had stopped there, but they continued to circle mercilessly around the child's appearance, and what he must have suffered. The missing teeth, the broken fingers.*

*As soon as the boy closed his eyes he saw himself shut away in a cramped, dark space. A door flung open, hands grabbing hold of him and dragging him out, kicks, blows, and even worse. Tools.*

*He couldn't shake off the images, but in the end he found a way to deal with them. Instead of being the one subjected to the abuse, he made himself the perpetrator. This was unpleasant too, but at least there was a glimmer of satisfaction in it. He had the power. This reassuring knowledge allowed him to fall asleep at last.*

*

My polling card instructed me to cast my vote at Blackeberg School. It would be fifteen years before I set some of the narrative of *Let the Right One In* inside that very building, but when I woke up feeling groggy from a lack of sleep on the morning of election day, I felt a nagging sense of horror.

I was far from done with my childhood, and not just the events surrounding the child in the forest. More 'normal' things still lay like muddy silt in my mind, and I avoided stirring it up if I possibly could.

Isolation leads to egocentricity. In the absence of outside influence, it is easy to imagine that the world is a machine, created to focus on oneself. As I walked out of Blackeberg's subway station towards the brick colossus on Björnsonsgatan, I thought everything was about me and the school, how we would handle our reunion.

I don't know if it was a disappointment or a relief when it turned out that this particular day wasn't in fact about 'Young man returns to his past', but about the election of the Swedish parliament, councils and local authorities. The schoolyard was full of people with party banners, handing me leaflets that meant nothing to me.

Someone explained the procedure to me, and I placed my votes in three envelopes. When I handed them over to the returning officer and he ticked me off on his list, for a brief moment I experienced a sense of *belonging*, of being a part of something bigger, and I realised that I really wanted the Social Democrats to win. Not because of any deep conviction, but because they were *my team*. I had voted for them, after all. There and then I made up my mind to stay up and watch the results come in on TV.

The sense of belonging faded away when I left the polling room and went upstairs to my old corridor. It hadn't changed, and the smell was exactly the same—a mixture of perspiration, paper, misery and hormones. I sat down on the bench outside the classroom and tried to feel something. There was nothing apart from a misdirected nostalgia, so instead I took out my notepad and thought about the not-too-distant past.

*

*The next day was a bad day. Jimmy became obsessed with the idea that 'the air is free', and during every break his hands fluttered and flapped in front of the boy's eyes. As soon as the boy blinked or tried to turn his head away, he got a smack on the cheek. Conny and Andreas helped out with pinches and name-calling just to increase the level of difficulty.*

*It wasn't the bullying itself that was the worst thing. The boy had learned to let his thoughts drift away while it was going on, let time pass until it was over. The constant feeling of persecution was much harder to handle, though—the knowledge that the schoolyard, the corridors and classrooms were unsafe places where the next attack could come at any moment, from any direction and in any way. The boy could never relax, and the constant tension, combined with poor sleep at night, meant that he was utterly exhausted.*

*During maths, the last lesson of the day, the boy was sitting there solving a simple equation when blood began to drip onto the squared paper in front of him. His immediate thought was that Jimmy had come up with something new, but the drops came faster and faster, and when he raised his head they trickled down into his mouth.*

*He was given permission to leave the room and ran to the toilets, where he stuffed plugs of toilet paper into his nostrils. By this time it was only twenty minutes to the end of the school day, and he had the golden opportunity to gather up his things and put on his outdoor clothes in peace. He made the most of it.*

*It was nice to walk home without having to look over his shoulder, and most of the tension in his body eased. The boy touched the lumpy plugs in his nose and thought about the black substance that had oozed out of the child's nostrils. What was it? He had never seen anything like it. It had looked like a black snake, poking its head out and trying to escape. Something special, something* different.

*

I spent the evening working with my coins and manipulating my cards in the glow of the desk lamp as something behind my back strove to take shape.

*The pressure. It's getting stronger.*

The busker's words had confirmed what I had suspected, and once I started thinking about it, it was more or less impossible to stop. I took my bearings, trying to locate the growing pressure. At nine o'clock I gave up and got ready to go to Monte Carlo. I slipped a pack of cards and a thumb tip in my pocket in case I had the opportunity to do some magic.

The Monte Carlo club at the junction of Sveavägen and Kungsgatan was a den of iniquity. I could feel it, just as I could feel the seedy atmosphere in my house. The appearance, attire and attitude of the clients were part of it, but it was also the way people looked at one another, how they conducted their conversations. Money, wariness and power play were circulating away from the roulette and blackjack tables too.

The large-screen TV, which normally showed music videos or sport, was tuned to the election results with the sound turned off. I bought a beer and sat down at the only free table as pie charts flickered on the screen. The forecasts indicated victory for the left. I raised my glass and toasted the image of Olof Palme that had just appeared.

Behind me I heard someone declaim with the exaggerated emphasis of the drunk: 'This whole fucking country will soon be part of the Soviet Union, just you wait and see. Spetsnaz units on the streets, U-boats in the Baltic, while Palme sits there grinning and rubbing his hands as the money pours into the funds controlled by the unions and disappears to Moscow. Fucking hell.' I turned around and saw a man who looked like a yuppie shaking his fist at the screen, where a smiling Olof Palme was now making his way through a crowd of people, a bouquet of red roses in his arms.

The angry man's friend, who had an identical haircut and was dressed exactly the same, was trying to get him to sit back down, but to no avail. When the friend said something, the angry man replied, 'I'll say what I want. If someone took out that arsehole I'd dance on his grave.'

A barrage of flashing lights from the TV as Palme stepped up onto a stage, raised the bouquet in the air and leaned towards a microphone. I could read the first word on his lips: 'Comrades!'

A whistling sound started up between my temples. I was caught in the crossfire between the joy on the screen in front of me and the anger behind my back.

*The pressure. It's getting stronger*

and it felt contradictory and *dirty* in a way that made me feel slightly sick. I stood up and left the club. When I got out into the street I took a few deep breaths and the nausea subsided a little.

*I have to practise.*

I had to practise my magic. I had to pass the coins more skilfully, make every movement smoother. It had to be cleaner, cleverer. I had to get *there.* I had to get away.

*

Transcendence. All my life I have striven to achieve it, in different ways. I am not sufficiently educated in philosophy to understand how Kant, Kierkegaard or de Beauvoir define it, but I know what it means to me. I believe that most people are striving for transcendence, whether they use that term or not.

The world and our existence are on the one hand wonderful, a miracle. On the other hand they are an insult, like being promised a buffet and receiving nothing more than a few cold potatoes. Of course no one promises us anything; it is we ourselves who are responsible for making the most of what we are given. Life is insufficient because we make it insufficient and regard it as a disappointment. And so it spins around and in the worst-case scenario gradually becomes a spiral. A downward spiral.

The only way to escape from this velodrome of the soul is through transcendence. To continue the analogy: it doesn't help if the cyclist begins to wobble as he or she travels around, pedals faster or repeatedly rings the bell. He or she is still following the circuit. It's all about getting the parts to blend together or to dissolve so that the movement continues without the help of either the circuit or the bicycle. This can be achieved. You just have to believe it.

With the help of Han Ping Chien, for example. When I returned from Monte Carlo I sat down at the desk in front of the mirror and switched on the light. I'd been practising a routine in which four coins are magically transported from the left hand to the right hand using the manoeuvre known as Han Ping Chien, but now I put the routine aside and concentrated on the manoeuvre itself.

One coin is on the upturned palm of the right hand, another in the closed fist of the left. Turn the right hand downward so that the coin ought to fall, but instead you palm the coin. At the same time the left hand slides over to the left and imperceptibly drops its coin in the spot where the coin from the right hand should have landed.

The manoeuvre takes two seconds to execute, and in its simplicity demands that a range of different muscles work together in a complex way in order to become totally harmonious and to make the illusion complete.

The left hand can move too fast and draw the attention of the observer, the right hand can acquire an unnatural appearance; the coin can land a centimetre away from the spot where it ought to have landed. Even if the observer can't say exactly what is wrong, there is a sense that *aha, something dodgy happened there*, and the whole thing is ruined.

I practised getting the right-hand coin in the perfect spot where it could be palmed most easily; I tried using different speeds for the movement of the left hand. I varied the height of my hands above the table, and the distance between them when the movement began and when it ended. I worked on exactly where the borderline lay when it came to applied pressure from the flaps of skin on my right palm so that the coin was held in place while my hand remained as relaxed as possible, and on how tightly I could weave the fingers of my left hand over the coin that was to be dropped. And so on.

I had been practising for over an hour when I began to enter the state I was trying so hard to achieve. Until then the turbulent emotions I'd felt at Monte Carlo had stayed with me like a background hum, but it had faded away without my noticing, leaving only my hands, the coins, the movement.

As I threw the coin from my right hand, my body and mind told me that I was actually throwing it, and that my left hand was naturally pulling away, nothing more. It was as if even I couldn't believe that the coin remained in my right hand while the left was empty. It was like *magic*, and for a brief period of grace I was on the other side of the borderline.

My fingers were stiff when I eventually put aside my equipment and picked up my pen to carry on writing the story of the child in the forest, the story of the time when I really *had* transcended and finished up somewhere else.

*

*When the boy got home he felt a strong urge to collapse on his bed and drift off for a couple of hours, but curiosity won out over tiredness. He wondered whether the child was still in the tree house, and if so, what he was doing. And there was something more, a pull he couldn't put into words.*

*He took a spare pillow out of the wardrobe and looked in the fridge to see what he could take without arousing suspicion. He settled on a tomato, two carrots and half a jar of jam that was lurking at the back of the shelf. He put these paltry offerings in a plastic bag and weighed it in his hand. In the freezer he found a foil tray containing a portion of lasagne, left over from a couple of weeks ago. It should be edible when it defrosted. He set off for the forest to see what had happened to his pet overnight.*

*It was a lovely afternoon. The deciduous trees shimmered in different shades of green, tucked in among the dark conifers. It was just warm enough, and soft sunlight found its way down between the treetops, scattering patches of brightness across the ground. The boy moved from one patch to the next, telling himself that he had to find the right one, the one that would beam him up to the mothership. He was so preoccupied with his quest that he didn't notice the uniformed man until he almost bumped into him.*

*'Steady on now,' the police officer said, placing a heavy hand on the boy's shoulder. 'Let's just take it easy, shall we?'*

*Ever since the boy had been picked up for shoplifting, the police had joined the list of things he was afraid of. It wasn't just their appearance and attitude, but also the thought that from that moment on, every single cop knew precisely who and what he was.*

*The man standing in front of him didn't exactly help matters. For a start he was very tall, almost two metres, and his muscular build made him seem like a giant in the boy's eyes. His hands were so big that he could easily place one of them on top of the boy's head, squeeze hard and lift him straight up in the air like a basketball. Or crush his skull.*

*'So where are you off to?'*

*His voice was deep and lacked any trace of friendliness. When the boy glanced up and met the policeman's gaze, it was like looking into two camera lenses, and for a moment he got the idea that the policeman was a robot. He lowered his eyes and muttered, 'Nowhere special.'*

*'What have you got there?'*

*'Just some stuff.'*

*'Can I see.'*

*It wasn't a question, and as the boy held out the bag with one hand, he clutched the pillow to his stomach with the other.*

*The policeman peered into the bag and asked, 'What are you going to do with all this?'*

*The boy shrugged. 'Eat it.'*

*'Look at me when I'm talking to you.'*

*A magnetic force was drawing the boy's eyes to the ground, and it took enormous effort to lift his head high enough to do as he was told.*

*'Let me ask you again. What are you going to do with all this?'*

*The magnetic force shifted and took up residence between the boy's jaws. His teeth chattered as he managed to part them just enough to say, 'Eat it.'*

*The camera lenses scrutinised him, and the boy scanned the ground. If he could just find the right patch of sunlight the mothership would be able to beam him up and rescue him from the evil robot. The plastic bag swung into view as the policeman held it out to him. The boy took it with a trembling hand. He turned to walk away, but a colossal hand stopped him.*

*'The thing is,' the policeman said, 'we're searching for a boy. A little boy, no more than a child, and we think he might have got lost in the forest. Do you know anything about that?'*

*The boy shook his head, his neck crunching as bones and muscles were unlocked.*

*'What did you say?'*

*The boy managed a whisper: 'No.'*

*'No, what?'*

*'No, I don't know anything.'*

*The policeman gripped the boy's chin, and it felt like being caught in the fork of a branch as his face was forced upwards. 'I hope you realise this is a serious crime. Withholding information. Do you understand?'*

*The boy nodded as best he could with his chin clamped in the policeman's hand. He had never been so scared in his whole life, and something was about to spill out—piss, shit, a confession. He didn't know why it hadn't already happened, particularly the confession. His tree house was three hundred metres away—he didn't even need to say anything, all he had to do was point. But as soon as he saw the policeman*

Dadda police

*it was as if all knowledge of the child had slipped down into the darkness. He knew and did not know at the same time, and it was doubtful if he could have told the policeman anything even if he'd wanted to.*

*The policeman contemplated him with those glassy eyes, then let go of his chin. The boy stood there with the pillow pressed against his stomach and thought about Mr Spock, about the Vulcan nerve pinch, about anything other than the man in front of him.*

*'Run along and play,' the policeman said.*

*The boy's legs wouldn't obey him well enough to allow him to follow the instruction, but he did manage to move away, one step at a time. He didn't head for the tree house, but took a detour down towards Råcksta Lake in a wide arc, and when he got there he sat on a bench and waited.*

*He sat on that bench for two hours. It was an hour before he had recovered sufficiently to think of sitting on the pillow to make himself more comfortable.*

*He was intimately acquainted with nastiness, spite and sheer cruelty. But evil was an abstract concept he had never encountered; he hadn't even believed that it existed, except in films and on TV. Now he thought differently.*

*The policeman who had come when he was caught stealing had been hard on him, and stupid, but the guy in the forest was something else. He was evil.*

Evil?

*The policeman had done nothing but ask a few questions and hold him by the chin. That was all. So how could the boy be so sure he had been faced with pure evil?*

*For a start, all he had to do was think of the child. He was pretty sure that it was the policeman who had hurt him, the policeman he had run away from. And yet that wasn't conclusive. The boy wracked his brains, trying to formulate something that would enable him to make sense of it all.*

*Yes. Got it. The boy and his mother had once gone on a skiing trip to Norway. There had been a sturdy rail alongside one of the runs. The boy had gone over to see what was on the other side. When he leaned forward, his stomach contracted. Half a metre in front of him there was a steep drop of at least a hundred metres, ending in a lake so deep in shadow that the ice looked black. If the boy simply lay down on his back and wriggled under the rail, he would fall straight down into the lake.*

*The feeling when he faced the policeman in the forest had been very similar: as if he were standing on the edge of an abyss and could fall at any moment. And just as on a particularly bad day when he was waiting in the subway and felt the urge to throw himself in front of the train, there was a* pull*...*

*The boy straightened up. Come to think of it, that same pull had emanated from the child. And yet he didn't feel that the child was evil.*

*Or did he?*

*

It was gone two in the morning by the time I put down my pen and closed my notepad without having reached the part about transcendence. No doubt there were celebrations going on all over the city—three more years for the Social Democrats. Sweaty faces, red flags and bunches of roses. I tried to feel happy—my team had won—but the only thing I felt was the pressure in my skull and a loneliness as deep as the ocean.

I took out *Some Great Reward* by Depeche Mode and placed the needle on track one, side two: 'Somebody'. I had nothing against

Dave Gahan, but at a moment like this it was Martin Gore's voice I needed. I sat cross-legged on the floor in front of the speakers and closed my eyes.

Gore had only just started singing when the needle jumped and made a hissing noise as it scraped along the outer edge of the record. I carefully lifted the arm with my index finger, but when I tried to drop it on the first track it skidded away and landed outside the grooves once more, as if the vinyl was charged with static electricity that was repelling the needle.

The night had to be endured without consolation. I laid out the mattress and made up my bed, then lay awake for a long time thinking about Olof Palme. All that joy around him, but at the same time the loathing of the yuppie in the bar—irreconcilable opposites. My thoughts drifted on to fire and water, life and death, and at some point I fell asleep.

I was woken early in the morning by the sound of something falling on the floor. In the grey light filtering through the blinds I saw it was the little cup I had won at the National Championships the previous year; I kept it on the window ledge. Then I went back to sleep.

With hindsight I might think it strange that I didn't see the signs, didn't put two and two together. And yet it was perfectly understandable. What's the point of putting this and that together when the final result is something hitherto overlooked, something abnormal?

*

I had toyed with the idea that the pressure I was experiencing, the sense of an approaching change or disaster, was in fact a *social* pressure linked to the election. Something that had been in the making had reached its conclusion.

On the morning after the election there was a notice on the main door, asking the residents to attend a meeting to discuss switching from rental rights to residential rights. I had only a vague idea of what this meant and wasn't really interested; instead I went into the city searching for signs of change.

I was young. I was looking for big, emotional movements—I didn't care about trivial matters written on bits of paper. I was both perceptive and easily fooled. I walked the streets and sat in cafes, studying people's faces and posture. Was there anything to indicate that we had started to care about one another a little more?

No. Maybe I was projecting my own loneliness onto my fellow human beings, but the only thing I saw was isolation, everyone enclosed in their own little world. Perhaps the sense of community the Social Democrats talked about was nothing more than a dream inside Olof Palme's head, a bunch of wilting roses.

Preoccupied with gloomy thoughts, I returned home. In the courtyard I caught up with Elsa. This time she was accompanied by a girl about the same age as Dennis, clutching a helium balloon in the shape of a rabbit. Elsa explained that they'd been to the Skansen amusement park, and were now on their way home for cakes and juice. Bearing in mind how things had gone with Dennis, I made no attempt to converse with the girl; I simply said something appreciative about the balloon, and headed for my house.

When I was halfway up the steps I heard a scream, and turned around. Through the railing I could see that the girl had let go of the balloon, and it was slowly floating upwards with the string dangling beneath it.

I leapt down the steps in a couple of strides thinking that as I was a few centimetres taller and many years younger than Elsa, I might be able to jump up and grab the balloon before it was too late. I had hardly covered any distance when I came to a halt and stared.

The balloon had stopped. It hung there motionless in the air in the middle of the courtyard, three metres above the ground. Elsa and the girl stretched their arms up high, but couldn't reach it. I went over to them, stood on tiptoe and grabbed the string, then returned it to the girl.

Elsa and I gazed at the spot where the balloon had just been, as if we might see an invisible glass roof, a spider's web—something. But there was no sign of anything.

'It must be the air pressure,' Elsa said, rubbing her temple. 'I can feel it in my head.'

'Yes,' I said. Only then did I become aware of an oppressive humming inside my skull. I rubbed my forehead and said, 'You kind of get used to it.'

Elsa and the girl went up to the next floor, the balloon dangling by the girl's side. When they reached the landing above my roof, the balloon tugged at the string again, pulling it straight as it strove to reach the sky.

*

*It was still daylight when the boy left the bench by the lake and cautiously returned to the forest. Patches of sunlight still dappled the ground, but the boy had lost interest in games. The forest was no longer a playground; instead, like almost everywhere else, it had become a place where danger lurked.*

*A faint gust of wind carried the rancid smell of a muddy stream through the air, and the boy got it into his head that it was the stench of a corpse. The policeman had found the tree house, found the child, and what had he done? The stench provided the answer.*

*The boy moved slowly, taking care not to snap any twigs. He wrapped the plastic bag around his hand to stop it from making any unnecessary noise. He was looking around all the time, terrified of spotting that dark blue uniform among the trees. When he got close to the tree house, he crouched down and shuffled along.*

*'Psst,' he whispered. 'Psst.'*

*Not a sound, not a movement. Bearing in mind the size of the policeman, it was unlikely that he was inside the cabin. The tree would have been bending sideways, if it was even capable of carrying his weight. The boy scanned the trunk, looking for signs that an adult had climbed up. It was impossible to tell. Maybe the policeman was up there after all, and would grab hold of him with those hands as soon as he showed his face.*

*There was an alternative, a good alternative. He could run home as fast as possible and never come back. And he might have done it if it hadn't been for that...pull. The tree house was drawing him in. It was possible to resist the pull, but he chose not to. He heaved himself up onto the lowest branch.*

*The whole cabin was filled with dark, odourless smoke that didn't disperse when the boy tried to wave it away. It wasn't too dense for him to see that the policeman wasn't there. The only things inside were the bucket, the water bottle and the sleeping-bag, rolled into a bundle.*

*'Psst,' the boy said again, but the bundle didn't move. The boy shuddered. What if the child was lying there hurt, dead, his body dismembered? And the smoke? Was it dangerous to inhale? The boy leaned forward and took a shallow breath. A warmth entered his chest, but it wasn't unpleasant—more as if he had been lying on a rock warmed by the sun on a summer's day.*

*It was pointless hanging there in the tree weighing up the pros and cons, when he knew he was going to clamber up into the cabin eventually. He glanced over his shoulder one last time, scanned the forest without seeing anything untoward. Then he climbed in.*

*'He's gone,' the boy informed the bundle. 'The policeman. Dadda. He's gone.'*

*It was a relief when the bundle finally moved. The boy took a deep breath, and for a moment he wasn't on his knees inside the tree house—he was on a TV-series green lawn, an empty field stretching in all directions as far as the eye could see. Above him was a clear blue sky without a single cloud. He exhaled in a long sigh, and was back in the tree house, where the child's head was poking out of the sleeping-bag. The smoke began to disperse.*

*'I've brought...food,' the boy said, dropping the carrier bag on the floor in front of the child. Then he sat there open-mouthed, watching as the child gobbled up the tomato and munched on a carrot. The inside of his head felt grey and dirty. He couldn't cope with any more*

*right now. It was too much—he was too tired. He made his way down the tree as if in a dream, and staggered home through the forest. When he reached his room he collapsed headfirst on the bed and fell asleep right away.*

*

That was a wonderful sentence to write: 'When he reached his room he collapsed headfirst on the bed and fell asleep right away'. To think I had once been capable of doing something like that. I sat at my desk. I passed my coins, I laid out my cards, I practised hard to make the impossible appear probable and I felt a faint madness approaching, a bowling ball moving in slow motion towards my head.

I crouched down by the record-player. I wanted to play 'People Are People' just so I could hear Martin Gore telling me that he couldn't understand what makes a man hate another man, but the needle behaved as it had done the night before, and skidded off the album.

I wept for a while; I hit my head with my hands; I realised that life is very, very long. There were three days left before I was due to travel to Copenhagen, but just then I didn't know how I was going to endure even that amount of time. I rolled around on the floor, I hugged myself, and the hours passed. Eventually I lay there exhausted, staring into the corner, where there was a connection point for a TV aerial.

I gave up. I couldn't do this any more. I had decided to live without a television in order to focus on what was important, but I just couldn't carry on. I needed to see faces and hear voices, even if it was only from a box. I had seen on the noticeboard by the main door that someone was selling a small TV. I was just about to get up so that I could check out the number and call right away when I realised it was after midnight. It would have to wait until tomorrow.

Like someone who has a party to look forward to and can therefore survive a few miserable days, the thought of the TV had calmed me sufficiently that I was able to practise my magic for an hour or so, then go to bed.

*

Collapsing headfirst on the bed, falling asleep right away. All that rolling around on the floor had made me so tired that sleeping seemed like an entirely reasonable proposition, but it was made impossible by a crackling noise in my ears, like when you exhale and allow yourself to sink in a swimming pool.

I sat up on the mattress and wrapped my arms around my legs. The crackling came and went with a stubborn, pulsating rhythm, and I tried to distract myself by going through my magic act in my head, movement by movement, each carried out with a precision of which I was incapable in real life.

I had almost reached the end, the finale where I produced a giant coin from a purse that was far too small, when the phone rang. I sat and stared at it, let it ring ten times before I crawled onto my desk chair, picked up the receiver and said, 'Hello?'

'You took your time.'

'Yes, I...Sigge isn't here.'

'No. I know.'

'You know?'

'Well, I can't be sure. But if you say so.'

I tried to imagine the room the man was calling from. The only thing I could say for sure was that it wasn't a public place. There were no other voices or sounds. Eventually I asked, 'So why are you calling me?'

He sighed. 'Why do we do this or that? Can you always answer that question? Anyway, what are you up to?'

'I was trying to sleep.'

'I'm guessing that didn't go too well.'

I might have been clutching at straws, but I couldn't help asking, 'Do you know what's wrong with this house?'

'What house?'

'The house where I live.'

'You live in a *house*?'

I shook my head at myself and said, 'It doesn't matter. Did you want anything in particular?'

'You were trying to sleep?'

'Yes.'

There was such a long silence that I thought he'd lost interest. I said, 'Goodnight,' and was about to hang up when he said, 'Wait a minute. Couldn't you just…lay the receiver down beside you?'

'What do you mean?'

'When you lie down to sleep. I won't talk or anything, I promise.'

'I'm not sure if…'

'Oh, come on—what does it matter?'

'What are you going to do?'

'Sleep, of course.'

On any other evening I would probably have reacted differently, but the combination of my search for a sense of community during the day and the thumbscrews of loneliness during the evening had weakened my defences.

'Do you snore?' I asked.

'No, I fucking don't. No way.'

'Okay. Goodnight, then.'

'Goodnight.'

I lifted the phone down from the desk and put it on the floor next to the mattress. I placed the receiver on my pillow, then lay down and looked at it for a while. Via that piece of plastic I was in touch with another human being somewhere. I think I might even have stroked the receiver with my index finger.

There wasn't a sound from the other end, and when I felt myself drifting into sleep, I murmured, 'Are you there?' but there was no response. Then I must have dropped off.

*

I slept unusually well that night. The first thing I saw when I woke up was the receiver lying beside me. What had happened the previous night seemed like something entirely detached from reality.

Reality? What did I know about reality?

I picked up the receiver and listened. There wasn't a sound. I tentatively whispered 'Hello?' so as not to wake the person on the other end if they were sleeping. No answer. When I replaced the receiver in its cradle and then lifted it again, I heard the dial tone.

I sat naked on my chair, trying to orientate myself in the world. It didn't go too well. I told myself it was because of the forthcoming Nordic Championships, that all my practising had caused me to lose touch with *reality*—but I had been in more or less the same state since I was twelve years old. The odd visit, brief periods of intimacy with life—like a pig glancing up from its trough and taking in its surroundings—then back to the vagueness, back to the swill.

I was no longer sure that the idea of writing down the story of the child in the forest was such a good idea. In a way it merely reinforced my lack of contact with normality. However, the narrative had been started, so it would be completed. If there's one good thing you can say about me, it's that I finish whatever I start. I see things through.

My mood was well suited to describing the hallucinatory state I had entered following my experience in the tree house, so I picked up my pen and carried on writing.

*

*He didn't wake up until his mother knocked on the door and said that dinner was ready. He went into the kitchen and chewed his way through a meal of stuffed cabbage leaves without even noticing what he was eating. He gave monosyllabic answers to his mother's questions about his day, lying out of sheer habit. His mother asked if he was sick and the boy replied that yes, he was probably sick.*

*And maybe that was true. Later on, when he and his mother were watching* Little House on the Prairie, *he had started shivering. The sight of the Ingalls' warm and simple lives almost made him cry, and he was on the point of telling his mother everything that had happened, but was prevented by her verbose lamentations over the state he was in. She tucked him up in bed, a cup of tea with honey on his bedside table.*

*The boy lay on his side, studying the steam rising from the cup. The greyness in his head began to clear, like when you rub your hand over the condensation on a window. He contemplated the steam and thought about the smoke in the tree house. What had actually happened?*

*He had inhaled the smoke, and been transported to a field. It wasn't as if he had seen the field in a fleeting vision, in passing—no, he had actually been there. He knew this because the field and the blue sky weren't just as real as the bed in which he was lying. They were much more real.*

*For a long time the boy had experienced the world as unreal. If someone had told him that life was a stage set and all the people were aliens in disguise it would have been hard to believe, but at the same time it would have confirmed a feeling he had, a suspicion if you like. That everything was pretend.*

*The field was different. During the few seconds the boy had been there, he had felt entirely present. The experience had been much too short for him to get a proper grip on it, but one thing he knew for sure: he wanted to go there again.*

*He was totally certain that he'd been in contact with something mysterious and possibly dangerous, but at the same time it offered the possibility of* something else. *If there was something he wanted out of life, it was something different. He took a couple of sips of the tea, which was lukewarm by now, then fell asleep.*

*He woke up terrified in the middle of the night and sat up in bed. It took a horrific minute before he managed to convince himself that what he had just dreamed wasn't a memory, that it hadn't actually happened.*

*When he slumped back on the pillow he still wasn't sure, and couldn't settle. He swung his legs over the side of the bed, drank some of the cold tea and looked around the dark room. His eyes settled on the poster of Gene Simmons from Kiss. The monster mask, the long tongue. There was pretend fear, and there was real fear.*

*The boy had dreamed that he had killed the child, and he remembered why he had done it. To become a different person. To stop being a kid who was bullied, and to become a murderer instead. To step over the boundary, to be transformed. In the dream something had happened to him when he stuck the knife in the child. Something that wasn't good, yet it was desirable.*

*The conviction he'd felt in the dream was jammed there in his chest, black and sticky, and he drank more tea in an attempt to wash it down. He got up and went over to the window, resting his hands on the warm marble shelf above the radiator, and looked out across the courtyard.*

*There wasn't a soul in sight. The lamps above the doors were lit, but the yard with its play area and climbing frame lay in shadow. The boy had felt this way on a couple of previous occasions when he woke up in the night and went to stand by the window, and now it came over him again: the sense that something was about to happen. Something unheard of, an approaching revelation, or rather the perception that* someone was going to come.

*He waited, motionless, by the window. No one came. Nothing happened. The perception faded and disappeared altogether. It hadn't happened this time either. Or maybe it had, but not here.*

*The boy crawled back into bed. The tea had made him feel wide awake, and he lay there for a long time thinking about the forces that move in the darkness. Inside us and beyond us. He thought 'hand' and was amazed that he could see a hand inside his head. Whose hand was it? And what was that knife it was holding? What is real? What is important?*

*

Those questions hadn't changed during the seven years that had passed, and the answers were still notable by their absence. I sat there glaring at the dirty dishes in the sink and tried to imagine a future in which I would have found peace and would be living in the world. The only picture that appeared was the Ingalls family in *Little House on the Prairie*, and the Moomin family. I had no starting point for a fantasy of my own. No doubt this contributed to my inability to feel any kind of connection or sense of community, to the fact that I didn't see myself as part of a greater movement, my life.

*My life.*

The most banal insights are often the most important. Like the realisation that we have one life, only one, and that we have to take care of it. Self-evident, of course, but there's a difference between knowing something theoretically and being struck by its essential truth.

*My life.*

I felt a wave of dizziness as I sat there on my chair, staring at the washing-up. I had a life—my disconnected days were links in a chain reaching backwards and forwards. I was on my way somewhere, and this trivial thought excited me.

For example, I was going to get myself a television. I got dressed, went down to the main door and made a note of the number on the ad: *FOR SALE—SMALL TV. PERFECT WORKING ORDER. 500KR.* It was handwritten, but the lines were so straight and even that it could have been printed by a machine. I would ring in the afternoon, but first I decided to have a shower before tackling the day and the city.

As I crossed the courtyard, the sky looked like a bright blue lid on top of the roofs. The sun lit up the top two floors of the four-storey buildings, making the window panes flash like the goodness of God, or signals from someone in distress at sea. I thought about the Ingalls family—how as far as I recalled, a large part of the action consisted of them sitting around the dinner table, discussing everything under the sun. My mind wandered freely and idly until I unlocked the door of the laundry block and stepped into the room, which smelled of softener.

*Run!*

Like an animal sensing danger, I instinctively cowered, trying to make myself a smaller target. I took several deep breaths and stood there motionless. Nothing happened, and I cautiously straightened up. Everything looked perfectly normal, but the awareness of a threat remained. I don't know if 'threat' is the right word. It was more like the feeling I had when I stood by the window in Blackeberg with my hands resting on the warm marble shelf, the feeling that someone is going to come. Like that, but more powerful, and the difference now was that this someone, or something, had an evil intent. 'Evil' isn't the right word either. When we are faced with certain experiences, language falls short.

I moved warily through the laundry towards the shower room. The blissful feeling of expansion I'd felt that morning evaporated, and I was now reduced to what was contained within my skin. A network of nerves and a pounding heart.

The threat didn't diminish when I opened the door of the shower room. Quite the reverse. I reached in to switch on the light; the bulb flickered twice, then went out. I gasped and slammed the door, backing away slowly.

*The crack.*

An image had burned itself on my retina during those brief flickers. Something was squeezing its way out through the crack in the ceiling, directly above the bath. Since I had recently been writing about the child in the forest, the association was inevitable: it reminded me of the thing that had emerged from the child's nose. But much, much bigger.

I stood with my back to the outside door trying to reshape the image into something else, but it continued to insist that it was what it was: a dense, black mass with the unmistakable nature of *life*, forcing its way out through the crack in the plaster.

I opened the door and went outside, stood beneath the blue sky. Glowing dots danced before my eyes. I rubbed my face, and when I looked at the palm of my right hand, it was streaked with red. My nose was bleeding. Only now did I become aware that what I thought of as 'the pressure' had been stronger than ever inside the laundry block.

*

I have no recollection of how I left the courtyard and got out into the street. I must have put down my towel and underclothes somewhere, because I wasn't carrying them when I found myself standing outside Dekorima's display window.

I didn't know where to go. People passing by stared at me, and only then did I realise that the metallic taste in my mouth came from the fact that my nose was still bleeding. A small pool had formed at my feet, and the sight of the blood oozing into a crack in the pavement made me shudder. I found an old receipt in my pocket, crumpled it up until it was soft, then tore it in half and rolled it into two plugs, which I shoved up my nose. I spat on my hand and scrubbed my face clean as best I could. Then I set off.

Without thinking about where my feet were taking me, I walked down Kungsgatan towards Stureplan. Wherever I looked I saw cracks. In the facades of the buildings, in the pavement, and in people's faces. Cracks where it could seep in.

*What? What?*

That was what I didn't know, that was what frightened me, and that is what I am still investigating to this day. What it is that seeps in and what it does to us. The other, in its shifting manifestations.

I turned onto Birger Jarlsgatan, drawn by the smell of the sea from Nybroviken. My head was beginning to clear, and the cracks in people's faces became wrinkles, mouths, eye sockets. When I reached the quayside and stood gazing out across the water, I took a deep breath and everything became a little easier.

What was it I had seen in the crack in the ceiling? Apart from its resemblance to that thing in the child's nose, what was so frightening about it? Nothing. There was a crack in the ceiling, and something was oozing out. What did it have to do with me?

As I stood there contemplating the gently bobbing Waxholm ferries, inhaling the fresh smell of Lake Mälaren, the whole thing seemed like yet another trick played by my closed-in, overheated pressure cooker of a brain. The sun was sparkling on the water, and cheerful people on their way over to Djurgården were walking past me.

I tentatively removed the paper plugs from my nose, and discovered that I'd stopped bleeding. I tossed them in the water, and a couple of ducks immediately showed an interest. I turned back towards the city.

*Okay.*

Regardless of how successfully I had reduced the thing in the shower room to something that had nothing to do with me, one thing was very clear: I had *no* intention of standing underneath it while I took a shower. I would have to come up with an alternative plan.

When I reached Hötorget I went into John Wall, where I found a bright red thirty-litre plastic tub for seventy-nine kronor. Not even I thought I could shoplift something that big. I also paid for a sponge, and then headed home clutching my purchases.

Now that I knew the source of the pressure, I could clearly feel it emanating from the northern area of the courtyard, from the laundry block. I avoided looking in that direction and hurried up the steps to my house.

I placed the tub on the floor in front of the washbasin and sluiced myself down as best I could. I held the sponge under the tap and squeezed it over my body, then soaped my skin and repeated the procedure. It worked pretty well. At least I was clean. When I had dried myself I emptied the tub into the toilet, then spent some time staring at myself in the mirror.

After all, there was an alternative way to explain everything that was happening to me, and I searched for something in my eyes, a sign that I was losing my mind. But what does such a sign look like, and can it even be spotted by a person who is losing the plot?

I realised I was heading for another of those damned circular arguments. Enough. I was fit and clean and I smelled good. Everything would be fine, if I could just get myself a television.

*

A woman answered the phone when I rang in the afternoon. Yes, they still had the TV. Yes, I could come up and see it right now, if I so wished. Something in the way she used her words made me think that she was the one who had written the ad. Her voice was rounded, definitive, and she said 'Third floor—it says Holmgren on the door' as if she were providing statistical information.

I put on a white short-sleeved shirt, because I felt I was on *official business*. To tell the truth I was pretty nervous, because I didn't really know how I should behave. I needn't have worried. The woman who opened the door showed no interest in me whatsoever. She merely gave me a brief nod and said, 'Come in.'

She was around thirty, with medium-length fair hair and clearly defined facial features. I found it difficult to concentrate on the TV she showed me, a smallish wooden box with no remote control, because a clichéd sexual fantasy had begun to play out in the back of my mind.

*Young man, older woman, a TV for sale, they end up on the sofa and…*

'I expect you want to see what the picture's like?' she said.

As she switched on the set I heard a door open. A man about the same age as the woman came into the room, and I breathed a sigh of relief—I could abandon the fantasy. He was wearing a bathrobe, and his cropped dark hair was wet. He was exactly as good-looking as the woman. We shook hands; his grip was stronger than mine.

The picture on the TV was fine. There was a children's program on, with figures cut out of paper making their way up a hill, dragging a plank of wood behind them. 'Great,' I said. 'That's great.'

The man asked if I'd like a beer, and I said, 'Yes, please,' because I assumed that was the right thing to do. The woman waved me towards an armchair that looked both new and uncomfortable. Which indeed it was. There was a highly polished glass table in front of me, with a single lily in a vase.

I looked around the room, because I had never seen anything like it in real life. It was sparsely furnished. A picture of a geometric figure hung on the wall above the straight-backed sofa. A narrow bookcase held books that appeared to have been chosen for the colour of their spines. A square, chalk-white rug lay between the sofa and the window. It was hard to imagine that anyone actually *lived* there.

The only object that diverged from the carefully thought out lines and colours was the television set, which seemed as misplaced as a jukebox in an operating theatre. The woman, who had sat down in the armchair opposite me, must have noticed my expression, because she said, 'We've decided to stop watching TV.'

'Right,' I said. 'I've decided to start.'

The woman smiled and something shifted in the room, as if a piano wire had passed through the air and sliced off a layer. Her smile wasn't a smile. The man came in with two glasses of beer and two coasters. He placed the coasters neatly on the table before putting down the glasses, then he sat down on the sofa.

I took a sip, taking care not to spill a drop, and had to suppress the urge to knock the whole lot back in one. My hand was shaking slightly when I replaced the glass in the centre of the coaster. I rubbed my forehead, and noticed that beads of sweat had broken out along my hairline.

*Pull yourself together!* I thought. *Calm down!*

'It's a good TV,' the man said. 'We've had it for three years. Never had a problem with it.'

'We haven't watched it much,' the woman said.

'No, that's true. But when we have watched it, it's worked perfectly.'

'It has.'

I nodded mechanically. A reasonable response would be to ask what they used to watch, but I didn't want to know, didn't want the conversation to carry on. I would have preferred to drop my money on the table, grab the TV and run down the stairs, like an animal returning to its lair with its prey. I realised that my impulses were socially unacceptable, and that I had to say something, so I asked, 'Have you lived here long?'

'Seven years,' the man replied.

'Our first home together.'

'After our wedding.'

That, at least, told me something about them. Who the hell refers to their marriage as 'our wedding'? As if it were nothing more than a fixed point in time that had been labelled in that way.

I wish I had more fine-tuned stylistic instruments with which to paint the picture, but in the absence of such tools I will simply say that I perceived the man and woman as *dead*. Their apartment was dead; their conversation lacked any sign of life; their gestures and expressions were stiff.

The erotic fantasy involving the woman had been nothing more than a projection. She radiated as much sexuality as the sound produced by an air guitarist. There was nothing there, and I finished off my beer with impolite speed.

The Dead Couple got their cash and I got my TV. Picking it up in a double grip meant I could avoid shaking hands. As I made my way down the stairs clutching my purchase, I had the feeling that they were standing watching me through the peephole. Both of them. At the same time. I sped up, anxious to get out of sight.

*

When I got home it became clear that there was another explanation for my highly strung behaviour. I was sweating as I connected up the TV, and by the time I had balanced it on top of three telephone books and run an extension lead from the socket, I was completely exhausted. My temperature soared, and I had to sit down and rest for five minutes before I could summon the energy to lay out my mattress. Then I crashed.

I have only vague memories of the next two days. I just about managed to crawl to the toilet, and I couldn't even think about food.

Curled up on my side and shaking, I watched TV, letting the images flicker past my eyes. The only thing I remember is that *The Brothers Lionheart* was on, and that the fluffy feeling in Körsbärsdalen was a great comfort. *Falcon Crest* was probably on too, but I might be getting mixed up there, because I remember seeing Angela Channing on a horse, pulling a papier-mâché kite along behind her. The theme tune from *Hill Street Blues* also penetrates the fever-fog. Black-and-white Swedish films. Time passed.

At some point I must have gathered enough strength to pick up my pen and carry on with the story of the child in the forest. The narrative is disjointed and hard to read, and it has taken a significant amount of editing to make it comprehensible.

*

*The following day the boy had to stay home from school. His eyes were bloodshot, his cheeks bright red. When his mother had gone to work, he got up and wandered aimlessly around the apartment. The fever was throbbing and swaying inside his head, and he felt curiously excited.*

*He spent a while leafing through the Hobbex catalogue, then fetched the cellar key and went downstairs. After searching through a couple of boxes looking for something to give the child, he finally found the one that held his old cuddly toys.*

*He chose a shaggy dog; it was the only one he couldn't remember the name of, and therefore the easiest to part with. He stroked the other animals' soft fur and whispered their names, which gave him a little pain in his chest. He closed the box carefully and went back upstairs with the dog—Raffe? Ruff? Riffe?—under his arm, then checked out the contents of the fridge.*

*He would be expected to eat during the day anyway, so it wouldn't arouse any suspicion if he made a few cheese sandwiches. He put them in a plastic bag, along with two apples. Something told him he ought to take milk too, that small children were supposed to have milk, for their bones or their brain or something, so he rinsed out a soft drink bottle and filled it up with milk. He placed the dog on top of the food, then weighed the bag in his hand. There was something missing.*

*He opened the bottom kitchen drawer and rummaged around until he found an almost new Mora knife in its sheath. He slid it out and ran his thumb over the blade. Super sharp. He put it back in its sheath and added it to the bag. Good. Now it was…complete.*

*Once again he approached the tree house cautiously, keeping an eye out in all directions. If he saw the policeman from far enough away, he would run, and if the policeman turned up at close quarters, he would play dead. Shut himself down inside, just as he did when the boys in his class started on him. He wouldn't let the policeman get to him.*

*The boy stopped, swinging the bag back and forth. Was that what the child had done? If the boy's suspicions were correct, and he had been systematically abused by the policeman or someone else, had the child employed the same strategy and shut down, but in a more fundamental way than the boy had ever done?*

*Jimmy, Conny and Andreas had once tied the boy to a tree and whipped his arms and legs with hazel branches. On that occasion the boy had managed to shut down and removed himself so effectively that he had found it difficult to come back when it was all over. He had felt no pain, and had hardly known where he was when they untied him and left him lying at the foot of the tree. There had been nothing but darkness, and it had taken him some time to escape from it. Had the child gone so far into the darkness that…*

*The boy swung the bag, whirled it around in circles. He felt desperately sorry for the child, and yet the child possessed something that the boy really wanted. Something that was* beyond.

*When he reached the tree he whispered 'psst' even though he didn't expect a response. But this time he got one. A faint 'ss' came from inside the tree house. The boy glanced around once more, then clambered up.*

*The child ate the cheese sandwiches while the boy munched on an apple, then he drank the milk. He had to clutch the bottle in both hands because his fingers were so crooked. A trickle of milk ran down his neck and under his jacket.*

*'What actually happened to you?' the boy asked. 'Did someone beat you?'*

*The child lowered the bottle, which was empty now, and nodded.*

*'Often?'*

*The child nodded again and said, 'Bam, bam. Bam, bam. Bam, bam.'*

*The boy picked up the carrier bag and took out the toy dog. 'Here,' he said, holding it out to the child. 'You can have it if you want.'*

*The child tilted his head to one side and stared at the dog—Roffe? Raff-Raff?—as if he had never seen anything like it. Maybe he hadn't. He reached out a finger that ended in a congealed lump of pus instead of a nail, and touched the dog's nose as if it might burn him. When that didn't happen, the child ran the palm of his hand over the dog's head.*

*'That business with the darkness,' the boy said. 'How did you do that?'*

*By now the child had plucked up enough courage to stroke the dog's fur properly, and was making a sound not unlike a cat's purr. The boy tapped on the wall of the tree house, and the child looked up.*

*'I mean, seriously? How do you do that?'*

*The child pulled up one sleeve of his jacket. His skin was covered in a network of lines. Older, white scars, brown scabs, and sores that still showed red.*

*'Blood,' the child said. 'Whoosh, whoosh. Blood. Evil.' He pulled down his sleeve and turned his attention back to the dog.*

*The boy finished off the apple and tossed the core outside. The child's purring turned into a soft crooning; it was a tune the boy recognised, because his mother had it on a record.*

*'Somebody Up There Must Like Me.'*

*

During Thursday night the fog in my head began to disperse, and when I woke up on Friday morning I was fine—stronger now, as if I'd passed through a furnace and come out the other side—and absolutely ravenous. My breakfast consisted of a big plate of spaghetti with ketchup. I say plate, but I actually ate it straight out of the pan, sitting on my mattress.

While I was sick I had been painfully aware that the train to Copenhagen and the Nordic Championships left on Friday afternoon. Now it was looking as if I might be able to go after all. I finished off my breakfast, put away the mattress and had a quick swill in the tub, then I sat down at the desk with my magic paraphernalia. I soon realised it was pointless. A few hours' practice would only serve to increase my anxiety, and I really didn't want to stay in the house. Now the illness had loosened its grip, I was once again free to feel the pressure. It had grown stronger, and my skull felt as if it were slowly being encased in a helmet made of lead.

*It can't go on like this.*

If the worst came to the worst, I would have to use all my savings and let the landlord keep his nine thousand—the current month's rent plus two months' notice—without staying on in the house. Move back to Blackeberg. It was a gloomy prospect, and I put it aside for the moment. First Copenhagen. I had booked a ticket on the train departing at 16.21, so I had plenty of time to get ready.

I started by carefully packing the items I needed for my act. The close-up mat, the deck of cards that had been used just enough, the four half-dollar coins with the shells that fitted over them, the purses, the oversized coin, plus the toy laser pistol I used instead of a magic wand. Then my stage clothes. Shirt, waistcoat, black trousers, bow tie.

The problem was underwear. I had nothing clean—no pants, socks, T-shirts. Right at the back of the wardrobe I found a pair of flimsy, washed-out pants and pushed them into my bag. Then I took them out again and threw them in the bin. There was still time for a little shoplifting trip to Åhlén's. I could pick up what I needed, nip home to finish packing, then head off to the Nordic Championships wreathed in the smell of new clothes.

Before I went out I flicked through my notepad and discovered that while I was ill I had written about giving the child the toy dog. As I said earlier, the narrative was unclear and unstructured, but it was crying out for me to carry on. I was getting close to the really terrible part, the part I wasn't even sure I could write down.

I put my notepad and pen in a plastic bag that could also be used for gathering up my 'shopping', then I set off to find a second, more conventional breakfast. I sat in Kungstornet for a long time with my coffee going cold; I didn't stop writing until I reached the point where it really began to hurt.

*

*The child carried on humming 'Somebody Up There Must Like Me' as he stroked and hugged the dog. The boy sat opposite, feeling more and more listless. He had felt feverishly enthusiastic on the way to the tree house, but now he was here it was no fun at all.*

*It was no fun having a pet that knew nothing, no fun having a tree house. Life was horrendous at school and boring at home. He was twelve years old and had never thought about his existence as a whole concept. He was doing that now, and he could see that it was total crap. All of it. His head drooped, drawn towards the floor as he saw himself wading through days as heavy as black, sticky mud.*

*Suddenly he straightened up. Everything might be crap, but he never thought that way. Was it the child making him do it? If so, it didn't appear to be something he was doing consciously. The child was still humming and stroking the dog. Maybe it happened automatically, just as a magnet is always a magnet.*

*It didn't matter. The boy couldn't fight against the images passing through his mind, and his head began to droop once more, weighed down by things that had happened at school, the fear he carried with him every minute he was there, the misery when he got back to his room at home, the emptiness on the streets of Blackeberg, where he didn't have a single friend to visit. He was a failure, an insignificant victim of bullying whom nobody liked. Fact.*

*He took the knife out of the carrier bag, slid it out of its sheath and studied the clean, shiny steel. The child stopped humming and moved as far back as possible, staring with huge eyes as the boy gently ran his index finger along the blade.*

To cut. *It was strange, really. The fact that you could hone a piece of steel until it was so thin that it could penetrate another substance.*

*The boy pointed the knife at the child. 'Are you scared of this? Are you? Do they cut you?'*

*The boy could feel the darkness growing inside him, or perhaps he was simply reflecting the child's darkness—it was irrelevant. It was there, and it was growing. He remembered his dream, the dream he had thought was a memory, but might have been a warning. He edged closer to the child as the images of his worthless life whirled by faster and faster, merging together into pure, unbearable pain.*

A murderer. I am…a murderer.

*No. It was impossible. Before the boy could stop himself he had slashed his right palm with the knife. Something of the throbbing darkness-pain in his chest eased, rushing towards the wound where blood was seeping out. The boy exhaled, gasped.*

*A drop of blood landed on the floor of the tree house. The boy frowned, and when the next drop fell, he watched more closely. The idea of a magnet hadn't been far off the mark: the drops changed course in midair and landed a few centimetres closer to the child than they should have done. They were drawn towards him. The boy grabbed the roll of toilet paper, tore off a sheet and pressed it to the cut.*

Why did I do that?

*On several occasions he had stolen things he didn't want, and thrown them in a bin outside the shop. Why? Because it had felt like a compulsion. Same with the knife—it was something he had to do.*

*He pressed the soft paper against the wound as the darkness began to well up inside him again. Slowly the child leaned forward, reached out and placed one deformed hand on the bloodstain. The boy's chest contracted and he found it hard to breathe. He shuffled back towards the opening as the child lifted his hand. The blood was gone.*

*The boy's limbs felt heavy by the time he made his way back down to the ground, dizzy with the lack of oxygen. After a few steps the pain in his chest began to ebb away and he was able to take a few breaths, which made the dizziness subside. He had escaped.*

*He was halfway home when he caught sight of the policeman, facing away from him and staring towards Råcksta Lake. The boy looked around, utterly panic-stricken, and crept behind a large rock before the policeman had time to turn around.*

*He kept perfectly still, listening hard. It didn't sound as if the policeman was coming closer. After a couple of minutes he dared to peep out, and saw the policeman walking towards the tree house. The boy clasped his hands together and pressed them against his stomach, feeling like a rabbit in the headlights. Everything around him was much too big, incomprehensible and terrifying.*

*He would run straight home. Lock the door behind him, defrost a portion of meatballs, sit on the balcony and read Spiderman, have a glass of juice with his meatballs and forget that any of this had happened. Unlike the rabbit, he had that possibility.*

*The boy had left the safety of the rock and scuttled several metres closer to home and safety when he heard a scream from the forest. From the tree house. If he hadn't known better he would have thought it was the scream of an animal, an animal caught in some terrible trap. But he did know better. Unfortunately. The boy stood there with his back bowed, digging his nails into his palms. His right hand started bleeding again.*

*Perhaps the most important decisions in our lives are made without the aid of our intelligence. There is good reason to suspect that this is the case. So is it possible to talk about something that resembles the concept of* fate? *Maybe it is.*

*The boy turned and headed back to the tree house.*

*

I came to a stop there, and I didn't know when I would have the courage to write the rest. I took a deep breath and wrote: *As he had thought, the slender trees were just capable of bearing the policeman's weight.* Then I noticed the time. It was almost two; I had completely lost track. Quickly I put the pad and pen back in the carrier bag, finished my cold coffee and hurried along Kungsgatan. I turned into Drottninggatan and made a beeline for Åhlén's.

I was hot and flustered as I approached the revolving doors leading into the perfume department, so I stopped for a while, allowing my heart to slow down. I assumed it wasn't good to look stressed if I was going to steal stuff.

I say *assumed* because I had no experience of what was right and wrong. I hadn't been caught since I was eleven, and all I'd taken then was a bar of chocolate from the corner shop in Blackeberg. Since then I had never been stopped, in spite of the fact that I'd helped myself to records, clothes, books and magazines worth many thousands of kronor.

As I mentioned earlier, my method was very simple. I picked up whatever I wanted and marched out of the department. If anyone stopped me I could claim absent-mindedness and pay for the goods in question. But that had happened only once. The shop assistant had definitely been suspicious, but she had no proof. I should add that only the more expensive items had security tags back then.

I hid my bag behind a suitcase in the luggage department, which wasn't exactly heaving with customers, and set off on my mission. After three trips up to the men's department I had gathered what I needed in terms of underwear, plus a new jumper. The bag was so full that it just fitted behind the suitcase. It was only quarter to three, so I treated myself to a visit to the record department.

I could see from some distance away that the Depeche Mode section was fuller than usual, and when I looked through I discovered they'd acquired Japanese pressings of both *Some Great Reward* and *Construction Time Again*, which cost three times as much as the normal pressings. As if that mattered. I tucked the two albums under my arm and walked out.

When I got back down to the luggage department, the LPs wouldn't fit into the carrier bag. That didn't matter either, because I was three floors away from the record department. I gathered up my loot and headed just purposefully enough towards the exit.

I went through the revolving doors and out into the street, and that's when I got the real kick. Every time I stole something from a department within a store I experienced a slight euphoria, but the real endorphin rush didn't come until I was outside and safely back in the harbour, so to speak. I let out a long breath and felt the carbon dioxide fizzing in my blood.

And that was when...

There is a line by Morrissey that I've carried with me through life, just waiting for the right opportunity to use it. That came in a story I called 'Majken', which is about shoplifting. The feeling stems from that moment outside Åhlén's. It's from 'Shoplifters of the World Unite', and it refers to a heartless hand on the shoulder, a push and it's over.

And that's exactly what happened. A heavy hand fell on my shoulder, and I heard a deep voice behind me: 'Stop right there. Can I have a look in your bag?'

The bubbles in my blood burst in a nanosecond, and my guts fell through the floor. There was a brief moment when I could have dropped everything and run. Drottninggatan was busy, and I might have been able to disappear into the crowd. But then I'd have had to leave my notepad behind.

I'm not going to make myself out to be any tougher or smarter than I was. The truth is that the hand on my shoulder completely paralysed me. When I slowly turned around, a substantial part of me—about the size of a twelve-year-old—expected to see *that* policeman looming over me. Which he wasn't, of course. The man in front of me was only fractionally taller than I was, and he was wearing perfectly ordinary clothes. A store detective. He produced his ID.

'The bag.'

I showed him the contents of the bag, the cellophane-wrapped T-shirts, the jumper.

'Have you paid for these items?'

I nodded.

'Do you have the receipts?'

'I...I didn't keep them.'

It was no more than a formality. It was clear from the man's attitude that he knew exactly what the situation was. He placed a large hand between my shoulder blades and guided me back into the store. We went down the escalator to the food hall, then into a room where I was asked to tip out the contents of my bag onto a table.

'And you say you've paid for all this?'

I nodded. I couldn't do anything else.

'Okay, let me explain. I can request printouts from the tills in the relevant departments to check if these items have been paid for. Are you with me?'

I was.

'But that takes time. A hell of a long time. And both you and I know that time will be wasted, because you *haven't* paid for them. Are you with me?'

Nod. Nod.

'Okay, good. So you admit you've taken these items without paying for them?'

I didn't know how the system worked. Printouts from the tills? Was that even possible? And of course there was always the chance that someone else had bought items for the same price at the same time. So I shook my head. The man's shoulders slumped and his expression hardened.

'You're not admitting it?'

'No. I've paid.'

The man let out a long sigh and shook his head. He looked at me as if he were about to say something a lot less pleasant, then he picked up the bag, stuffed everything back inside it, turned on his heel and left the room, slamming the door behind him. When I got up and tried it after a couple of minutes, it was locked.

I don't remember what I thought about during the long period while he was away. I followed the movement of the minute hand on the clock on the wall. My own movement, which had been focused on 16.21 for the past few weeks, had come to a standstill.

*Fuck*, I probably thought. *Fucking hell.*

It was ten to four by the time the man came back. He was carrying several strips of paper, which he placed on the table in front of me. With deliberate slowness he examined the items in my bag one by one, comparing them with the strips of paper and then jotting down notes. I cleared my throat.

'Excuse me, but...I've got a train to catch.'

The man looked up and stared at me. He didn't even deign to reply before returning to his task. I should have owned up, I realised. If I'd done that, everything might have been sorted out by now.

There were fifteen minutes to go before my train left by the time the man pushed aside the strips of paper and summarised the situation: 'So—we have goods to the value of 1872 kronor which have not been paid for at any till. Do you know what that means?'

Yes. I wasn't that stupid. I had been caught out, and there was no point in pretending any longer. I was about to say something along those lines when it turned out that the man had a surprise up his sleeve, one he was only too happy to share with me. 'Since the value of the goods in question exceeds 1500 kronor, this is no longer a question of shoplifting—we're looking at *theft*. Are you with me?'

Not any more, no—but the very sound of the word, *theft*, didn't bode well. I made a quick calculation in my head and worked out that the Japanese pressings were to blame, because they cost 200 kronor each.

'Which means,' the man went on, leaning back in his chair with undisguised pleasure, 'that this is now a police matter.' He looked at me and nodded slowly, as if to emphasise that what he had said was in accordance with the truth. Then he got up and left the room.

Once again I was left alone for a long while, but this time I remember what I was thinking. Those fucking Japanese pressings. Why did I have to have them? The sound was a fraction clearer, the bass a fraction deeper, but the main reason was that the Japanese writing on the sleeve looked cool. A status symbol. Who the fuck did I have to show off to? And for that I had crossed a line I didn't even know existed and had become a *police matter*, whatever that meant.

It was gone five o'clock by now. The competition in Copenhagen was due to start at three o'clock on Saturday. There was an overnight train and an early-morning train that could get me there in time. Without new underwear.

The more I thought about it, the more I realised this wasn't just about the competition itself. I had severed the few social ties I had with the rest of humanity, with one exception: the world of magicians. I still had a few friends there, and I had been looking forward to seeing them.

Mika from Finland with his amusing accent and his skilful side steals; Charly from Gothenburg, who might be every bit as crazy as he seemed. Magnus, Peter. And a few others. They would still have been up and about when I arrived in Copenhagen in the middle of the night, sitting in some hotel room drinking beer and showing each other card tricks until their eyelids began to droop. I should have been on my way there. Fuck. But it still wasn't too late.

Just before six o'clock the door opened and the man came in, accompanied by two uniformed police officers.

'Is that him?' one of the policemen asked, and I stupidly glanced behind me as if I thought they might be referring to someone else. When I turned back, both officers were looking expectantly at me.

'Let's go,' one of them said.

'Go where?' I asked.

'You'll find out.'

*

We emerged onto the street via a back door. I was hustled into a police van. A scruffy, skinny man with a bushy beard was already sitting inside, and the smell of his breath filled the space with alcohol fumes. The two officers got in the front and we set off along Klarabergsgatan. When we passed the central train terminal and I saw that the clock outside was showing ten past six, I began to cry. It was so upsetting; I should have been on the train now, practising my magic, on the way to people and light.

I pressed my fingertips to my forehead, digging my nails into the skin, and gave myself up to the misery that poured out of me in great hulking sobs. After a while I felt the opposite of a heartless hand on my shoulder. The bearded man patted me gently and said, 'You'll be okay. It'll be all right.'

At that moment it felt like the kindest thing anyone had ever done for me. The man's life was no doubt considerably more fucked-up than mine, and yet he had reached out to comfort me. I collapsed with my head on his chest, and remained there, enveloped in a miasma of booze and urine, until we reached the police station. He spent the whole time stroking my hair.

At the station the plastic bag containing my notepad and pen was taken off me, and I was told to empty my pockets. The duty officer was particularly interested in the thumb tip; I always pick it up before I leave home, out of sheer habit.

'What's this?'

'A thumb tip.'

'What's it for?'

'Magic.'

'Magic?'

'Yes. I'm a magician.'

For a second I hoped this information would make him realise that I didn't belong here, or at least make him a little more sympathetic towards me, but it didn't. He tossed the thumb tip in a box along with my wallet, my keys and my belt, and I was led deeper into the station.

I don't know if the way the police treated me on that occasion was routine, or if they were making a special effort to scare me and thus put me off a life of crime. Or maybe that *was* routine when it came to first-time offenders.

I was taken to a small room where I was ordered to drop my pants. A man slowly pulled on a pair of latex gloves, and I knew what was coming. I stood there with the palms of my hands on the wall as the man parted my buttocks, and I thought: *I'm a long way down right now.* He didn't go any further, though. If the police were aiming to intimidate and humiliate me, they had succeeded. I was at rock bottom as I was led along the blue-grey corridors.

My memory fails me at this point. I might have been interviewed; I might have signed something. But what follows is the part I remember best, and is the real reason I am including this scene.

There were corridors and a lift. New corridors. Eventually I was shown into a cell. When I turned around to ask how long I would have to stay there, the door slammed behind me.

The cell measured five or six square metres, and held nothing but a table fixed to the wall—no chair—and a bunk with a plastic-covered mattress. The silence was even more palpable than at home, and the door was so effectively sound-proofed that I couldn't even hear footsteps in the corridor.

I sat down on the bunk, rested my elbows on my knees and stared at a spot on the cement wall where someone had managed to scratch: *Palme is dead. Elvis is alive.* After a couple of hours I needed a piss, so I banged on the door. To my surprise a guard came and opened it and allowed me to go to the toilet.

Before he locked me in again I asked how long I would be there. He said he didn't know, but probably until early the following morning. I didn't even bother mentioning trains or Copenhagen, and the door closed behind me once more.

I lay down on the bunk with my right arm covering my eyes and gave up. I tossed my hope and my will aside and abandoned myself. That's the only way I can describe it. I accepted the fact that the small room with its fluorescent tubes was all I had, that the figure lying on the bunk was me, and that this was what had become of me. Does it make sense if I say it was a relief? If I was nothing and had nothing, then I had nothing to lose. I became as still and silent deep inside as the room surrounding me.

Time passed. The night came and went. I didn't sleep. At some point I began to write the final part of the story of the child in the forest. I wrote it in my head. Later on I wrote it down on paper too, but it was during that night in the cell that I really wrote it, because it was only then that I found the courage, when all hope had gone.

*

*As he had thought, the slender trees were just capable of bearing the policeman's weight. The tree house tilted and rocked as if it were in a fierce, shifting gale, while the sound of movement could be heard from inside. The boy stopped a few metres away, unsure of what to do. Once again his mind had led him astray. Why had he come back? There was nothing he could do, nothing he dared do. The best thing would have been to run home and call…*

*The police?*

*Before the boy had time to reflect on the impossibility of the situation, the policeman appeared at the opening to the tree house. He was holding the child in both hands, and the boy just had time to see that the child was clutching the toy dog before the policeman hurled him into the air.*

*The tree house was about four metres from the ground, and the child fell towards the boy in a wide arc. As he came down he began to blur and dim, his contours became unclear and the boy could see that his eyes were closed. The boy instinctively stepped back, and the child crashed to the ground in front of him.*

*Two things happened at virtually the same time. One of the child's feet was bent sideways at an unnatural angle, and the boy heard a dry sound like a cap gun. The child screamed with pain, and black smoke exploded from his body in a cloud, enveloping the boy and rushing down into his lungs when he took a deep breath so that he could scream too.*

*Before he could push up the air past his taut vocal chords, they relaxed and the scream turned into a gasp. He was back in the field. The grass was green, the sky blue. At his feet lay a five-year-old boy, barely recognisable as the child from the tree house. This boy had clear brown eyes and rounded cheeks. His skin was smooth and clean, and his fingers looked like the fingers of any other child, with neatly clipped nails.*

*The child shook his head and got to his feet. The toy dog fell from his chest and landed on the grass. His eyes met the boy's, and the only question the boy could come up with was: 'Where...where are we?'*

*The child shrugged. 'In the other place. It's better here.'*

*'But what place is it?'*

*This seemed to bother the child. He looked around with a slight frown, as if he were wondering too. Then his face cleared and he rubbed his nose.*

*'Don't know. Maybe I invented it. Don't know. It's not finished. There's not much here.'*

*Too right. The grass extended towards the horizon in all directions, with not a hint of unevenness to be seen beneath the cloudless blue sky. And yet the boy didn't find this place frightening—quite the reverse. Accustomed as he was to keeping an eye open, fearing attack from every possible hiding place, it was liberating to be able to see in all directions, to breathe in an open space with no risk of a punch in the stomach or a gob of spit landing on his face. When the boy inhaled the clean air of this place, it was as if over the past few years he had forgotten what it was like not to feel tense or to be afraid, but simply to exist. To breathe.*

*He was about to ask the child another question when something invisible seized hold of his cheeks and prevented him from opening his mouth. It hurt, and he screwed his eyes shut. When he opened them he was back in the forest. The policeman was looming over him, and the boy's face was clamped in the iron grip of one enormous hand. The child was lying at his feet, legs bent. The boy noticed that the toy dog was gone before the policeman forced his head back and said, 'Do you hear me?'*

*The boy tried to shake his head, but it was no more than a faint movement. His body felt unreal, split between two worlds. It was only when he saw the Mora knife in the policeman's other hand that he had to accept he was in this world, in the forest, and that he was in deep trouble.*

*However scared he was of the kicks and blows, the pinches and punches in school, he knew the other boys in his class would never think of killing him, whatever they might say about the piggy going to the slaughter. This was different. His limbs went cold and limp when he saw the blade coming closer in his peripheral vision.*

*'I said this hasn't happened,' the policeman said. 'Do you understand?'*

*The man could have asked absolutely anything that required a positive response, and the boy would have squeezed out the same 'Yes' as he did now.*

*'You haven't seen anything, you've never met anyone, you're going to forget this whole thing. And above all...above all you are never going to say anything to anyone.'*

*The boy's mind was paralysed with fear, and he couldn't work out what the right answer was supposed to be. Yes or no?*

*'Are you?' the policeman said, squeezing the boy's face even harder. The boy made a noise that could have meant just about anything, but the policeman nodded and showed him the knife.*

*'I will find you. Remember that. And just so you don't forget, here's a little reminder.'*

*He let go of the boy's face and grabbed his right wrist. Two rapid slashes with the knife and the boy felt a burning sensation in his arm. He didn't dare move a muscle. He saw the policeman pick up the child and carry him off over his shoulder, paying no attention to his broken leg, which was dangling and bouncing as if there were no bones beneath the skin. The child's eyes were still closed, so at least the boy didn't have to meet his gaze.*

*The policeman marched away with the lifeless child. The boy remained where he was for several minutes with one meaningless thought running through his mind.*

The dog was left behind. The dog was left behind. The dog...

*'Rebus,' the boy said eventually, and the sound of his own voice broke the paralysis. 'Rebus, that was his name.' Slowly he raised his right arm and examined the burning, stinging flesh.*

*Two lines scored the skin between his wrist and elbow, two cuts at right angles to one another forming an 'X'. He was marked. He walked home, one step at a time. He never went back to the tree house; he never saw the child again. He never said a word about what had happened. Not to anyone.*

*

I raised the arm covering my eyes, pulled up my shirtsleeve and studied the white scar, the cross that still disfigured my skin. I ran my index finger over the smooth scar tissue, and that was when it happened. Something juddered and shifted, as if a cold draught had passed through the earth's crust, as if the planet itself had *shuddered*. Later on I came to the conclusion that the movement must have happened at that precise moment.

The morning light had been seeping in through the barred window for a couple of hours when I was finally let out. It was past eight o'clock, too late to go to Copenhagen. It didn't matter any more. I was informed that I would receive a summons by post, and that I would be required to attend court at some point in the future. I signed a piece of paper.

A different officer was on duty at the desk where I'd handed in my possessions the previous evening, and he too was interested in the thumb tip.

'What's this?'

'A thumb tip.'

'What's it for?'

'Drug smuggling.'

The joke was not appreciated, but I was allowed to reclaim my belongings, sign another piece of paper and leave Kronoberg. Because of the early hour the car park was virtually empty, and seemed enormous. Though I had spent only half a day in custody, it felt fantastic to walk down the streets in whatever direction I wanted. I have no hesitation in calling the state in which I found myself *happiness*—it was the first time I had experienced it for what seemed like an eternity.

I stopped by the railings at Sergels torg, watching some kids practising their skateboarding skills. The city looked brand-new to me, a gift to enjoy. I assumed that the feeling would soon subside, and I wanted to hang on to it for as long as possible.

I bought a coffee and a croissant at a cafe overlooking the glass obelisk in the fountain. As I sat there gazing at it I realised I'd never actually *seen* it, and what an amazing creation it was. How many meetings must there have been before they decided to put up that particular monstrosity? The things people came up with!

I let my eyes wander over all the people on their way somewhere, still half-asleep or not, carrying bags or not, and I experienced an unusual surge of tenderness—as if I were watching a film, and all those passing by were the minor characters we identify with just a little bit more.

It was only when I got up from the table that I realised how tired I was. I hadn't slept at all during the night, and there was a rushing sound inside my head. The feeling of happiness did indeed begin to fade as I walked along Sveavägen towards Luntmakargatan. I was dreading getting back to my house, to the courtyard and the pressure. No doubt the disappointment at missing the Nordic Championships would also hit me when I returned to my normal abnormal life. The journey from Kronoberg to home had been nothing more than a breathing space, and my movements were heavy as I keyed in the code and pushed open the main door.

As soon as I entered the stairwell I noticed that something was different, and this was confirmed when I stepped out into the yard. The pressure was gone. The blue sky that had covered the rooftops like a tightly sealed lid was now open and distant.

Something crunched beneath my feet as I crossed the courtyard. Fragments of something resembling gravel were scattered across the tarmac. I crouched down and picked up a few pieces to examine them more closely.

There were a couple of small chunks of cement, I could see that, but the others were trickier. I turned them over and squeezed them for a little while before I eventually realised they were lumps of putty from the windows.

*

I slept right through my day of freedom. I must have been mentally exhausted, because when I woke at dusk I got up to go to the toilet, then curled up on my mattress and went straight back to sleep. I didn't wake up properly until eight o'clock in the evening, and that was because something was banging above my head.

I lay there listening with the covers pulled right up to my chin. I heard something sliding across the roof, then a faint thud as it hit the ground. It sounded soft, like a piece of rotten fruit. The thought of fruit made me realise I was starving, so I shuffled over to the fridge, opened the door and squinted into the bright light.

I found a chunk of Falun sausage, half a jar of lingonberry jam and a tube of fish roe, with just about enough left to make one sandwich. A shrivelled carrot lay all alone in the vegetable drawer. I picked up the sausage, dipped it in the jam and ate it raw. This increased rather than diminished my hunger, so I got dressed. Potatoes. I would go and buy some potatoes. I had never cooked potatoes, but it was time to cross the borderline into the adult world. Potatoes. The very word encapsulated maturity, responsibility.

It was gloomy when I got outside; maybe the light had been broken by the same movement that had loosened the putty. I had only the glow from my neighbours' windows to guide me as I made my way down, and I almost stood on something that was lying on the bottom step.

At first I thought it was a stone, but when I crouched down and took a closer look I saw that it was a bird. A small bird. I've never been much good at that kind of thing, and as I said, it was getting dark, but maybe...a bullfinch? I nudged it with my foot, but it didn't move.

Apart from the fact that it was obviously dead it looked unharmed, which suggested that a cat wasn't to blame. Not that I'd ever seen a cat around. It crossed my mind that birds must die of old age at some point, and maybe this bird had done just that. In fact it was pretty strange that you didn't see more dead animals in general.

I edged the little bird off the step with the toe of my shoe and carried on across the courtyard. I hadn't gone more than a couple of paces when I saw a dark lump in front of my feet. Another bird. Only now did I connect the phenomenon with the thudding sound I had heard, and I walked around the house to where it had come from.

I was right. A gull lay flat out on the black tarmac. Its white wings glowed in the darkness, and a sour taste filled my mouth when I realised it wasn't dead. The tips of its wings were twitching spasmodically, and its beak opened and closed as it gasped for air. When I sat down beside it, it moved its head a fraction and made a faint hissing noise. A star was reflected in its black eye, and I looked up at the night sky hoping to find some clue to what had happened.

The sky looked perfectly normal, a dark blue blanket studded with stars—nothing that might explain why a number of birds had plummeted to the ground. The gull kept on hissing and cheeping as its wings flexed.

*Can I?*

No, I couldn't bring myself to grab hold of the bird and wring its neck, though it was clearly suffering. I stood up, feeling dizzy as I made my way to the door leading to the street. I stopped, turned around. The gull looked horribly lonely as it lay there in agony in the dark courtyard. I knew that white shape would remain seared into my retina like an open sore if I didn't do something.

I was irresistibly drawn towards the laundry block. It was easy, as if a moving walkway was helping me along. I unlocked the door, switched on the light and went inside. My eyes immediately went to the shower room door. There was something stuck on it. A note.

*Closed for maintenance until further notice*, it said in the same neat letters I recognised from the TV ad; the woman from the Dead Couple must have written it. I took a deep breath and pushed down the handle. Locked. I put my ear to the door and listened. Nothing—but when I covered my other ear I thought I could hear a rhythmic rushing sound, like waves retreating from the shoreline.

I knew what I had seen a few days earlier: the crack in the ceiling and something emerging from it. And yet I was seized by a compulsion to *get into that room*, a pull that I experienced on a purely physical level, as if something had taken hold of my arteries and tried to reel me in. The image of the gull flashed before my eyes, and I remembered why I had come into the laundry block in the first place.

The only thing I could find that might be of any use was a floor-scraper, a rubber blade attached to a long handle, used to sweep water towards the drain. I picked it up and went back outside, hoping the gull had died while I was gone.

No such luck. The wings were still moving pointlessly across the tarmac with a dry, lifeless sound. I went over, trying to swallow the lump in my throat without success. Then I placed the rubber blade on its neck. The gull's feet paddled, and it gave a sad, strangled cry. I gritted my teeth and pressed down. I heard a brittle crunch. The feet twitched a couple of times, then the bird lay still.

I propped the scraper against the wall; I didn't want to go back to the laundry block. Then I stood there with my head down, contemplating the dead bird. I held a minute's vigil as I sent up a silent, pathetic prayer: *May you soar across an endless sky*, or something like that.

*

During the days that followed I began to sort out my life, bit by bit. I did a big shop and filled up the fridge, I went through the phone book making a note of restaurants that might be suitable for table magic, and I put together a folder of photographs and testimonial letters. I also started practising a close-up routine focused on entertainment rather than pure technical skill, something more like the magic I often performed on the street.

Birds kept falling from the sky. From time to time I heard a thud as yet another feathered body landed on the tarmac. When I went out in the mornings there were usually several corpses littering the courtyard. At about two o'clock a man came along and cleared them away.

One day I sat by the window and watched him. He was around sixty years old, with puffy cheeks and a beer belly. A circlet of grey hair framed an otherwise bald pate. With a sorrowful expression and slow movements he shuffled from one dead bird to the next, placing them gently in a supermarket carrier bag. There was something of the fairytale or everyday mythology about the scene, which the man concluded by tying together the handles of the bag and dropping it in the garbage chute.

Gradually the number of dead birds diminished, and after a week the phenomenon had more or less come to an end. Maybe the birds had worked it out, just as eider ducks learn to avoid islands where there are hunters. The thuds grew more and more infrequent.

Once, and only once, I witnessed the actual event. I was on my way home from my daily visit to Kungstornet, and when I opened the door to the courtyard I glanced up at the sky just as a crow appeared between the roofs. I stood there open-mouthed as I saw it lose its ability to fly.

The best comparison I can come up with is that of a fish in an aquarium when the water suddenly drains away and the fish falls to the bottom. It doesn't matter how much it thrashes around—it has lost a medium against which to brace itself.

That's exactly what happened to the crow. Suddenly and for no apparent reason, it dropped like a stone. It flapped its wings frenetically, trying to gain height, but it was if it couldn't get a grip on the air. Nothing slowed its acceleration towards the ground, and after a couple of seconds it landed headfirst a couple of metres in front of me, then lay mercifully still.

As I believe this narrative has already shown, the extent to which people are prepared to close their eyes to anything unusual or downright abnormal is astonishing—as long as it doesn't directly affect them. Admittedly the dead birds in the courtyard were unpleasant, but not so unpleasant or weird that I considered giving up my house. I kept on going.

*

I had visited most restaurants in the Norrmalm area of the city, produced my folder and given a few examples of how I could entertain their clients, but no one was interested. The general view was that people wanted to eat in peace, rather than having—as one unpleasant owner put it—some buffoon spoiling their enjoyment over coffee.

It was depressing, but I hadn't given up. A couple of places had shown a vague interest and had liked my tricks, but they didn't have the nerve to go for something so different, even though I was asking for little more than a token sum as payment, in the hope that there would be tips. But no. Not just at the moment. Not quite like that.

I still intended to do the same in Östermalm before I abandoned the project. One evening in early October I was sitting at my desk going through the phone book when I heard raised voices. I went over to the window and opened the blind a fraction.

The door to the laundry block was ajar, and a strip of light sliced across the yard. That was where the voices were coming from. I couldn't make out who was talking or what was being said, but from the tone it sounded like an argument.

The evening air was chilly when I stepped outside, crept down the stairs and towards the strip of light. By now I could hear disjointed phrases: 'Not some kind of exclusive deal just to…have to work out a plan…no idea how much it costs…don't know what the consequences might be…'

I was only a couple of metres from the door when it flew open. The woman who had sold the TV to me came out, but stopped dead when she caught sight of me. I couldn't read her expression because the light was behind her, but her stance suggested that anger outweighed surprise.

'Are you eavesdropping?'

I could have stood up for myself, pointed out that this was a communal area and that I was perfectly entitled to be there, but the sharpness in her voice made me shrink.

'I was just…going to book a slot,' I said.

'Right. So where's your key?'

I desperately needed to do some washing. I had more or less run out of clean underwear, but I could hardly use that as proof of my intentions. A key in my hand would have been better.

Behind the woman I could see that the door to the shower room was ajar. I also saw that there were at least three other people in the laundry room: the woman's husband, Elsa, and the man who had cleared away the dead birds. They had all turned to face the door.

In spite of the raised voices, there was something *blissful* about their faces, and Elsa appeared several years younger. The harsh light from the fluorescent tube on the ceiling was transformed when it caught her skin, making her look as if she was lit from the inside.

And then there was that pull. The pull from inside the shower room that made me take a step towards the woman in the doorway, even though her body language made it clear that I needed to keep away.

'What are you doing?' she said, also taking a step forward so that we were face to face.

'I need…a shower,' I said, pointing to the laundry block. The woman shook her head. 'The shower room is closed. For an indefinite period.'

With those words she turned on her heel, went back inside and slammed the door behind her, as if she had forgotten that she was on her way out. I remained standing there for a few seconds; I could feel the pull, but I didn't dare move any closer to the door.

*

That was the evening when I gathered what strength I had and wrote down what I had formulated in my mind during my night in the cell. After I had written the concluding sentences—*He never said a word about what had happened. Not to anyone*—I read through the whole thing from beginning to end.

Loneliness has a tendency to make us into interpreters of signs. We see connections and symmetries; we attribute significance to meaningless coincidences. I'm convinced that the first astrologers were hermits with only the stars for company, and that their observations were elevated to the status of a national religion at a much later stage.

We seek meaning in whatever is in front of us. That's how it was for me, anyway, as I sat there with that terrible story on the desk before me. I became more and more certain that it was somehow linked to what was happening in the laundry block, that the two phenomena were branches of the same tree.

It would eventually transpire that I was right, but on that night in October it was no more than a feeling, filling me with a presentiment of evil as I sat there leafing back and forth through my notepad.

I had heard my neighbours leaving the laundry block, and when I peered out through the slats of the blind, I could see that it was in darkness. I was on my way out in defiance of the warnings to find out what was going on when the phone rang. I picked up the receiver and said, 'Hello, John here.'

'He's turned up, hasn't he?'

'Who?'

'You know who.'

'Sigge?'

'M-hmm.'

'Not as far as I know. So what does he look like, this Sigge?'

'How the hell should I know?'

'You haven't met him either?'

'How could I possibly have met him? I mean, he hasn't arrived yet. I've asked you over and over again: *Is Sigge there? Has Sigge arrived yet?* No, you've said. Every time. Have you been lying to me?'

'No, I...'

'No. So how the hell could I have met him?'

'I just assumed...'

'Well, don't. Don't assume anything. That makes life simpler in every possible way.'

He hung up. Even if I was still convinced he was really looking for someone else, there was something familiar about his voice. I lay awake for a long time, going through everyone in my past and trying to work out who that voice could possibly belong to. When that didn't help I moved on to voices on the radio and TV, but I had no luck there either. He remained a stranger who had chosen to contact me, for some reason.

*

The following morning, before I went over to Östermalm, I gathered up enough underwear, trousers and shirts to make up a load and crossed the courtyard with a full IKEA bag over my shoulder.

The laundry block looked just the same as always, except for one thing. The flimsy lock on the shower room door had been reinforced with a new bar from which a heavy padlock dangled. The notice was still there: *Closed for maintenance until further notice.*

The current laundry slot was free, so I booked it. Before I loaded my washing into the machine, I went over to the shower room door, put my ear against it and closed my eyes. I could just make out the distant surge of waves, an enormous machine, or the breathing of the rock. The darkness behind my eyelids deepened, and gradually my breathing started to match the rhythm of the sound.

As the perception of my own body—its weight and reality—diminished, another began to grow, and yet I was still able to think and to define the fragile sense that crept up on me, like the scent of a flower far away in a dark forest.

It was similar to the feeling that had come over me on election day when I cast my vote. *Belonging.* The realisation that I was a part of something much bigger, that I was connected to all the people on earth, and that my life was neither lonely nor meaningless, because I was a part of the greater community within the darkness that surrounds us all.

It was a pleasant sensation and I wanted to hang on to it, but it faded away inexorably and my breathing rose to the surface, until I was breathing only for myself and my body's need for oxygen. When I pulled back from the door my ear was hurting; it had been sucked hard against the silent surface.

I felt dizzy, and swayed where I stood. I slumped down onto the IKEA bag to stop myself from falling over, and sat there for a while on top of my dirty clothes before I pulled myself together sufficiently to load the machine, add detergent and close the door. As the drum began to rotate, the water inside making a noise not unlike the one I had heard from inside the shower room, I left the laundry block and went home to sluice myself down.

As I stood naked in my tub in front of the bathroom mirror, squeezing the sponge over my skin, I tried to make sense of what I had just experienced. Given the circumstances I never ruled out autosuggestion—the idea that the rushing sound came from the water pipes, for example. But if that was the case, why were my neighbours behaving so strangely?

I dried myself with a towel that smelled musty, and decided that the only reasonable explanation was that there was something in the shower room. Something that had forced its way out of the crack, something that caused the birds to fall from the sky, and made the neighbours uncooperative, because they wanted to keep it for themselves.

But what? *What*?

The question continued to occupy my mind as I unloaded the machine and distributed the clothes between two tumble dryers to speed things up. There was a silent, watchful presence behind my back. Something that wanted me, for some reason. I tugged at the padlock, but the bar was bolted to the door and impossible to force without proper tools. I gave up and went back to my house, where I tried to come up with some suitable patter to accompany the trick known as Invisible Palm.

At one-thirty I returned to the laundry room and retrieved my clothes. I was just cleaning one of the filters when the outside door opened. I closed the dryer and stood there with a ball of fluff clutched in my fist.

The person who walked in with a laundry basket under his arm was the smartly dressed man who had said it was nice to see a light on in my house in the evenings. He didn't notice me, because his eyes were fixed on the shower room door. It would be an exaggeration to say that he was looking scruffy, but in comparison to his previous standard, he had deteriorated. Several strands of hair were sticking out, his shirt was creased, and he had dirt under the fingernails of his right hand, which was wrapped in a bandage.

I cleared my throat and he gave a start, as if I had interrupted an internal dialogue. Something in his eyes made me focus on his forehead as I said, 'Hello again.'

'I'm sorry, do we know one another?'

'I live in the house over there.'

He appeared to be retrieving information from an archive right at the back of his mind, and something of the deep glow in his eyes disappeared as he said, 'Oh, yes, of course. How's it going?'

'Fine,' I said. 'Although I no longer have a shower.' I nodded at the padlock.

The man glanced at the door and pursed his lips. I ventured a step further, and asked, 'Do you know what's happened?'

He widened his eyes and shook his head, a gesture so obviously false that the needle on a lie detector would have gone crazy. It's possible to untangle small lies, but big lies are knots so tightly tied that you need an axe to undo them. I took out my axe and got straight to the point: 'What are you actually doing in here? What's in the shower room?'

The man put his finger to his lips and hissed: 'Sssh! Sssh!' He glanced at his laundry basket. I was about to push him harder, when he suddenly yelled, 'Get out of here! Get out of here! You're young! Get out of here!'

'What does the fact that I'm young have to do with...'

The man waved his hand in the air as if to add weight to his words, 'Get out of here! Just do as I say!'

We stood there staring at one another, then I picked up my IKEA bag and headed for the door. As I passed the man I looked down into his basket. The clothes that had been folded last time were now in a heap, although they didn't look dirty.

Something glinted at the bottom of the basket. The clothes were only there to hide the fact that the man had brought a knife with him, a knife he had glanced at when I started to question him. I decided it was best to leave it for now.

I gave him a nod as I walked out, but he just stood there with trembling lips and refused to look at me.

*

Before I started to sort out my life, my existence had resembled that of a jellyfish. The currents carried me wherever they wished, and external impulses were immediately transmitted to the very heart of me. This amoeba-like tendency remained, but I was fighting it. I refused to allow the incident in the laundry block to take over my thoughts, but instead stuck to my plan for the day. I gathered up my publicity material, my magic paraphernalia and my list of addresses. My first port of call was the Mona Lisa restaurant on Birger Jarlsgatan, a mid-range Italian place.

What kind of person do you have to be to *sell yourself*? It's a question of promising too much and painting a glowing picture of how things will be if someone decides to hire you. I have never had that skill; instead I prefer to deliver a gloomy prognosis, suggesting that the ship is more than likely to sink with me at the helm. It went against my nature to show off and promise success.

And yet it had to be done, because I really, really wanted to do magic. I loved magic. The moment of amazement when the audience's grasp of reality is called into question, when the object that was *here* has in some impossible way ended up *there*. Those priceless seconds before they ask themselves, 'So how did he do that?'—the seconds when magic actually exists.

I headed for Birger Jarlsgatan through the Brunkeberg Tunnel, giving myself a good talking-to and trying to think positively. Twenty metres into the tunnel I felt as if something was trying to get inside my head, like another person's distant voice when you're in a deep sleep. I stopped and tried to work out which direction it was coming from.

I pinned it down to a section of the rock face, and then, picturing it from above, I worked out that the shower room must be directly behind it. Only a few metres of the Brunkeberg Ridge separated me from whatever was in there. There was no sign of anyone else in the tunnel, so I went over and laid my hand and my cheek on the cold surface of the rock.

At the risk of appearing inconsistent, I must revise my earlier reference to sleep. It was as if I myself was fully alert, yet a dream was trying to penetrate my consciousness by osmosis. A sleeper calling to someone who was awake. The image that came into my mind was as fragile as a butterfly's wing, but it glowed with absolute clarity.

I was sitting in a shabby, comfortable armchair. On my knee sat a young man in Doc Martens, jeans with turned-up cuffs, and a bomber jacket. His head was shaved. A skinhead. In his eyes I could see latent violence but also a certain intelligence.

It was as if I had been split in two. The larger part of me was standing with my cheek resting on a cold, damp wall of rock, while the remainder was in the armchair with the skinhead's considerable weight pressing down on my thighs. My right hand appeared in my mind's eye. It was wrapped in a bandage, and there was dirt under my fingernails. I was the smartly dressed man who was no longer quite so smart.

My hand tenderly caressed the skinhead's cheek. He looked into my eyes and gave me a smile filled with love, then leaned forward and hugged me. I felt his arms around my neck, heard the rustle of the bomber jacket as he held me close. His cheek touched mine and then there was nothing but the cold rock. The image was gone.

I stood there in the tunnel blinking, whole once more. I thought I understood two things. First of all, I had been given a glimpse into the smartly dressed man's fantasy. Secondly, the reality of that fantasy was probably considerably more powerful when it wasn't impeded by a two-metre thick wall of rock.

I am not in the habit of judging people, yet I found the dream quite repulsive. If I was forced to choose the kind of person I least wanted to snuggle up with, a skinhead would be pretty high on the list. I had encountered gangs of them a few times when I was performing street magic in the Old Town, and they really hadn't come across as being particularly cuddly.

Footsteps echoed through the tunnel from the direction of Östermalm. I detached myself from the wall and began to walk. After about thirty metres I met a guy with a sunbed tan in a yellow T-shirt so tight it made his bulging muscles look like a physical deformity. When he had gone past I turned around, curious as to whether he would react to the scene pouring out of the wall, or if I would be the only one to experience it.

I saw him slow down, like someone who thinks they can hear their name being called from far away. But he didn't stop, and within a couple of metres he was marching along purposefully once more, his meaty thighs swishing against one another, arms swinging. I guessed that, unlike me, he didn't concern himself with anything formless and difficult to comprehend. I carried on towards Birger Jarlsgatan.

*

The Mona Lisa restaurant had opened so recently that it wasn't in the phone book, but it had come to my attention through posters stuck up here and there. I didn't know whether its newness was a good thing or not; no doubt it depended on the owner, as usual.

When I pushed open the door I was informed by a man in a white shirt and black trousers that unfortunately lunch was over and they would be open again at five. He was vacuuming away, and I got the impression that lunch hadn't been particularly busy; only one table bore any trace of customers.

'That's not why I'm here,' I said. 'Would it be possible to have a word with the owner?'

The man straightened up and his expression changed as he switched from one role to another. 'That's me,' he said. 'What's it about?' I too changed from someone making a general enquiry to experienced entertainer. I walked towards the man holding out my hand, so that our new characters could meet.

'My name is John Lindqvist. I'm a magician.'

The man shook my hand and raised his coarse, dark eyebrows. It seemed likely that he really did come from Italian stock. He was around forty years old, with a short, compact physique and eyes that looked cunning, friendly and tired. A charmer who was past his prime, or a mummy's boy with unfulfilled ambitions.

'Roberto,' he said; his hand was small but surprisingly strong. 'A magician?'

'Yes. Or rather an entertainer who does magic. Can you spare a few minutes?'

Roberto shrugged, and we sat down opposite one another at a table. I showed him my credentials and my testimonial letters; I swept my arm around the room, visualising an evening with every table packed; and I explained how my magic could entertain customers while they were waiting for their food, or how it could be the icing on the cake at the end of a successful evening.

Roberto's gaze was distant, and I hoped he was lost in contemplation of the image I had conjured up. Maybe it was just the thought of a full restaurant that appealed to him, or maybe it was the whole package. He scratched the back of his neck and said, 'I don't know. How much are you asking for?'

This was the third time I had managed to get to this point, and I assured him that I would be happy with forty kronor an hour, plus tips. Pitching so low might have been a mistake, because Roberto frowned as if he smelled a rat. 'Forty?'

'Yes,' I said, correcting any possible miscalculation by adding: 'To start with. Then we can see how it goes. If it's a success, we can renegotiate.'

Roberto's expression cleared and he nodded. Once again he looked around the room as if he was finding it difficult to picture the scene I had described. Then he asked the devastating question, the one I knew would come up sooner or later: 'Have you done this before? At another restaurant?'

I had considered lying, even faking a letter from some non-existent restaurant, but it was far too easy to check up on that kind of thing, and if I was caught out, my chances of performing would be zero. The word might even spread among restaurant owners, warning each other to look out for a con artist going around asking for a job.

'No,' I said. 'Not in a restaurant, but I've done several hundred performances in front of an audience.'

I didn't mention the fact that at least ninety-five per cent of those performances had been in the street, in front of an audience that dispersed faster than it gathered. Roberto sat in silence for a while, his chin resting on his hand. I expected him to tell me he wasn't interested, but his words were a fraction more encouraging: 'So what exactly is it that you do?'

I am no longer a member of the Swedish Magic Circle, so I can't be thrown out. And yet the magician's etiquette remains, and it forces me to paraphrase words that might reveal the secret. I pretended to search my jacket pockets and hid the gimmick in my hand, then asked, 'Do you have a ten-kronor note?'

Roberto took out his wallet and handed me a note.

'Okay,' I said, folding it up in preparation. 'If I really was a magician, if I really could do magic...what would you want me to do with this ten-kronor note?'

Roberto thought for a moment, then much to my relief he gave the right answer—the one around sixty per cent of people give: 'Turn it into a hundred.'

I pretended to be worried at the prospect of this challenging task. Roberto folded his arms and leaned back, pleased at his own cleverness in putting me on the spot. I folded the note in the way I had practised so often, talking all the while about the difficulty of making something look like something else, but how, in the manner of an origami expert, I would try to make his ten-kronor note at least *resemble* a hundred.

The arms that Roberto had folded so confidently dropped to his sides and his smile disappeared from his lips as I opened out the hundred-kronor note and placed it on the table in front of him. Though I now risked going home ninety kronor down, I allowed him to pick it up and examine it. Fortunately he put it down again, and I was able to repeat the trick in reverse, explaining that the resemblance had now passed and he could have his ten kronor back.

The momentary confusion had lasted a few seconds longer than average in Roberto's case, but now the original note was on the table in front of him he asked the inevitable question: 'How the hell did you do that?'

I gave a modest shrug. 'Practice. And a little bit of magic.'

There was a brief silence, then Roberto said, 'Okay.'

'Okay, what?'

'Okay, you can do your magic here. We'll give it a go.'

My heart started pounding and I had to make a real effort to keep my voice steady as I said, as indifferently as possible, 'Great. When do you want me to start?'

We talked for a while and I forced myself to nod and murmur in agreement rather than jumping up and dancing around, waving my hands in the air. We agreed that he would put up a poster and insert a note in the menu announcing that from six o'clock on Thursday evening—in three days' time—the multi-talented award-winning magician John Lindqvist would be performing magic to entertain and amaze the clientele at Mona Lisa.

It was four o'clock by the time we stood up and shook hands. We exchanged phone numbers and wished each other all the best until we met again on Thursday.

When I stepped out onto Birger Jarlsgatan, the city had changed completely, as if a telescopic lens had been switched for a wide-angle. Buildings that had seemed flat and nondescript a little while ago were now three-dimensional and full of elaborate detail, while the people passing by were no longer extras but leading characters, each one involved in a drama of their own.

I dared to see the world as diverse and full of promise because at long last I was on the way to taking my place within it, to becoming someone. John Lindqvist, magician and entertainer at the Mona Lisa Restaurant!

*

I didn't want to go back through the Brunkeberg Tunnel; in fact I didn't even want to go home. In a burst of lightheartedness I went into the Rigoletto and bought a ticket for *Rambo: First Blood Part II*. It was showing in one of the smaller cinemas in the basement, and I was all alone as I allowed myself to wallow in the images of Stallone racing around, killing people and blowing things up. I watched but didn't really see, because I was busy redefining my role in life.

By the time I emerged onto Kungsgatan as dusk was gathering, another veil had fallen from my eyes, and everything was so *clear*. The rigid, sprayed hairstyles bobbing by enveloped me in a wash of phthalates that made me feel nauseous. All my senses were on full alert, and the world seemed almost unbearably rich in detail. To get home faster and avoid too many faces, I went up the steps to Malmskillnadsgatan and then down to Tunnelgatan.

I hurried across the courtyard without even glancing at the laundry block, and when I had closed my door behind me I let out a long sigh. I didn't feel tired or trapped as I had on other days; on the contrary, I was fulfilled, I was happy, I was *happening*, and I felt like sweeping everything off my desk to start working on a new act right away.

I pulled myself together, though. I tidied away newspapers and cups, my notepad and pens. Wiped the desk with the dishcloth. Then I methodically set out my close-up mat and magic paraphernalia. I was about to sit down, then I remembered I would be standing up when I performed.

I replaced the desk with a restaurant table, turned the bookcase into five or six expectant faces looking up at me. I tossed three coins between my hands and said, 'Hi, my name is John Lindqvist. Through intensive practice I've learned how to teleport coins through my blood vessels…'

I went over Daryl's Elbow, Knee and Neck many times, changing my patter so that it flowed more smoothly, practising the movements and facial expressions, bowing to acknowledge imaginary applause and feeling happier than I had for a long time.

*

I don't remember much about what I did during those three days, apart from practising. Oh yes, one thing: one afternoon when my fingers were stiff after hours of manipulation and my head was spinning from the sound of my own voice, I took myself off to the City Library to read up about the Brunkeberg Tunnel.

My fingers had softened and my head had quietened down as I

walked along the rows of books about Stockholm, running my hand along their spines. It took me half an hour to amass the following information from a range of sources.

The tunnel had been excavated between 1884 and 1886 under the leadership of Knut Lindmark, who had achieved great success with the Katarina Lift a couple of years earlier. His aim was to make it easier for the residents of Stockholm to travel between different parts of the city. For a fee, of course.

The construction of the tunnel turned out to be a more difficult and more expensive project. There were serious complications on the west side, the side where I lived, because the walls repeatedly collapsed. Lindmark overcame the problem by hiring ridiculously expensive machines from England that ran all night, freezing the water in the unstable rock so that a small amount could be excavated the following day, until the water thawed and the machines had to be started up again.

What happened next is shrouded in darkness. A couple of people died or disappeared during the final phase of construction. When the tunnel was opened, hardly anybody wanted to use it, even though it made it much easier to move between Norrmalm and Östermalm. People preferred to cross the steep Brunkeberg Ridge rather than go through the tunnel.

Lindmark was worried about the tunnel, for some unknown reason. He didn't want people to use it, and in spite of the enormous sums of money he had spent, he actually tried to get it closed. He failed, and eventually took his own life.

It was just after six when I strolled home along Sveavägen. The leaves on the trees down below the Observatory shimmered in shades of yellow, and a few kids were hanging around by the empty pool. From the McDonald's behind me I heard someone shout: 'I need ketchup!'

My mood was the polar opposite of the feeling I had had on Kungsgatan. I was numb, mute. The impressions drifted by without becoming anything other than what they were: yellow trees, kids smoking, someone who wanted ketchup.

One of the lectures being advertised on the Workers' Educational Association noticeboard was 'A New Social Democracy?', and suddenly it seemed to me that the election in which I had voted with such enthusiasm had been totally unnecessary. If things are only themselves, and people too in the long run, then how can concepts such as solidarity and 'the people's home', the idea that society should be like a family where everyone contributes, have any meaning? This is all built on a mystification of society itself, the idea that it can be spiritualised, when in fact nothing exists but kids, trees and ketchup, silently changing colour and place.

As I turned into Tunnelgatan and ambled towards the black mouth of the Brunkeberg Tunnel, I was struck by a new respect for this anomaly in our city—a respect that wasn't easy to separate from fear. I saw the steam-driven freezing machines pumping away night after night in the darkness of the tunnel, and the labourers hacking away at the rock, one swing of the pickaxe and one thrust with the spade at a time, constantly terrified that the walls would collapse. What had they seen? What had they encountered? What was it that had driven Knut Lindmark to ultimate despair and down into the depths of Lake Mälaren?

Just as I was about to turn off Tunnelgatan and up into Luntmakargatan, the tunnel doors opened and a fat woman with a small flowering pot plant in one hand emerged. I caught a couple of lines of a song from inside the tunnel. The busker was in his spot, singing 'Somebody Up There Must Like Me'.

The world shifted, and for a moment it seemed unpleasantly significant and coherent. I stood there with my mouth hanging open and the woman with the pot plant stopped in front of me. She looked at me, then back at the tunnel, before asking, 'Are you all right?'

With her generous bosom and belly and the flower in her hand, she reminded me of the subject of a Rubens' painting who had ended up in the wrong century. A face that might have been pretty was lost in puffy cheeks. I nodded and said, 'Fine, thanks. How about you?'

'Not so good, since you ask.'

The question had been automatic, and I didn't want an answer, but it turned out that the woman lived in the same place as me, and as we walked she told me she had just moved into a one-room apartment. Her previous home had been much bigger, but long-term illness and a dispute with the national insurance office had left her broke.

She refused to let me go, and stood there in the stairwell listing all her problems: obesity, heart failure, bullying at work...Eventually she started to cry. It was terrible.

What would I have done if I had known then that I would sleep with this woman just a few months later? Screamed, probably. But people change. I didn't scream when it happened. Well, I did, but not for that reason.

In a brief pause between her sobs I gabbled, 'Lots to do!' and left her weeping and clutching her little plant. My empathy was seriously underdeveloped at that time, and a while later I had more or less forgotten the encounter. I spent the rest of the evening practising. Getting ready for my premiere.

*

That Thursday was a big deal for me. I had done hundreds of street performances, sometimes as many as ten or twelve in one day, and my throat would feel like minced beef afterwards—all I could do was whisper. But street magic is different. You have to use big gestures, hammer home the key points and effects at regular intervals to capture and hold the audience's attention. They have to stay until the performance is over, otherwise you don't make any money. Okay, occasionally people would drop some cash in the hat earlier on, but the real clinking of coins—or, if you were lucky, the rustle of notes—came after the final bow.

Things would be different at the Mona Lisa. I would be able to do what I was best at, close-up magic, and have time to build up the effects with only a minimal risk that someone would leave before I'd finished. It was a privilege and a responsibility. I was already yawning by three o'clock; that's what I do when I'm nervous.

At quarter past five I was dressed—black trousers, white shirt, waistcoat, bow tie—and had packed what I needed in my doctor's bag—decks of cards, four five-kronor coins, foam balls in a range of colours, the specially prepared salt pot, the close-up mat and the laser pistol. Before heading off, I allowed myself five minutes sitting at my desk. I placed my hands on my knees, closed my eyes and tried to visualise a successful evening.

It didn't go well. Instead of beaming faces and deafening applause, a room pushed its way in. The cell where I had spent the night. However hard I tried to conjure up the restaurant and its clientele, I kept coming back to the loneliness of the cell, the night that had ended in clarity.

Perhaps it was just as well. When I got to my feet I was calmer than I had been all day. Even the yawning had stopped.

Ten minutes later I arrived at the restaurant, and got a kick I hadn't been expecting. Behind the glass door I saw a beautiful handwritten notice.

*This Evening:*
*Magical Entertainment*
*From*
*John Lindqvist*
*At Your Table!*
*Welcome*

I stood there for quite a while, staring at the words. It wasn't exactly a jumbotron, but it was the first time I'd seen my name in writing like that, a message to the world: *Here he is! Come and see him!* When I had finished gazing I went inside and complimented Roberto on the sign. He smiled and told me it was his mother's work. Of course. However, the corners of his mouth drooped when he said, 'Only two reservations tonight. A party of six and a party of four.'

'So what's it usually like?'

He shrugged, and I could tell that he'd been hoping for a more immediate effect now that he'd hired a magician. The place was empty, and I realised how naive I'd been. Maybe it was the street magic that had led me astray, because I had kind of assumed that people would come. There are always people around; you just have to capture their interest.

Roberto disappeared into the kitchen and I was at something of a loss, unsure of what to do. I considered going to sit in the corner at the back, but that felt weird. When the customers came in I would be waiting there like a vulture observing a lion, biding my time until it finished so that I could do my vulture-thing.

I went around the bar and into the kitchen, where I found Roberto deep in conversation with the cook. There was a chair next to the dishwasher, plus a table with a half-full ashtray on it. I sat down, opened my bag and rummaged among my things. Roberto was on his way back into the restaurant when he caught sight of me and nodded. I nodded back; I was obviously in the right place.

The cook came over and introduced himself as Miguel. I stood up and gestured towards the chair. 'Have I taken your seat?'

'No problem. You are...magician?'

He had a strong Spanish accent: 'a' became 'e', and he pronounced words with the stress on the final syllable. Probl*em*. Magici*an*.

'That's right.'

Miguel had a broad face with small eyes; he looked almost Indian. He nodded slowly, as if we shared a secret. Then he held his hands up in the air and said, 'Hocus pocus!' I responded with 'Abracadabra!' With that our conversation was over, and Miguel returned to his kitchen.

Six o'clock. I wished I'd brought something to read, my walkman, anything. I didn't feel good, just sitting here waiting. My fingers had been supple and ready to amaze; now they were beginning to stiffen. I took out my deck of cards and began to play patience—Aces Up.

At six-thirty Roberto came into the kitchen and said, 'Okay.'

'Okay?'

'They're waiting.'

Three men and a woman, casually dressed, were sitting at a window table. As I walked towards them with three five-kronor coins in my hand, I couldn't help thinking: *What the hell am I doing? This is crazy!* Pushing the thought aside, I plastered on a self-assured smile as I took up my position at the end of the table and said, 'Good evening—welcome! My name is John, and I'm pleased to offer you some magical entertainment.'

From the guests' reaction I realised they hadn't seen the sign on the door or the note in the menu. They looked at one another as if trying to ascertain whether this was okay or not.

If there was one thing I'd learned while performing on the street, it was never apologise, never hesitate. I had intended to begin with Elbow, Knee and Neck, but that trick required a thirty-second build-up before anything magical happened. I needed something more immediate right now to stop them deciding that no, it wasn't okay.

I slipped two of the coins in my pocket and passed the third from one hand to the other as I asked, 'If I went to Australia and did this, the Australians would probably fall off their chairs—do you know why?'

The question aroused their interest enough to stop them wondering—temporarily at least—whether they really wanted to be entertained. I placed the coin between the painfully acquired calluses on my right hand, sent up a rapid silent prayer that it would fly, then said, 'Well, they live on the other side of the world, so when they do it, it looks like this,' and then I squeezed. My hands were slightly sweaty, which was an advantage for this particular trick. The coin shot half a metre up in the air and landed perfectly in my left hand.

The group relaxed as if a cooling breeze had blown over them, and a couple of them smiled in a mixture of relief and admiration. I might be an unexpected adjunct to their meal, but at least I seemed to know what I was doing. The atmosphere changed as they leaned back and became receptive. I took out the other two coins and said, 'Through years of practice I've learned how to teleport coins through my blood vessels. Could I borrow a hand? It doesn't matter if it's still attached to an arm...'

And so on.

I finished off with the ten-kronor note that turns into a hundred, bowed in acknowledgement of their applause, said, 'Enjoy your evening,' and left the table. When I got back to the kitchen I felt as if I'd done an entire evening on stage at the famous Hamburger Börs, even though I'd only been gone for eight minutes, according to the clock. Only then did I realise that I hadn't received any tips. Not necessarily because the people I'd performed for were mean—it was just that there was nothing in what I said or did to suggest that tips might be appropriate. No hat, so to speak.

I would have to think about that. For the moment I was just happy that everything had gone well, and that I was actually capable of entertaining people under these conditions.

When Roberto came in twenty minutes later to tell me that the larger group had arrived, my fingers had already begun to itch; I couldn't wait to get started again. Like all other forms of pleasure, performing magic is addictive, thanks to the kick you get from people's amazement and appreciation.

The second round went even better than the first. These clients were relatively well dressed, and seemed to have come straight from some kind of conference. They were after something cool, and I can confidently say that I delivered. I was feeling relaxed after having broken down the barrier with my first performance, and I was able to push things further, include the audience in more of my tricks. They didn't seem to know each other all that well, but experiencing my illusions together drew them a little closer, and I could feel it.

When it was over and they had applauded warmly, the man who seemed to be the informal leader of the group said, 'I've seen this kind of thing before, in LA, but you were much better. I'm Hasse, by the way.'

I shook his outstretched hand, gave a modest shrug and was about to walk away when Hasse touched my arm and asked, 'Are you here on Saturday?'

'Yes...why?'

'A gang of us from work are having a night out, about ten of us—I was thinking we could come here, if you're performing then?'

I was about to go and check with Roberto, but he was standing behind the bar and had obviously heard the conversation, because he raised his eyebrows and nodded.

'No problem,' I said. 'I'll be here.'

'Great,' Hasse said, reaching into his inside pocket. I thought he was going to give me his business card, but he brought out his wallet. 'Are you allowed to accept tips?'

'Absolutely,' I said, which made Hasse laugh. I could see that he was trying to impress his companions with his worldly ways and his generosity, but I was quite happy to go along with him as he picked out a fifty-kronor note and gave it to me with the words: 'There you go. You can turn it into a thousand when you get home!'

I laughed politely and left the group, wishing them a pleasant evening and saying that I looked forward to seeing them on Saturday. As I passed the bar Roberto patted me discreetly on the back and whispered, 'Yesss!'

Only four more customers came in that evening, two couples at separate tables. One pair wanted to be entertained; the others didn't, because they were totally absorbed in each other. When the group I had performed for at the beginning of the evening paid their bill they added an extra twenty kronor for me, possibly inspired by what they had seen and heard at Hasse's table.

Okay, so it wasn't exactly Springsteen at Ullevi, but when I sat down in the kitchen after my final performance, I could describe the evening as a success. When Roberto came to pay me I told him that a hundred was enough, because I hadn't done many performances. I wanted to show him some goodwill, and it was clearly appreciated. We toasted each other with a beer: 'Here's to the future!' At that moment I couldn't imagine it was anything but glowing.

*

I walked home over the Brunkeberg Ridge. The tunnel was closed for the night, and in any case I wouldn't have wanted to go that way. I whistled to myself, and it was only when I was on my way down the steps leading to Tunnelgatan that I realised the tune was 'Somebody Up There Must Like Me'.

I was just outside the entrance to the tunnel. Beside me was a cast-iron plaque that read:

1886
KNUT LINDMARK
ENGINEER

I thought about all the material that had been removed during construction. The ridge had been sliced away in several different stages , Kungsgatan had been excavated and the tunnel dug out, so what had they done with the millions of tonnes of rock? Dumped the lot in Lake Mälaren? Built something else?

As I stood there on that misty October evening, it was difficult to imagine the enormous amount of activity that had gone on around this spot at different periods of time. The transportation. The movement. All in order to leave this place to me and me alone as I stood there on the steps, leaning on the railing and contemplating the memorial plaque, which resembled a shield.

Maybe the successes of the evening had evoked a mindset of unreasonable egocentricity, because I thought I felt a vibration in the railing, the echo of hundreds of years of effort, leading to me, right here and right now. Nothing dies or disappears, it simply metamorphoses and moves forward, and somebody up there must like me. I let go of the railing and carried on down the steps.

I had decided to ignore whatever was going on in the laundry block, but that night it was impossible. When I walked into the courtyard I could see that the light was on in there, and I heard faint but unmistakable noises.

I went over to the door and listened. The sound didn't seem to be coming from the laundry room itself, but from further in. Silently I took out my keys, opened the door. The outer room was indeed empty, and the noises grew louder when I stepped inside. In spite of the fact that I was alone, my face flushed red as I quietly closed the door behind me.

Someone was making love in the shower room. No, I have to use another word. They were fucking. Violently. A man was grunting and groaning while a woman screamed in short bursts; it was impossible to distinguish pleasure from pain. The usual pull was emanating from the room. I didn't resist, but allowed myself to be drawn closer until I was standing right next to the door, my face burning.

I heard thuds as bodies repeatedly banged against one another, a wet smacking accompanied by humming, whimpering and screams. It was hard to decode the animalistic noises, but in the brief pauses I could make out human voices, and I was more or less sure they belonged to the couple who had sold me the television. The cold couple. The dead.

They were neither cold nor dead now. I carried on listening as they went at one another with something close to violence. Beyond their howls I could hear something else, something that couldn't possibly be coming from their bodies: a sluggish splashing that rose and fell. Stamping on a frog, mashing it into a slimy mess beneath the sole of your shoe. That sound, but deeper and following a different, slower rhythm than the Dead Couple's increasingly frenetic activity.

I looked down at the floor and my throat contracted as a wave of nausea came over me. The linoleum was dotted with several small pools of blood, and I was standing right in the middle of one of them. I gasped and brought a clenched fist up to my chest. This was 1985, remember, and coming into contact with blood was regarded with the same horror as exposure to radioactive material, if not worse. The police wore thick gloves whenever they were called out, and any room in which an HIV-positive person had been held was fumigated with corrosive chemicals. Blood was death, and I was standing in it.

The Dead Couple's pleasure and agony were building to a climax, but I stopped paying them any attention as I backed away towards the door, my bag clutched to my stomach, leaving behind a disgusting trail of blood smeared across the floor. When I got outside the door slammed behind me, but I didn't care.

I went over to the steps, took off my shoes and left them at the bottom. When I got into my house I washed my hands and examined my nails to make sure no lethal traces of blood had got stuck underneath.

Through the fear I realised with absolute clarity that I was overreacting. You couldn't be infected just by being near blood. I sluiced my face with cold water and had almost convinced myself that there was nothing to worry about when someone knocked on my door.

I grabbed the edge of the washbasin and stood there motionless, hardly daring to breathe, childishly thinking *I'm not here.* The knocking came again, harder this time. Driven by another infantile reflex, I turned the key in the toilet door, so that there would be two locked doors between me and whoever was outside.

It could only be the Dead Couple. No one had ever knocked on my door before. They had seen the footprints in the blood and my shoes at the bottom of the steps. Now they wanted to get hold of me and...Fear has a tendency to evoke childish reactions, and yet another one popped up now. When I heard knocking for the third time, a rhyme started running through my head, a song from the previous year's student parties, with alternate parts sung by girls and boys:

*GIRLS: 'Who's knocking on my door? Who's knocking on my door? Who's knocking on my door?' said the beautiful virgins.*

*BOYS: 'Me and my boys are on parade, and we want to get laid,' said Scout Leader Frasse.*

I didn't want to know what the Dead Couple might have in mind. The song about Scout Leader Frasse was running on a loop, accompanied by the animalistic grunts and yells from the shower room. I could easily imagine the worst, so I clung to the basin and waited for the moment to pass.

The knocking stopped, but I didn't hear any feet descending the steps, so I stayed where I was. After five minutes I finally plucked up the courage to unlock the toilet door as quietly as possible. My inner child was still in charge, so I checked the room: nothing had changed, the front door looked the same as usual and there were no faces at the window. I didn't know what else to do then, so I sat down at the desk and rested my hands on its surface.

My gaze settled on the scar on my right arm. I often rolled up my sleeves when I performed, because many people mistakenly believe that's where we magicians hide things. Occasionally someone would ask about the scar, and I always lied. A childhood accident, et cetera, et cetera.

Sitting there now, all alone, I suddenly got the idea that it was the cross that had put me in this situation. I was marked, chosen—*I will find you*—and now it had caught up with me like one of the Hounds of Tindalos, pursuing their quarry through time and space in order to devour him.

Intuition is a strange phenomenon. A momentary cohesion of impressions stored in the subconscious creates a conviction without the help of sentient reasoning. So I can't explain which connection of the synapses led me to the conclusion that the scar on my skin and what was happening in the shower room were linked. It was unfortunate, because I would eventually be proved right.

I made an effort to think about the cell instead. It had worked earlier in the evening, and it worked again. The image of that bare, silent little room cocooned my naked heart in soft material, and peace crept in. I breathed more calmly, opening and closing my magician's hands.

It had gone so well. *That* was what the evening was about. Success, being on my way, a bright future.

*Me and my boys are on parade*

No. No chance. I had nothing unresolved with anyone; I hadn't harmed a fly. Outside my walls, in the city around me, was an audience that would grow, one couple at a time, one table at a time, and soon my skills would be in demand. *Are you here on Saturday? Are you here next week? Do you work in any other restaurants?*

There you go.

*

I slept well that night, in spite of everything. Once I had managed to shake off the suggestions with the help of other suggestions, I realised how tired I was from the exertions of the day and the evening, and I fell asleep around midnight after playing 'Somebody' without the needle jumping. The lyrics followed me down into slumber, and I dreamed about this somebody who could make me see things in a different light.

When I woke up the events of the previous evening had been sent to the slagheap with a sign that said: *Nothing to do with me*. It was quite a busy route these days. Big cars with tinted windows.

There were only two days to go until Saturday's performance, and I didn't think I could do the same act when there would be at least one person in the audience who'd seen it before. I hadn't felt comfortable repeating the same effects at the larger table when I'd already shown them to the smaller table. What I needed was a number of tricks to choose from, so that I could vary my performances, making each one different—at least during the same evening.

After a cup of coffee and a cheese spread sandwich, I turned to the bookshelf for inspiration. As usual I homed in on Paul Harris. I took out *Close-Up Entertainer*, *Supermagic* and *Las Vegas Close-Up*, and spent a couple of hours making a list of possible tricks that could be included in a more flexible act.

To a layman it might seem over-ambitious to learn several new tricks in just a couple of days, but the truth is that the lion's share of all magic tricks is based on the same hand movements. If you can master five or six card manoeuvres and two or three coin manoeuvres, you can do most things. It's about combinations of these movements, plus the presentation—the spiel around the trick.

There are exceptions, of course—tricks based on complex manoeuvres that require hundreds of hours of practice. On the other hand, there's no guarantee that these tricks are any more striking or entertaining than the basic ones. Often the reverse is true.

Paul Harris has come up with some complex moves, but in my opinion his greatness lies in what he's done with the simple moves. The illusion known as Reflex is a nerve-jangling battle between the magician and a member of the audience that culminates in something that appears to be completely impossible. All achieved with a couple of double lifts and a palming.

The day ran away as I sat or stood at my desk with my cards and coins. I took some of Paul Harris's patter, added my own and modified the trick accordingly. By four o'clock I had expanded my act by six or seven minutes, and decided I could break for a late lunch or early dinner.

I had managed to distance myself so successfully from the events of the previous evening that there was a moment of confusion when I was ready to go out and couldn't find my shoes. Then I remembered. I opened the door and looked out. They were exactly where I had left them. I felt stupid for having overreacted so badly, but I still filled a jug with water to clean the soles, then padded down the steps in my stocking feet.

When I had rinsed off the dried blood, I found a folded piece of paper inside the right shoe. I opened it up and read *WE'LL BE BACK*, written in the same neat capitals as the ad for the television and the note on the shower room door. The woman might have set aside her human dignity, but she had retained her faultless handwriting.

A threat, a promise or merely a statement? If this was meant to scare me, it had the opposite effect. The bellowing, bleeding spectres who had knocked on my door last night turned into ordinary people who could write notes, then fold them tidily and tuck them into my shoe.

*

Nothing special happened on Friday, and the Dead Couple didn't fulfil their promise. I practised my double lift and my Elmsley Count, came up with a new presentation based on the concept of hiding things in the air, watched a documentary about *Viking*, the Swedish space probe, slept.

I carried on practising on Saturday. Perhaps too many card tricks had sneaked into my act, so I worked on a variation of the Coin in the Bottle. After a dozen or so attempts the elastic band in the gimmick I was using snapped, and I had to give up, so I decided to go out for a coffee.

When I stepped into the street and the main door slammed shut behind me, someone shouted, 'Hey, you there!' I turned around and recoiled.

Coming towards me along Luntmakargatan was a skinhead. Under his open bomber jacket I could just see a T-shirt bearing the Odal rune, and his black boots thumped on the pavement as he marched along with an aggressive look on his face. He didn't just look like the shaven-headed guy I had seen sitting on the smartly dressed man's knee, on *my* knee, that day in the tunnel; he *was* that guy. He stopped a metre away from me and jerked his thumb towards the door. 'What's the entry code?'

Even under normal circumstances I wouldn't have given the code to someone like him, and the memory of him sitting on my knee left me standing there at a total loss, as he frowned irritably. His face was smooth, and the lack of hair made his eyes and lips stand out as if he were a mime artist. A difficult-to-read mixture of hardness and innocence. He waved his arm and said, 'The code! For the door!'

I looked at the door as if I needed a visual aid to understand what he was talking about. I was about to say something when he clicked his fingers, pointed at me and said, 'You're a magician, aren't you?'

'Yes…yes, I am.'

He wagged his finger in front of me as if this was something for which I needed to be chastised, and said, 'Saw you in the Old Town last summer. Fucking fantastic!'

'Thanks...'

I remembered a Friday evening when so many people had gathered that Västerlånggatan had been completely blocked by my audience. A group of four skinheads had pushed their way through the crowd, which obediently parted. They came and stood right at the front, glaring at me, their faces immobile. I performed my last two tricks with a growing sense of panic as the audience drifted away. When I finished and bowed, bending my body over the bad feeling in my belly, there was no one left but the four of them, standing there with their arms folded.

There is no shortage of stories about people who have been beaten up by gangs of skinheads who've tired of hanging out around the Helicopter Platform in the Old Town and have taken to the narrow streets searching for some fun. Maybe I had been selected to provide the evening's entertainment as a punishment for having blocked their route.

*Arms over the head, fists tightly clenched. Not the skull, not the fingers.*

Occasionally the police would come and move me on for causing an obstruction, but there was no sign of them or anyone else in the extensive no-go area that had formed around me and the skinheads. I was alone.

The biggest member of the group slowly began to applaud. The others joined in. I stood there with my arms dangling by my sides as the big guy reached into his pocket and took out an unopened can of beer, which he placed in my hat. 'Fucking hell,' he said, and then they walked away. I sank down on a nearby step, opened the beer and took a couple of swigs.

I have never been good with faces, and the skinheads' uniform makes things even more difficult, so I couldn't say if the guy asking me for the door code now had been part of that group. Anyway, the fact that he recognised me had softened his attitude: 'Come on, man. I really need to get in.'

Did I have any real reason to deny him? Did I care what he

might get up to? Besides which, there was something about him that suggested he might have more going on inside his head than *Sweden for the Swedes, tra-la-la-la-laa*. It might have been an excuse to avoid any unpleasantness, but I said, 'Nineteen nineteen.'

He grinned. 'Votes for women, right?'

'Wasn't that...1921?'

He shook his head. 'That was the first time they actually voted. The decision was taken in 1919. Read up on your history, for fuck's sake.'

There was no aggression in his last comment; it was more of a joke. I watched him go over to the keypad, enter the numbers and open the door. As if I didn't have enough to think about.

I had decided to meditate on my act over lunch, see if any weaknesses spontaneously occurred to me, elements that could be improved. Then I would come home and work on them. But when I sat down with my chicken salad, my mind kept returning to the skinhead, as I had feared.

It was partly his character. I had never spoken to a skinhead before, but judging from their general behaviour, he didn't seem to me to be typical. Women's suffrage was hardly likely to be the main topic of conversation among the beer cans on the Helicopter Platform. Once when I was passing on the way to a street magic session I had heard someone bawling out a filthy song about tits and arses.

Then there was the question of his role in the smartly dressed man's fantasies. Was he a rent boy, on his way to do his job? That was one step too far for me. An intellectual skinhead who was also a prostitute. Maybe in a song by Marc Almond, but not in the street outside my door.

When I had eaten my salad and drunk my coffee, I did what I always did in those days: consigned my thoughts to the slagheap. Rubbish that I could dig up and examine if the opportunity arose, but not now. I had a show to do.

*

Like Donald Duck, when we are children we have the propensity to switch from sadness to joy to anger within the course of one minute. *Quack, splat, hiss, ho ho!* These mood swings become less pronounced as we grow older, because our internal processor has more to keep on top of, and works more slowly. Impressions are chewed over and manipulated until they result in a more considered response. The older we get, the less we resemble Donald Duck.

I still had Donald's ability to shake off anything incomprehensible or alarming, and to face any new situation with confidence. Not completely, but enough to be able to put the skinhead, the blood and the bad feeling behind me as I set off across the ridge at five-fifteen to do my act. My thoughts were solely focused on the tricks I was going to do, the words I was going to say.

I opened the door bearing the sign with my name on it, and said hello to Roberto and Miguel. There were three bookings this evening in addition to the party of ten who were coming especially to see me; they were due at seven.

I don't need to go through the evening in detail, because my account of Thursday gives the general picture. The new tricks worked well, and Reflex in particular captured the attention of the whole table; everyone wanted to see if the hand really can be faster than the eye. At ten past seven the large group arrived, much to my relief, led by Hasse. He patted me on the shoulder and introduced me to his colleagues as if I were a rare ape he'd discovered in the big city jungle.

'Here he is! The man, the legend!'

He and his party had had plenty to drink before they came out, and Hasse's gestures were wild, his eyes glazed. The party noisily took their seats at the table they'd booked.

You might think it's easier to perform magic for people who are drunk, because their observational skills are impaired. Quite the reverse. Many tricks depend on what is known as misdirection, which means using words and/or gestures to divert attention from something you don't want the audience to see. Drunks are unpredictable. Their eyes dart around all over the place, and in the worst-case scenario can land on exactly what you don't want them to notice.

Alcohol also has a tendency to erode social conventions and normal, everyday politeness. If sober people see something a little bit suspect, they usually keep quiet out of consideration for the performer, or because they're not absolutely sure of their ground. Not the drunk. The eyes flicker, pause, and a second later the finger is pointing and out come the words: *Hey, look at that!*

It took a while for Hasse's group to place their order, and meanwhile I worked out an act that depended as little as possible on misdirection. Once their drinks had been served I was called in, and against all expectations the performance went brilliantly. Hasse must have built me up to his colleagues in advance, and maybe he was the boss, because they all reacted to my minor miracles with the same enthusiasm as him. In fact it almost became embarrassing as they cheered every little twist and turn.

I was worried about how the other customers would react to having such a boisterous group in the middle of the restaurant, and looked around apologetically. I happened to glance through the window, and saw a number of people peering in, curious to find out what all the noise was about. Before I moved on to my next trick, I saw the people outside moving towards the door.

At the end Hasse collected money from everyone in his group—'At least ten kronor each!'—and I walked away two hundred kronor better off. I sat down in the kitchen and let out a long breath. After a while Roberto came in and gave me the thumbs up.

'Sorry,' I said. 'It got a bit crazy there.'

Roberto shrugged. 'As long as they're spending money like those guys, it's fine. Champagne before dinner. And an expensive one at that. The only kind I had. I love yuppies. It's cool.'

He knocked three times on the table as if to protect himself from bad luck, and said, 'Listen, another table has asked for a performance too.'

'Fine,' I said. 'I'll just let the big group calm down a bit. Five minutes.'

'Okay.'

To tell the truth, I was the one who needed to recharge my batteries. Wipe the slate clean, reboot ready to meet the next audience as something new and exciting. I leaned back and closed my eyes, using the same method I employed when I had a headache. Give the pain a shape, a colour and a precise location, and imagine a hole in your skull directly above the pain. Then slowly tilt your head and allow the pain to run out through the hole. I did that now, although I was tipping out noise and impressions instead of pain.

After a couple of minutes I was empty, creatively speaking. I got to my feet and went back into the restaurant, and into a new phase in this narrative. (Or rather a parenthesis.)

*

You might think that the longing for love and sex is noticeably absent from this story about a young man. Of course I felt such a longing, I just don't want to describe it. Literature is overflowing with lost, horny young people, all of them devastatingly dull, and I don't think I'm capable of producing anything different. Or maybe I'm just a prude.

However, I must now mention Sofia. She was part of the group I had inadvertently enticed in from the street, and after I had performed at her table, we started chatting. She was a year older than me, she was at college, and she looked remarkably like Anna Lindh, chair of the Social Democratic Youth League. An ordinary girl, if such a person exists. The unusual thing about her was that she appeared to be interested in me.

I have never managed to *pursue* someone to the point where they give in. That would require a completely different self-image, and possibly a different idea of love. How can you trust someone if you have forced them to love you through sheer exhaustion? I don't know—I've never tried.

But Sofia was giving out subtle signals that I picked up, and I heard myself ask, 'What are you doing tomorrow?' Apparently she was planning to spend part of Sunday shopping for a new microwave at John Wall, a stone's throw from my home. A world record stone's throw, admittedly, but I asked if she'd like some company. She said yes, and we arranged a time and place to meet.

To summarise, the evening was a great success. Hasse's party had eaten and drunk as if there were fifteen of them rather than ten, and in general Roberto had done well. Another beer, another toast, another stroll home through dark streets after we had confirmed that I would work Wednesdays and Saturdays.

There was a light on in the laundry block that night too, but whatever they were doing in there, they were doing it in silence. I went indoors and dug out an old copy of *Expressen* with a picture of Anna Lindh in it. The resemblance was striking. Sofia's glasses weren't quite so large, the eyes behind them were a different shape and the face wasn't so noticeably square, but otherwise she could have acted as a look-alike. I wasn't sure whether I found this attractive or not.

And was I ready for a relationship? How do you know if you're ready for *anything*? It's only when something is under way that you find out whether you can cope with it or not; up to that point you can only guess.

I switched on the TV and found myself in the middle of *Nattsudd*. Svante and Björn were sitting around talking rubbish, interspersed with black-and-white music videos. It was strangely relaxing and I felt kind of abandoned when it was over. I folded the newspaper so that it would stand up on its own on the table with the photograph facing me. Then I talked to it. After a while I realised what I was doing, and put the paper aside. Maybe it was time to break out of my loneliness after all. There was every indication that this was the case.

*

One of these days I will write a completely normal love story. One of these days, but not now. What happened between Sofia and me cannot be called love, and yet it occupies a certain period of time in this story and must be told, albeit briefly.

We met at Carl Milles' Orpheus fountain on Hötorget and had coffee at Kungstornet before we went to John Wall. I found out that Sofia was training to be a childminder, that she had her own apartment in Traneberg, preferred cats to dogs, and had seen every episode of *Dallas* bar one. When she had qualified she was planning to work for a couple of years before continuing her studies to become an after-school recreation tutor.

When we ran out of conversation, I went over to the jukebox and put on 'Everything Counts'. It turned out that Sofia was a big Depeche fan, and that 'Somebody' was her favourite song. I think that was the critical moment. Definitely.

Sofia bought her microwave and we hugged when we said goodbye at the subway station after swapping phone numbers. When I went home the image of her was imprinted in my head, and I was humming 'Somebody'. The blue duffel coat with the matching blue woolly hat. She was really pretty, in her own way.

I can't say I was in love, but by the time I walked into my house I felt a certain sense of liberation, like a shipwrecked sailor who has been drifting on the open sea for a long time, and finally thinks he can see something on the horizon. It might only be a skerry, or an illusion, but at least it gives him a provisional direction. Something small to hold on to.

I spent the evening cleaning. I'm ashamed to say I hadn't touched the place since I moved in. The hose of the vacuum cleaner rattled away like crazy as I went over the carpet, and it took me several hours to get rid of the layers of dust that had gathered in the corners and on top of all my books. I even changed the sheets, because it was possible that someone might stay over. At some point.

It wasn't until eleven o'clock that I was able to make a start on myself. I did a thorough job there too, giving myself a good scrub with the sponge, changing the water in the tub, cutting my nails. I had just started shaving when there was a knock on the door.

I lowered the razor and looked in the mirror. My face was covered in shaving foam, and there was no fear in my eyes. In a way this was a good time to tackle the confrontation I had been dreading. The lather on my cheeks was a convenient excuse to keep it short, so I pulled on my bathrobe and went to answer the door.

Elsa was standing outside. I had been expecting the woman with the cold eyes, and had to make a mental adjustment to adopt the right tone of voice. 'Oh...good evening?'

Elsa looked at my foam-covered face and asked, 'Am I disturbing you?'

'No, I was just...'

The bulb in the outside light still hadn't been changed, so Elsa was illuminated only by the faint glow of my desk lamp. It took a few seconds for my eyes to adjust, but then human shapes began to appear in the darkness behind her, on the steps. Three, four, five—possibly more. Elsa took a step forward so that I couldn't close the door.

*Me and my boys are on parade.*

I was still holding the razor, and for a stressed moment I clutched it more tightly, regarding it as a weapon. Then I realised it was a plastic Bic I was gripping, not a cutthroat, and it dropped to the floor. Elsa and I looked down at the razor, and my tough guy act was shot.

'Do you want to join us?' she asked.

'Join you in...what?'

'In what we're doing.'

'And what are you doing?'

'It's hard to explain. You have to see it. Experience it.'

Once again it was as if an inner light had been switched on behind her eyes, making them glitter as she looked up at me. I found the line of dark figures behind her disturbing, and it was difficult to speak. Elsa made an impatient gesture and said, 'It's not appropriate for you to live here. Unless you're with us.'

I assumed the Dead Couple had told the others what had happened two nights ago. Hence the delegation. It's not *appropriate*. It wasn't hard to detect a hidden threat behind Elsa's choice of words. I glanced over at the laundry block, where the light was on.

'But what is it?'

'It's impossible to explain. But you won't be disappointed. It's wonderful.'

If this was about whatever had squeezed out through the crack in the ceiling, then it was hard to make sense of what Elsa was saying. Had I misunderstood? Was this about something else? Something… wonderful? I couldn't believe it. The glow in Elsa's eyes, the silent, waiting group. There was nothing healthy about it, and nothing wonderful either.

'Okay,' I said. 'I'll come.' I gestured towards my bathroom and my face. 'I just need to…'

Elsa smiled and the light in her eyes was turned up a notch as she said, 'Excellent, that's excellent. We'll be waiting for you. Welcome.' She took a step back and I reached for the handle. Before I could close the door, she said, 'John?'

'Yes?'

'Something else is beginning now. Believe me.'

'Okay. I'll be there in a minute.'

I closed the door and heard a crunching sound as the razor was crushed. It didn't matter—I had no intention of finishing shaving. I went into the bathroom and rinsed my face, then dug Sofia's number out of my wallet and called her. I jammed the receiver between my shoulder and ear so that I could pull on my underpants and trousers.

*Please be home. Please be home.*

Sofia answered on the fifth ring. Her voice was hesitant; she probably wasn't used to getting calls at this late hour.

'Hi?'

'Sofia, it's John.'

'Oh…hi.'

'Listen, I need to ask you a favour. I know this is…a bit weird, but can I come over to your place?'

Pause.

'Now?'

'Yes, now. I wouldn't ask if it wasn't absolutely necessary. Something's happened.'

'What kind of something? I was just going to bed—I have to be up early in the morning.'

'Please, Sofia. It'll take too long to explain, but I can't stay here, and I don't have anywhere else to go. It's urgent.'

I could understand her hesitation. A guy she had met only once had called her up in the middle of the night, begging to come over in a tone of voice that suggested the Mafia were hot on his heels. I got it. But either she was keener on me than I thought, or she was less conventional than she appeared to be, because she said, 'Okay, come over.' She gave me the address, and I thanked her from the bottom of my heart before hanging up.

I threw on a T-shirt, jumper and jacket. As I tied my shoelaces I peered out through the gap in the blind. It seemed as if my neighbours had gathered in the laundry block, and I thanked my lucky stars they hadn't left anyone on guard in the courtyard.

I had no intention of participating in whatever they were up to, because I instinctively knew it had to be something sick to make their eyes shine like that. Something beyond what human beings should be getting involved in. The question was whether they had sensed my attitude, and taken measures to prevent me from getting away.

I switched off the desk lamp and allowed my eyes to adjust to the darkness before I opened the door as quietly as possible. I could hear the low hum of voices from the laundry block, but there didn't seem to be anyone outside. I locked the door behind me and crept down the steps.

There was no way of reaching the main door without passing the fan of light emanating from the half-open door of the laundry block. I pressed myself against the wall and took a couple of deep breaths, then I made a dash for it.

As I suspected, they were keeping an eye out for me. As I shot past the light I heard someone shout, 'Hey! Stop! Where are you...'

I yanked open the door and raced through the foyer. I opened the door leading into the street and heard the courtyard door slam shut behind me, then the sound of footsteps pattering across the marble floor. I didn't stop running until I reached the subway. Ten minutes later I was on my way to Traneberg.

*

This journey marked the beginning of a period of my life that doesn't have much to do with this story. The most important thing about those two months is how they ended, and for that to make sense, I have to give an outline of what went on.

Sofia met me outside the door of her apartment block, which was usually locked at that time of night. She took me up to her tidy little apartment and offered me a cup of tea. I told her about the threat from my neighbours without giving an explanation. Then we went to bed. Yes, we slept together. No, I'm not going to go into detail, for the reasons I gave earlier.

Sofia got up at six-thirty, and I could see she wasn't entirely comfortable with the thought of leaving her apartment in the hands of a stranger. But that's what she did. I went back to sleep, and when I woke at about ten I abused her trust by rummaging through her drawers, searching for short cuts to help me understand who she was.

My search confirmed what I already suspected: Sofia was completely unartificial. I don't even think that word exists, and yet it's the most suitable. A little bit different, a little bit complex, but basically unartificial. Let me mention just one detail.

In a corner of the living room stood a decent-sized music system. Amplifier, equaliser, record deck and a double cassette deck. Next to this was something that I first thought was a poster, but when I took a closer look, I found it was a cassette shelf.

Sofia had taken a poster of a sunset with palm trees in the foreground and cut it up into one hundred and twenty pieces, which she had then inserted into the spines of one hundred and twenty cassette tapes. She thus had a collection of tapes that together formed a panorama. There was nothing written on the spines, but when I took out a tape at random, there was a neatly written track list.

A mixtape. Dead or Alive, Madonna, Wham!, Modern Talking and so on. Depeche, of course. I looked at several more cassettes, and they were all mixtapes. Some tracks were repeated two or even three times. Since the record case contained only a few albums, I guessed that Sofia recorded songs from the radio, then edited with the help of the double tape deck. That says something about her, even if I'm not entirely sure what.

I found milk in the fridge and muesli in the cupboard, and ate a bowl sitting at a tiny kitchen table as I tried to decide what to do next. Sofia and I hadn't discussed how we were going to proceed. Moving into her apartment didn't feel right, but I couldn't see any other option. In which case I would need to fetch a few things from home, in spite of the fact that I would have preferred not to go anywhere near the place. I needed my magic paraphernalia, though, if nothing else.

I hung around until the afternoon, then wrote Sofia a note: *Thanks for last night. I'll come back this evening if that's okay. Not as late as yesterday.* After a moment's hesitation I added *Kiss kiss, John* and placed the note on the kitchen table. I washed up my bowl, made the bed and left the apartment.

*

The raid went well. I was alert with every step I took, and anxious while I was inside the house, gathering up my things faster than necessary. But no one knocked, and as far as I'm aware, no one saw me. Even if my neighbours were displaying behaviour typical of a cult, they hadn't yet reached the paranoid stage. I left Luntmakargatan with four plastic carrier bags filled with clothes, toiletries, my magic paraphernalia and a few LPs.

I stopped at the intersection of Tunnelgatan and Sveavägen. I hadn't grasped how desperate my situation was until that moment. There I stood, homeless and at a complete loss, with my belongings stuffed into four carrier bags. I didn't want to be in Sofia's apartment when she got home—I wanted to give her time to see the note, realise I hadn't stolen or broken anything, maybe start to miss me a little bit. Or at least wonder what had become of me.

For the want of a better option, I hauled my bags off to the City Library. The October wind sliced through my clothes, and I remembered my thoughts of a week or so earlier. The lack of cohesion and meaning, the essential numbness of life. At least then I had been on the way home to my house; now I was even more disconnected. I could be blown away like an autumn leaf, and no one would care. *Fucking neighbours. Fucking crazy sick-in-the-head Scout Leader neighbours.*

I sat in the reading room getting warm for quite a while before I took a stroll around, picking out a book here and there. *Malone Dies* by Beckett, *Nausea* by Sartre, and *The Autists* by Stig Larsson. Among others. The choice says something, about both my state of mind and my pretensions. I sat down at the table where I had left my bags and started reading *Malone Dies.*

The effect was unexpected. I had chosen to wallow in misery, but the book was so rich in black humour that I began to feel excited. *I shall soon be quite dead at last in spite of all.* The tone seemed like a possible approach to life. I had finished reading it by the time the library closed, but took it out on loan along with the other books so that I could read it again. Yet another carrier bag.

I called Sofia from a phone box, and there was no hesitation in her voice when she said that I was welcome. I fought my way to the Odenplan subway station in the biting wind, and things didn't seem quite so depressing.

That evening we had a proper conversation. I told her I knew things had moved way too fast, but this was due to circumstances beyond my control. I explained that my neighbours were giving me a hard time because I didn't have a legal tenancy contract.

Sofia didn't seem entirely convinced, but said it was okay for me to stay with her for the time being. I offered to pay a share of the rent—I felt I had no choice—but fortunately she said that would be putting things on too much of a formal footing. We would wait and see.

The entire discussion had such a practical tone that I thought maybe we should shake hands when it was over. Instead we kissed, and so on. Afterwards we stayed in bed and I showed Sofia the books I'd borrowed. She hadn't read any of them, and asked what they were about.

'It's hard to explain,' I said.

'But they must have a plot?'

'Not exactly.'

'So what happens?'

'Not much. It's mainly…ideas.'

'That doesn't sound very exciting.'

'No. You're probably right.'

It's hard to work out why we fall in love with someone, and almost equally hard to work out why we *don't*, even when we're trying to. And I really did try. I thought Sofia was sweet, I enjoyed her company and I liked living in her apartment, but during the two months our relationship lasted, I can't say I was in love.

I suppose it's the small things, character differences that pile up over time and become an insurmountable obstacle, until we realise that we're never going to reach one another. Not properly. Let me give you an example.

Sofia was involved with the Social Democratic Youth League in Sundbyberg. One evening a week or so after I'd moved in, she was on her way to a meeting about more or less the same topic as the lecture at the Workers' Educational Association: the future path of social democracy.

She was on a high when she got home; both the talk and the subsequent discussion had been exciting. The focus had been the current watered-down labour organisations versus Meidner's original vision, the possibilities inherent in collective ownership, the common responsibility that leads to a greater sense of community among people and to happiness in the long term. A wonderful opportunity that was being lost.

'But,' I asked her, 'can people really be together?'

'What are you talking about? Of course we can. It's all of us together who build this society.'

'Well, yes, obviously it's possible to carry through a project together, but...that sense of *belonging*, of *togetherness*, does it really exist?'

'That's what people feel when they're striving for common goals.'

'But isn't it like a football team? During the ninety minutes while the match is on, they all want the same thing. But when it's over, they all go home separately.'

'I don't understand where you're going with this.'

'Me neither. I just mean...that dream of a greater feeling of community, it's just a dream. It's not something that can happen in reality.'

Sofia's eyes narrowed as she looked at me and asked, 'How did you vote in the election?'

'Social Democrat. Your lot.'

'Why?'

I shrugged. 'I don't like the centre or the right.'

That conversation was typical of what happened whenever we discussed politics or related topics. I honestly believe that Sofia's attitude was both healthier and more sensible than mine, yet I still couldn't bring myself to share it, because I was far too convinced of man's fundamental isolation inside his own poor head. We are all standing on the edge of an abyss, and we are standing there alone. A solipsism perhaps, but that was my experience of life, and it differed significantly from Sofia's.

*

And yet we battled on. Sofia usually left early in the morning to go to her childminder's course in Solna. I slept later, and when I woke I would practise my magic, read newspapers and books, and go for walks in the area around the Traneberg Bridge as I tried to work out what to do with my future.

My job at the Mona Lisa was going okay, but no more than that. Roberto seemed disappointed that my appearances hadn't led to a surge in bookings, and after a couple of weeks I felt I had to forgo any kind of payment and just work for tips. On some evenings I came away with as little as a hundred kronor.

I still hadn't given notice on the house in Luntmakargatan. The situation would have been untenable if Sofia had asked for a contribution towards the rent, but she didn't, and I never mentioned it again. It didn't feel good, though. The glowing future that had shimmered before me just a few weeks ago was now at best a guiding light in the darkness.

Winter came with repeated falls of wet snow, and I got more and more depressed as the temperature dropped. When Tage Danielsson died in October it didn't really bother me, although I was a big fan. On the other hand, when the ice hockey goalkeeper Pelle Lindbergh smashed his car into a wall in the middle of November I was upset for several days, even though I'd only seen him play in a couple of matches in the '83 World Cup.

Why did Sofia put up with me? The only explanation I can think of is that she was just as lonely as I was. We spent the evenings watching TV and listening to music, mostly Depeche. Sofia liked to read aloud from *Winnie the Pooh*, which was her guide to life. Sometimes we played board games—Mastermind, Yahtzee, Othello, Monopoly. She loved games, and had a whole pile that she had brought from her childhood home, in spite of the fact that she hadn't had anyone to play with before I came along. At my lowest moments this seemed to me to be unbearably sad.

On my birthday, 2 December, she gave me a special backgammon board made of wood, and I did my best to look pleased, although I knew it was more of a present for her than me. In the evening we went out for a meal and I drank too much wine. Sofia paid.

During the journey home on the subway we sat opposite one another in silence. As we crossed the Traneberg Bridge I looked out of the window at the big snowflakes falling into the water, and I knew that the life I was living was not my real life. In my alcohol-befuddled state I thought I could see two parentheses made of cast iron slamming down on either side of me, trapping me.

It wasn't until a couple of weeks later that I decided to break free. No, that's wrong. Like so many other important steps, it was taken without any contribution from me. It *was decided* that I should break free, and that decision was passed on to me through despair.

*

It was a few days before Christmas Eve. A week earlier Roberto had informed me that he no longer had any use for my services, so I was pretty much unemployed. I had 1200 kronor in my bank account, and a hundred-kronor note and two tens in my wallet. I still hadn't paid the rent for January. It was some small consolation that I had been booked to appear at the Boilermakers' Association New Year party, which would pay 1500 kronor.

I wandered restlessly around Sofia's apartment. The twee neatness felt like a kind of menacing madness just then. The three soft toys on the bedspread, the china bunny rabbits on the chest of drawers, the bunch of dried flowers from her high school graduation, the cassette rack. She knew where every single tape was, even though there was nothing written on the spines.

When Sofia got home from college we made dinner together, and I fantasised about slicing off my fingers. As we ate we avoided talking about Christmas and what we were going to do. We watched a film on TV, and Sofia had to ask me more than once to stop jiggling my leg up and down, because it was getting on her nerves.

Sofia wanted to make love when we went to bed, strangely enough, and I couldn't do it until I'd asked her to put on her glasses. Then I managed it by pretending Anna Lindh was on top of me, and that I was Olof Palme. Sofia fell asleep, while I lay there wide awake. After an hour she started snoring gently. I couldn't bear it and a confused plan began to take shape in my head, a way of putting things right. I slid out of bed, got dressed, grabbed a bucket and a wooden scoop and went out into the night.

During that bitterly cold winter I had observed a strange phenomenon. Next to the doors leading into the subway station there was a ventilation drum, from which warm air poured out onto a flowerbed. At the exact spot where the air met the earth, there was a little rosebush, which, encouraged by the heat and the floodlights, had decided to start flowering in its temperate patch, surrounded by snow.

It was just after one o'clock, and I could see that the barriers in the station were unmanned. I started digging. The roots went deeper than I'd expected, and when a small group of travellers came up the escalator about fifteen minutes later, I had barely made any impact. I hid in the shadows, and when they had gone past, I carried on.

It took me just over an hour to dig out the bush and a decent clump of earth, with the help of the wooden scoop. Sweat was pouring down my back as I shovelled earth into the bucket and pressed the bush down on top of it. My hands were bleeding from countless scratches, but I picked up the bucket and hurried home in a state resembling intoxication. I had the rosebush—here I come with my rosebush beneath the glow of the street lamps.

By the time I stumbled in through the door, panting because I'd run up the stairs, my enthusiasm was already beginning to wane. I took off my jacket and boots and carried the bucket into the bedroom, where I placed it on the chest of drawers in front of the bunny rabbits. Then I stood and contemplated the outline of the half-metre-tall bush. It redefined the room, which had probably been my intention. I couldn't say for sure—it was just something that had to be done.

When I had finished looking I lay down on my side of the bed on top of the covers, without getting undressed. Half-formed thoughts and images ricocheted around in my head like a badly planned firework display. At some point it occurred to me that I ought to rearrange the furniture in the living room, but fortunately I fell asleep before I could act on that particular impulse.

*

'What have you done?'

It was still dark outside when I woke up, dizzy from the lack of sleep, and saw Sofia standing in the kitchen staring at the floor, which was streaked with dirt and littered with clods of earth. I rubbed my eyes and muttered, 'The rosebush...'

'Yes, I saw it. Why have you brought it here?'

I squinted at the bush, standing on the chest of drawers in its plastic bucket, which did it no favours. It was impossible to explain the compulsion that had made me dig it up, so I simply said, 'I just did.'

Sofia shook her head. She fetched a dustpan and brush and swept up the worst from the kitchen floor, then said, 'You can do the hallway. I have to go to college.'

She put on her coat, and when she appeared in the doorway to blow me a farewell kiss, I said, 'Have you looked at it? The rosebush?'

'Yes, John, I have. It looks ridiculous. We'll talk about it later. Bye.'

'Bye.'

The front door closed behind her, and I lay in bed gazing at the bush. Its tangled, thorny branches with their leaves and the odd flower billowed out from the chest of drawers like a confused train of thought frozen in the moment.

I got up and showered, then stood in front of the misted-up mirror with a towel around my hips. Like the rest of the apartment, the small bathroom was very tidy. Bottles of shampoo, conditioner and moisturiser were neatly arranged on a shelf. From hooks adorned with Winnie the Pooh characters hung three identical towels. There was a liquid soap dispenser covered in a floral pattern, and next to the washbasin was a brand-new body brush hanging from the nose of Winnie the Pooh himself.

I looked at the brush, which was never used, but was there because the space required that a body brush should hang there. From Winnie the Pooh's nose. I thought about the revolting bathroom in the laundry block. The ingrained dirt, the dim lighting, the cracks in the plaster.

*I know.*

A tiny dot of calmness grew until it took over my entire body. I knew. There was nothing to be done. However hard I tried, I would never fall in love with Sofia, or be able to live the life in which I now found myself. It was a parenthesis and an escape attempt. I remembered the last words Elsa had said to me: *Something else is beginning now. Believe me.*

Wasn't that what I had always waited for, searched for? *Something else.* For something else to begin, irrespective of what it might be. The chance had been offered to me, and I had recoiled in fear at the prospect. What did I have to lose? I had nothing.

I packed my plastic bags and wrote a note to Sofia, thanking her for everything and wishing her Merry Christmas and the happy life she deserved with someone better than me. The last thing I did before I left the apartment was to fetch the rosebush in its plastic bucket.

Over-burdened with bags and bucket I headed for the subway. When I had got halfway I began to hurry, and by the last bit I was almost running.

It was ridiculous, of course—after an absence of two months a minute here or there was unlikely to make any difference, but I longed for that *something else* to begin, and was horrified at the thought that it might be too late. So I ran.

# 2. Inside

When I got off at Hötorget, it turned out that the exit for Tunnelgatan was closed, so I went up the escalator to the central concourse, where as usual I was disorientated for a little while before I found the way out to Kungsgatan.

There was definitely a festive atmosphere. Christmas lights were strung between the buildings, and because it was lunchtime, people were taking the opportunity to shop for presents. Apart from the bucket containing the rosebush, I think I fitted in well as I went round the corner by Ström's clothes shop and continued down Sveavägen, laden with carrier bags.

A lot of snow had fallen and been trampled by hurrying crowds; it had then been sprinkled with sand so many times that it lay beneath my feet like an extra layer of tarmac. Everything was familiar yet at the same time quite alien; the streets were like old acquaintances you haven't seen for a long time who suddenly turn up with new clothes and a new haircut. The same but different.

Dekorima had set up their Christmas display in the window. A dummy dressed up as Santa Claus was standing at an easel with a brush in one hand and a palette in the other, busily painting a bowl of oranges adorned with carnations. I started wondering what the connection might be between all this and the birth of Jesus, but my train of thought was abruptly broken off as I turned into Tunnelgatan.

The street that had formed a link between Sveavägen and the tunnel was now dominated by four builders' huts stacked on top of one another in twos. The sign on the restaurant on the corner was hidden, and to make up for this they had put up a poster on the wall of one of the huts facing onto Sveavägen: *Bohemia Bar and Restaurant*.

When I had passed the huts, I found out why the builders were there. The whole of the side of my building adjoining the tunnel was covered in scaffolding and tarpaulin. Some of my neighbours' apartments, including Elsa's, must have been significantly darker as a result.

There was no sign of anyone working; maybe the builders were on their Christmas break. It seemed to be a renovation project, but why only on the side where the tunnel was? It was impossible not to think back to what I already knew. There had been a movement of some kind, and maybe something had cracked.

My arms were aching as I put down my burdens to key in the entry code. The date of women's suffrage still worked. I lumbered on, through the stairwell and out into the courtyard. Everything looked the same as usual, apart from the layer of snow covering every surface. There was a well-trodden path between the fire escape, the main door and the laundry block, but in front of my house the thick snow lay untouched. My eyes swept the apartments, the windows, but no faces had appeared, and no one seemed to have noticed my arrival. In a way I was disappointed. Here I am, everyone!

I plodded up the steps and scraped away the snow with my boots before fishing out my key and unlocking the door. A horrible smell hit me immediately, and I staggered back outside waving my hand in front of my nose.

It can be seen as a measure of my determination to return that I didn't follow my usual pattern and interpret the stench as sabotage or a sign that something terrible was going to happen, but assumed that it was what it was: rotting food in my overflowing kitchen bin.

I took a deep breath of fresh air, held my nose and then tackled the problem. The food scraps had metamorphosed into something else entirely, and the bag dripped all the way to the garbage chute in the yard.

I left the door open to air the house, and went across to the laundry block. There didn't seem to be anyone inside, and I hesitated with the key in my hand before deciding to wait a while. Better to get myself sorted first, then tackle whatever had brought me back. If there was anything to tackle. Maybe it was over

*something else is beginning now*

and I had lost my chance. The silence all around me, the sense that everything had turned away, suggested that was the case. With a sinking feeling I went back to my house and unpacked my bags. I placed the rosebush on top of the television. In my current situation it seemed like a friend.

*

When everything was as tidy as it could be, I was suddenly overcome by despair. I was so naive. I had run to the subway as if a wonderful revelation was waiting for me, but the only thing I had actually done was to *flee*. Not *to*, but *away from*. Away from the floral soap dispenser and the body brush hanging from Winnie the Pooh's nose.

I didn't have a job, I couldn't afford to pay the rent, and I had no plan. I wasn't even back to square one—I was back to square zero. From something to nothing. I really wanted to be a romantic, a seeker, but what was I? An idiot.

As I sat on my chair with my head in my hands berating myself, I heard the door of the laundry block open and close. I leapt up and peered through the blind, but all I could see was the light being switched on. Without any great hopes I pulled on my boots and went outside; dusk was already falling. It was minus ten degrees, and the snow crunched beneath my feet as I crossed the courtyard, turned the key and stepped inside the laundry block.

Even from the back I immediately recognised the person standing in front of the closed shower room door. The shaven head, the bomber jacket, the boots. The skinhead turned around and nodded in acknowledgement.

'Have you got a key?' he said, gesturing towards the door.

Maybe it wasn't over after all. The room was still secured with the same bar and heavy padlock. Someone had clearly tried to force the bar, but it hadn't given way.

'No. What's in there?'

'How the fuck should I know? That's what I'm trying to find out.'

'Why?'

'Because it's something, and it's making my dad crazy. Have you got a key, or what?'

'No, I don't have a key.'

'So what are you doing here?'

I could have said that I was there for the same reason as him, but for one thing I had no desire to form a team, and for another I was beginning to see a connection, so I asked as casually as I could: 'Does your dad live here?'

The skinhead had lost interest in me. He placed the palm of his hand on the door as if he were trying to feel a vibration. 'Mmm.'

'Does he usually wear a suit?'

'Yes, why?'

'I just wondered.'

I now saw the image that had filled my mind that day in the Brunkeberg Tunnel in a completely different light. What I had experienced was no erotic fantasy, but a father's longing for his son, the same son who had now turned back to face me, and was standing with his hands by his sides.

'Are you not a participant in this at all?' he asked.

'No.'

'Was it Elsa's recommendation you be excluded?'

'No.'

The way he spoke, his gestures and body language, were confusing. Words like 'participant' and 'recommendation' were not what I would have expected from a person like him, and there was something *polite* in his manner, as if he were a cultural correspondent working undercover as a skinhead. I must have been staring at him without realising, because he frowned and, as if to confound my suspicions, said, 'What the fuck are you looking at?'

'Nothing—it's just you're so different from others who...go for that style.'

'You mean skins?'

'Yes.'

'So you think that everyone who *looks* a certain way *is* a certain way? Bit bigoted, maybe?'

'Not as far as I'm aware.'

'Okay, but most people are, and they don't even know it.'

He snorted and shook his head, as if other people's prejudices never ceased to amaze him. I was about to ask what he was called, because I wanted to put a name to this contradictory apparition, but before I could speak he had walked out without saying goodbye. I glanced around and saw something glinting on the table where people folded their clean laundry. A smooth gold ring. I picked it up and read the inscription on the inside: *Kajsa & Erik 25/5/1904.*

I was about to put the ring back where I had found it when the door opened and the skinhead reappeared. Without a word he took the ring from me and put it in the pocket of his jeans. As he was on his way out again I managed to ask my question: 'What's your name?'

He stopped, his hand resting on the doorhandle. I expected a dismissive response, but instead he said, 'Thomas.'

'Okay,' I said, holding out my hand. 'Hi. John.'

Thomas looked me up and down, possibly wondering whether it would be best to shake my hand or punch me, but he contented himself with saying, 'Fucking nutcase,' as he walked out.

*Elsa.*

It was Elsa who had led the delegation the evening I fled, and it was on *Elsa's recommendation* that Thomas had been denied entry to the shower room. I waited a while to make sure he wasn't coming back, then I switched off the lights, went outside and headed up the fire escape to Elsa's door.

*

There was a green plastic wreath hanging next to the nameplate that said *Karlgren*. Thomas's assertion that his father had been driven crazy worried me a little, but my anxiety was allayed by the sight of the wreath, and I rang the bell. If you're raving mad, you're hardly likely to bother with Christmas decorations.

As I waited I questioned this conclusion. Maybe Christmas decorations are exactly the kind of thing you pay attention to if you're crazy—details that set the stage with an appearance of normality while you run amok in the wings. I tensed as I heard soft footsteps approaching.

Elsa was an elderly lady and there was no peephole, so I was expecting her to call out, 'Who is it?'—but while I was considering how to respond, the door opened and there she stood, dressed in a black tracksuit and sheepskin slippers.

The light in her eyes was still there, but now it was mixed with something else that made her seem slightly…I hesitate to use the word *depraved*, so instead I'll go for *tired*—like someone who has had the opportunity to live out their fantasies to the full, and has discovered that it's not enough. A worldliness bordering on weariness. I should add, however, that Elsa still looked several years younger than when I first met her.

'John.'

'Yes.'

'Come in.'

Her hallway had the smell that is fairly common in the homes of older people: mothballs, lavender bags, or the smell of ageing bodies and time going around in circles. A domesticated, unthreatening smell. I took off my boots and followed Elsa into the living room, where she sat down in an armchair with her hands resting in her lap. This room too was exactly as you might imagine the living room in the home of Elsa Karlgren, a lady in her seventies.

A sofa and two well-used armchairs around a glass table with a lace mat. A corner cabinet with glass doors, in which a number of ornaments were neatly arranged. A chest of drawers, also with a lace mat on top, and above it a cheap print of the sun setting over a mountain chalet. A dark wooden shelf displaying books with yellowing spines.

And yet there was something strange about the room, something outside the norm. It was only when I had sat down in the other armchair that I realised what it was: no photographs. Elsa had both children and grandchildren, yet there was no sign of any of them. As I covertly glanced around the walls I could just make out faint rectangular shadows where the wallpaper hadn't been faded by the sun, because something had been hanging there, something that had been removed quite recently.

Elsa said, 'So. You're back. How come?'

That question would take a long time to answer, and I wasn't even sure if I could do it. I presumed that wasn't really what Elsa wanted to know anyway, so I simply said, 'I want to be part of it.'

Elsa raised her eyebrows, which were more coloured pencil than hairs, and asked, 'Part of what?'

'Whatever it is you're all doing. In the laundry block.'

Since we sat down Elsa had been sitting with her hands in her lap, like a queen patiently listening to one of her subjects. Now she laced her fingers together, rested her elbows on her thighs and her chin on her hands, then sat and stared at me for a long time. I had to make an effort to stop my eyes darting across the walls, searching for more shadows of memories.

Eventually she said, 'I want you to answer one question. Why did you run away that night?'

I leaned back and ran my hands over my face before I gave the only possible answer: 'I don't know why I ran away and I don't know why I've come back. It just feels as if it's what I have to do.'

To my surprise Elsa smiled and nodded, as if she approved of my response. Her attitude softened as she asked, 'Do you have any idea at all? Of what this is about?'

'I think so, yes.'

'Tell me.'

Though I had spent my journey home on the subway speculating on this very issue, I hadn't been able to put my suspicions into words, and all I could come out with was: 'It's *something else*. Something that lies beyond. A road. Yes. A road.'

'And where do you think this road leads?'

'I don't know.'

Elsa frowned and her eyebrows lost their exaggerated symmetry, but I got the impression that I was doing okay. That my inarticulate responses were roughly what she wanted. 'So is it sensible,' she asked, 'to set off along a road when you don't know where it's taking you?'

'Yes. If you don't have a choice.'

Elsa laughed, a not entirely pleasant sound, and shook her head. She glanced around the walls as if she were looking at the photographs that were no longer there. She didn't make eye contact when she said, 'How old are you?'

'Twenty.'

'Twenty. And you're telling me you have no other roads to choose from. Except that one. From that room.'

My anxiety about seeing Elsa had subsided as we talked, and now her condescending attitude was starting to annoy me. Admittedly she was a lot older than me, she had taken down her photos and her eyes were filled with world-weariness, but that didn't mean she understood the depth of my feelings, or was entitled to sit in judgement.

'Forgive me,' I said, 'but I don't understand. Before you were very keen for me to be involved. What's changed?'

'A great deal. And you lived here then.'

'I'm intending to live here again.'

Another silence as Elsa weighed me up. I tried to calm myself, suppress the irritation that was making my cheeks burn. She got to her feet with surprising ease and said, 'Come into the kitchen.'

I didn't want to obey the queen's order immediately, so I stayed where I was, gazing at the tarpaulin outside the window. I didn't know what to think. I had expected the whole thing to be more… elevated.

I went into the kitchen and found Elsa sitting under the extractor fan with a cigarette in her hand. She blew a stream of smoke out of her mouth, aiming it carefully at the fan.

'You smoke?' I said stupidly.

Elsa shrugged. 'I gave up for forty years, but now I've started again.'

I looked around. It was a typical 1950s kitchen, and I see no reason to describe it in detail. The main colour scheme was yellow, and the room was shabby but clean. I sat down at the table, which was adorned by yet another lace mat. Elsa took a deep drag, enjoying every second, then sighed.

'I've lived for others,' she said. 'All my life. First my husband. And my children. Then my grandchildren.'

She tapped the ash into a clean ashtray. I guessed that she wasn't a heavy smoker, partly because she took such pleasure in it, and partly because the apartment didn't smell of smoke. Maybe she saved it for special occasions. Was this a special occasion?

'Do you know why I did it?'

I assumed the question was rhetorical, and shook my head. I noticed that she said 'did' rather than 'have done', as if it were something that was now concluded.

'Because I thought I'd get a reward.'

'What do you mean?'

'Not *that* kind of reward, not a tangible reward, not something waiting for me in heaven. But a sense of satisfaction. Being able to think, at some point in my life: *I've done all I can, and I'm where I'm supposed to be*. Do you understand me?'

'I think so.'

'You think so. Or maybe you actually do. Understand, I mean. But you can't know that it's possible to spend an entire lifetime longing for that harmony. That sense of completion and fulfilment. To sit in an armchair with all your grandchildren around you, the Christmas lights sparkling in their eyes, hearing them say *Grandma*...'

Elsa took a final drag, stubbed out the cigarette and checked that it really was out before switching off the fan. 'And then to find that wasn't it—it was something else.'

'How can a person know that?'

She picked up the stub and threw it in the bin, then rinsed the ashtray and placed it upside down on a tea towel. With her back towards me she said, 'Good question.' She turned around and for the first time she looked unsure, as if I had really made her think. Eventually she said, 'What we think we want isn't what we want. As it turns out.'

'But when?'

'When we start to...associate with what's in that room.'

'What is it?'

'I can't describe it. It has to be experienced.'

She opened the cupboard above the fan and took out a cocoa tin. Inside was a padlock key hanging from a red ribbon. She gave me one last long look, then said, 'Okay. Let's go.'

*

As I approach the dark core of this story, I am feeling unsure of myself. It's exactly as Elsa said: it can't be described, it has to be experienced. And yet I have to describe it as best I can, with the words at my disposal. My whole career as a horror writer stems from two locations: the tree house in the forest and the shower room on Luntmakargatan. Everything I have come up with since then is a projection or distortion of what was in those two places, and therefore it is with some trepidation that I now face up to the impossible task of describing it. I will try and I will fail again, but hopefully I will fail better.

*

I followed Elsa down the steps and into the courtyard, keeping my eyes fixed on the key on its red ribbon dangling from her hand. As we passed my window Elsa nodded towards it and said, 'What's it like in there?'

'Dark.'

We didn't say another word until we were standing in the laundry room and Elsa had switched on the fluorescent light. She handed me the key with a ceremonial air and said, 'There you go. You can get yourself a copy made afterwards. If you want to carry on.'

'Carry on with what?'

'Associating. As I said. With yourself.'

I went over to the shower room and inserted the key in the padlock. Before I opened the door there was a question I had to ask, however feeble it might sound. 'Is it dangerous?'

Elsa shrugged. 'I'm sure it can be. That depends on you.' She sat down on the only chair. 'I'll wait here. You can lock the door behind you if you want.'

I turned the key, removed the padlock and opened the hasp. As I reached for the doorhandle, Elsa said, 'You have to give it blood. You decide how much, but I'd recommend a small amount to start with. There's a knife in there.'

'You give...blood?'

Elsa pushed up the sleeve of her blouse. Her arm could have belonged to a self-harming teenager. A network of healed and more recent scars crisscrossed her wrinkled skin, and an image flashed through my mind. The child in the tree house pushing up his sleeve. *Blood. Whoosh, whoosh. Evil.* Elsa gave me a wan smile and said, 'Nothing's free, is it?'

I opened the door, thinking in passing about AIDS, but I was far too preoccupied with what I was going to see to let myself be afraid. I was already embarrassed because I'd asked if it was dangerous, so without further ado I stepped into the room, closing the door behind me and turning on the light.

The room was still lit by a naked bulb, but it was brighter than before. There was nothing to illuminate but the bathtub and a stool beside it, with a clean handtowel and a fruit knife lying on the stool. I took a step forward and looked into the bathtub.

So there it was. *The other.* From where I was standing, the bath appeared to be half full of pitch-black paint. That was all. I glanced up at the crack in the ceiling. Whatever it was had forced its way out, landed in the bath, and was now lying there. *Okay.* I put the towel and the knife on the floor, sat down on the stool and stared at the shiny black surface. I can't deny that I was disappointed. When I had had my fill of gazing at the nondescript substance, I reached out and dipped my fingertips into it.

The consistency was thicker than paint. At the risk of making an utterly ridiculous comparison, I have to say it reminded me of

Slime, the jelly-like stuff you can buy in a plastic tub that doesn't stick to your skin when you play around with it. Firm but fluid at the same time. When I pulled them out again, my fingers were unmarked. *Okay.* This amount of slime was definitely an experience, but not the one I had been expecting.

I picked up the knife, tested the blade on my thumbnail and found that it was as sharp as a cutthroat razor. A thin white scar had run across my right palm ever since the incident in the forest. I placed the blade along the line of the scar, took a deep breath and made a shallow cut. As the blood welled up I had to force back my fear of infection to make myself push my bleeding hand into the bath.

Something touched me down in that dark mass. When I reflexively recoiled and tried to withdraw my hand, it was held fast—as if another, much stronger hand had seized my own. But it wasn't a hand, unless you can imagine a hand that is simultaneously a tongue—a soft, inexorable muscle whisking over my palm while holding it in an iron grip.

My guts churned in terror as my head was filled with light and knowledge: *I can do magic.* My hand, down there in the slime, was a magical hand, able to manipulate physical reality. I saw it close around an egg, only to open a second later and release a fully grown hummingbird. I'm not talking about a vision, like seeing a film pass before your eyes—no, this really *happened*, and I was consumed by the glorious feeling that I could perform miracles with that hand.

All the hours I had spent making sure Han Ping Chien flowed smoothly were nothing more than a memory now that I could make coins dissolve, hover and appear from thin air with only the strength of my own willpower. Effects I had spent years of my life simulating could be made a reality, and I had never been happier. *Have* never been happier. Magic existed, and I was the master of it.

When I widened my vision I saw that I was standing in a field. Cropped green grass stretched towards the horizon in all directions, and high above was a clear blue sky. The last time I was in this place it had seemed sketchy and washed out. Now the colours were strong, the contours sharp.

There were other people here too. Diffuse echoes of my neighbours lingered on in the field, and I perceived them as upright shadows. I raised my hand in greeting—*here I am*—and found myself back in the shower room with my arm outstretched, my hand resting a couple of centimetres above the black surface.

The ecstasy drained from my body like a fading orgasm and disintegrated in the cold, harsh light. My right palm was as clean as if it had been washed with white spirit, and only a tiny drop of blood seeped out of the cut. I didn't know how long I'd been sitting there, but the muscles in my arm were aching. I stood up on unsteady legs.

*

'The knife,' was the first thing Elsa said when I emerged from the shower room. 'Each person washes it when they've finished.'

I went back in and fetched it; thin streaks of blood could be seen on the short blade. Half of me was still in the field as I went over to the sink. I scrubbed the knife and dried it on a tea towel that had been placed there for that very purpose, while trying to drag myself back to the reality in which I now found myself. Happily I didn't quite succeed. Bright, living fragments of the other place were still floating around in my body, and I felt almost weightless, as if my veins were filled with helium instead of blood.

Elsa produced a half-full bottle of whisky and two glasses, which she placed on the floor. I returned to the shower room and put the knife on the stool, then I came and sat cross-legged in front of Elsa. She poured a drop into each glass, handed me one and asked, 'So? How was it?'

I took a sip of whisky and the golden yellow spirit ran down my throat like liquid sunshine, suffusing my whole being with warmth. 'It was everything I could possibly wish for.'

Elsa nodded, and at the time I couldn't understand the fleeting look of sorrow in her eyes as she said, 'Mmm. And this is only the beginning.'

*

With a thick felt pen I wrote *THE OTHER PLACE* on a clean page in my notepad, in which I'd already written the story of the child in the forest, thereby confirming the link between what had happened when I was twelve and what was happening now. Chance had once again brought me into contact with the field, and I intended to keep a diary and write down what there was to see there. Shouldn't I have been questioning my sanity instead? Many people would have done.

Not me. All that was over now. Even at the age of twelve I had known that the other place existed, and I had lived ever since with the sense that something was missing, insufficient, within normal reality. The world of the field lacked almost everything on which our ordinary lives are based, but in spite of that, or because of it, I felt more alive, more present when I was there.

Being able to do magic was part of my character. In our world I couldn't do it—no one could—so instead I had spent my time *simulating* magic, like a person born to circumnavigate the globe who settles for whittling bark boats, sailing them in the washbasin and dreaming of the sea. In the field I didn't need to pretend. In the field I could do magic, and that made me *true*.

Many people can go through life without needing what lies beyond this world, but I wasn't one of them. Am not one of them. What I am is linked to things outside what can be seen. Now a path had revealed itself to me. I intended to follow it and document what I saw.

The story of the child filled just over a third of my notepad. I left a blank page after the words *not to anyone*, then described the experience of feeling the magic in my hands, the upright shadows of my neighbours, how the place had become more solid since I was last there.

When I had finished writing I heard a rustling sound behind me. I spun my chair around and saw that a leaf from the rosebush had fallen to the floor. The bush was wilting, and had lost its lustre. I filled a jug with water and poured it evenly over the surface of the soil, then let it sink in before carrying the bucket over to the window and opening the blind. Pointless. It was already dark. I closed the blind, but left the bush where it was. The next day I would make sure it got some light.

I looked around the room, my little fortress with its thick walls. The desk lamp shining on my notepad, the television, the mattress on the floor. This was mine and I didn't want to leave it—*couldn't* leave it since I had become a part of what was in the shower room. Somehow I had to make money so that I could stay here.

In a feverish desire to sort it out *now* I went through the pockets of every item of clothing that had pockets, and searched the desk drawers. The final result was thirty-two kronor and fifty öre. Together with the money I had, plus the fee from the Boilermakers' Association gig, that was almost enough for a month's rent. But that left nothing for food or anything else. That wasn't going to work.

The phone rang. I assumed it was Sofia, and got ready to explain the inexplicable. But it wasn't Sofia. The voice on the other end started speaking before I had even said my name.

'Where the hell have you been? I've called over and over again!'

'I didn't realise I was obliged to answer the phone.'

'What the fuck are you talking about? Obliged? What kind of a word is that?'

'Sorry. I've been away.'

I heard a snort, then the caller lowered his voice: 'Sigge's there, isn't he?'

'Okay, so this Sigge—is he a person?'

'A person?'

'Yes.'

'What's that supposed to mean?'

If we were really talking about the thing in the bathtub, it seemed absurd to call it 'Sigge', but I asked anyway: 'How do you know Sigge?'

I expected another evasive response, but the man on the other end said, 'I've chatted to him. Loads of times.'

'I thought you said you'd never met him?'

'Well, I've never met you either, have I—but we're sitting here chatting. Listen, I haven't got all day. Has he arrived or not?'

All the questions swirling around my head suddenly made me feel weary of language, and I just said, 'Yes. He's arrived.'

'Good! That wasn't so difficult, was it? Okay, so now I need to—'

'Just a minute. Can I ask...*where* have you spoken to him?'

'In the tunnel. The Brunkeberg Tunnel. I busk in there sometimes.'

Ever since the man had called the second time I'd had the feeling that I'd heard his voice before, but a voice on the phone isn't the same as a voice in real life. It was the busker I was speaking to. Before I had the chance to ask him anything else, he hung up.

*

The rosebush wasn't happy in its new home. When I woke up the next morning, the day before Christmas Eve, another dozen or so leaves had fallen off. I opened the blind, bathing the bush in the dirty grey light. I wanted it to survive, but didn't know what I could do to make that happen. As so often I found myself helpless in the face of powers beyond my control.

My right palm stung a little as I got dressed to go out and make a copy of Elsa's key. I wondered whether to put a bandaid on the cut, but there appeared to be no need. A thin scab had already formed, knitting the edges together. I decided to leave it alone.

When I stepped outside it was snowing silently, and the streets were beautifully made up for Christmas with a fine layer of powder. I cocked an ear towards the Brunkeberg Tunnel, but couldn't hear any music. As I walked along Tunnelgatan, I thought about the busker.

*I've chatted to him. Loads of times.*

There was something in the rock. Something that had been disturbed or had come to life when the tunnel was dug out. You didn't need to have read *Lord of the Rings* to have a bad feeling about whatever slumbers inside the mountains. But it was a form of prejudice, quite literally. *There is no evidence that whatever lies beyond means us any harm. It is far more likely that it's indifferent.* Not good or evil, simply a movement and a chaotic possibility. What I didn't understand was how the busker could communicate and *chat* to it. I would so love to do that!

Santa was still standing by his easel in the window of Dekorima. One of the staff must have been particularly conscientious, because the still life on the canvas was nearer completion than it had been the previous day. Almost done, in fact. Snowflakes drifted down between me and the painting. A rosy-cheeked lady clutching a big parcel was standing in the exact spot where Olof Palme would fall two months later. The Christmas atmosphere was intense.

I went down into the underground mall at Hötorget and found the shoe repairer and key cutter I knew would be there. It took him three minutes to make a copy of the key to the shower room, and he wished me Merry Christmas as he handed it over.

By the time I reached Kungsgatan, I had decided. To make some money quickly, I would do the only thing I was good at. It felt like a retrograde step, going back to street magic, but I couldn't see any other option. As I walked home I thought about suitable locations and finally settled on Galleria, a public place frequented by plenty of people, with the further advantage that it was heated.

It was just over six months since I had practised my street magic skills, and I felt a little rusty. I began to yawn as I got closer to home, as if to let the butterflies out of my stomach.

*

There were a couple of steps a few metres inside the main door from the street. I was so preoccupied with my thoughts that I didn't notice Thomas sitting there until he said 'Merry Christmas!' so loudly that I jumped and stopped dead.

He was wearing a woolly hat and a padded jacket, and only the turned-up jeans and the Doc Martens boots gave away his ideological homeland. His Christmas greeting had been barked at me in a tone that would just as easily have suited 'Achtung!', and I risked clicking my heels and giving a hint of a bow before answering unnecessarily loudly, 'Merry Christmas to you too!'

Thomas grinned and patted the step beside him. 'Come and sit down.'

The keys were burning in my pocket and I really didn't want to talk about the shower room, but snubbing Thomas didn't seem like a very good idea, so I went and joined him. He looked me up and down and asked, 'How's things?'

'Good. Well…okay. What about you?'

Once again Thomas looked me up and down. I became conscious of my bobbled jumper, my cheap jacket and my shabby boots, and his next question seemed entirely understandable: 'Do you need money?'

Maybe it wasn't just my clothes, but something that radiated from me when I was desperately short of cash. I shrugged. 'Yes. Kind of. Why?'

'Do you want to be in on something?'

'What kind of something?'

Thomas's expression clearly said *Come on, man, you know what I'm talking about*. To a certain extent I did, so I said, 'Specifically, I mean.'

'Picking up a few bits and pieces. From a house.'

'And the person who lives in the house doesn't know that these bits and pieces are going to be picked up?'

'You could say that. Should be worth around fifty thousand. You get twenty per cent.'

'For doing what?'

'Keeping watch. Outside.'

'Why me? You don't even know me.'

'I think I do. And you use what you have, as Kajsa Warg said. Have you got a pen?'

Taking out a pen and handing it to Thomas made me start to feel like a fellow criminal, something I definitely didn't intend to become. Thomas jotted down a phone number on the back of a subway ticket and gave it to me. 'Think about it. Call me by tomorrow evening at the latest.'

'Or?'

'Or I'll have to speak to some idiot instead.'

I couldn't help it. As I left Thomas sitting on the step, I felt flattered. We had only met a couple of times, but he had formed the impression that I wasn't an idiot. I suspected he thought most people fell into that category.

In spite of my extensive shoplifting career, I had never considered moving on to more serious crimes, such as break-ins, because they harmed individuals. I had no intention of getting involved in Thomas's enterprise, but I felt paradoxically buoyed up by the fact that he had even asked me, and my heart was a little lighter as I checked over my magic paraphernalia.

I put new batteries in the laser pistol and prepared a rope for the Jumping Knot, took the least crumpled white silk cloth and fed it into the gimmick, placed the foam rubber balls in their places and finished by testing the rubber band on my stool. I placed it on the floor, pushed it down with my foot, then let go. It obediently leapt into my hand as it was supposed to.

That left the problem of the hat. I had thrown away my old hat, because it had been so scruffy that it made me look like some kind of derelict. Street magic was shabby enough as it was. Now I regretted my vanity. A hat was a well-established marker indicating a desire for voluntary contributions, and a cap didn't carry the same weight at all. A cap suggested begging. Small signals, but these things are important.

I got a glass bowl out of the kitchen cupboard and tried tossing a few coins into it. A couple of them bounced out, so I spent ten minutes covering the bowl in aluminium foil. I sensed that what I was really doing was coming up with delaying tactics. The effect of

Thomas's words had passed, and my heart was heavy once more. I was worried about standing in the middle of a crowd making a fool of myself. *Look at me, see what I can do, give me some money!*

Twenty per cent. Ten thousand. Where had Thomas got the sum of fifty thousand from? I cut off the thoughts that had crept in—*no!*—and tried out the bowl. This time the coins stayed in. I packed everything into my doctor's bag and put on my shirt, waistcoat and bow tie.

Thomas was gone when I went out. Oh, well, I had his number. Not that I was going to call him, but still. I buttoned my jacket right up to the top and set off through the falling snow for Galleria on Hamngatan.

*

It went okay, but that's all. Inside Galleria, the Christmas atmosphere from the snow-covered streets turned into stress. People didn't have time to stop and watch a diversion from the consumer model. Those who did linger were generous, though, perhaps because they were already in the mood to spend money. The proportion of notes was greater than usual.

In fact I could have made a decent amount if it hadn't been for the shopkeepers. In two places they came out and told me to move, because I was causing a disturbance. One of them even called over a security guard, who stared at me and made it impossible for me to continue, so I ended up with 208 kronor. I took my revenge on the lot of them by stealing a pair of expensive sheepskin slippers as a Christmas present for my mother.

I made my way through the bustling crowds, longing for the field, but I still had two days to wait for my slot. For the time being I was stuck in this earthly crush, and in my jellyfish-like way I went with the flow, allowing it to carry me around Stockholm until evening came and the shops closed.

When I got home I felt restless and anxious. Sitting up late all alone in my little house could plunge me into a well of despair so deep that it would be difficult to climb out again. I had a quick wash standing in the plastic tub, put on clean clothes and took myself off to Monte Carlo.

They had made a token attempt to put up Christmas decorations. A few strands of tinsel dangled from the ceiling, and in one corner stood a plastic Christmas tree adorned with multicoloured flashing lights. Their effort didn't succeed in creating a festive atmosphere any more than one swallow makes a summer, and the place was just as dark and ominous as ever. I sat down at the bar and had a beer, then another. The wide-screen TV was showing Swedish Television's evening entertainment with the sound turned down. Famous people were sitting in a cosy-looking room with soft lighting, chatting and laughing. Occasionally one of them burst into song.

I was halfway through the third beer I really couldn't afford when I spotted a familiar face at a table near the back of the room. The smartly dressed man, Thomas's father, was sitting there with his fingers entwined around a glass containing at least a treble whisky, gazing listlessly up at the screen. I picked up my beer and went over to him.

'Anyone sitting here?'

He looked up. It was obvious that he had to make an effort to find me in the fog obscuring his vision, and he hesitantly waved a hand in the direction of the other chair. His clothes were well cared for but slightly old-fashioned, a dark blue three-piece suit with a matching tie in a small checked pattern. I sat down, raised my glass and said, 'Merry Christmas!'

The man raised his glass, the melting ice cubes clinking, and returned my festive greeting. His hand bore the marks of healed wounds. We sat for a while watching TV as one of Santa's Little Helpers joined the party and performed a Cossack dance, his beard bobbing up and down.

'My name is Lars,' the man said.

'John.' We raised our glasses once more.

'Do you come here often?' Lars asked.

'Now and again. When I feel a certain way.'

Which is?'

'Empty. Emptier than usual.'

I turned away from the screen and faced Lars as I asked, 'Why did you tell me to get out? That day in the shower room?'

I wasn't sure if he would remember what had happened several months earlier, but he shrugged and said, 'I don't know. I might have overreacted. You're young. I assume you haven't lost very much.'

'Has that got something to do with it?'

'For me it has.'

'In what way?'

Lars sighed and finished off his whisky. He stood up, using the table for support, and pointed to my almost empty beer glass. 'Can I get you another?' I nodded, and he made his way to the bar, his movements stilted and awkward. Santa's Little Helper had now sat down to join the others on screen. I looked out onto Sveavägen where cars were silently forging their way through the snowfall, and a feeling of cosiness came over me. I was sitting indoors in the warmth, and I had someone to talk to. I was about to get a free drink, and possibly a story.

Lars came back with my beer and another large whisky for himself. As I thanked him, he took a deep breath, searching for the right words to begin.

'I was happy,' he said eventually. 'I had a wife and a son whom I loved. I was a university lecturer in history, which I enjoyed very much. Life was as perfect as it could be. Then it ended. All at once, it ended.'

'What happened?'

'My wife died. Meningitis. It only took a couple of weeks, then she was gone. Just like that. As if it were...normal. The kind of thing that happens.'

Lars took a sip of his whisky and blinked hard a couple of times, as if he were trying to remove unwanted images from his retina before he went on.

'It *is* normal. It *is* the kind of thing that happens. But that doesn't mean we accept it. I didn't. I started to hate this life that had hurt me so badly. Everything we'd had, everything we'd done. It could all be taken away by tiny fucking bacteria.'

'And Thomas?'

Lars was about to take another sip, but lowered his glass. 'Do you know him?'

'I've spoken to him a couple of times.'

'So you know. What he's become. And it's my fault. He was eleven when Marianne died, and I began to hate life. We'd been close until then. I loved him. He was such a wonderful boy. He was interested in history even before he started school. He was reading Grimberg by second grade. We used to have long discussions—he wanted to know everything. Everything. Then it stopped. I stopped. Because there was no point any more.'

During his account Lars had slumped towards the table, little by little. He straightened up then, as if to bring himself back from the past, and said, 'He despises me. He stole from me. And I can't complain. I deserve it. I betrayed his trust. As if everything he and I had was just a sham, worth nothing when his mother was no longer around. That is my great sin, and I will never be free of it. It's too late.'

The scene I had experienced in the tunnel, with Thomas sitting on my knee, made more sense now. I didn't want to reveal that I had stolen a peek at Lars's secret, so I simply said, 'And the thing in the bath? In the shower room?'

Lars took a swig so deep that he half-emptied his glass. He turned his face towards Sveavägen, his eyes flickering as they followed the movements out in the street. I discreetly moved his glass a few inches to the side so that he wouldn't catch sight of it and be tempted to carry on drinking. I wanted to hold on to him for a while. When he answered, he was still facing the window, as if he were addressing the passers-by.

'The thing in the shower room allows me to pretend. That I can be free. That there's a possibility. That…love still exists. I believe in it for a little while, because I can see it. Because it is shown to me.'

He dragged his attention away from the window and started picking at a patch of candle wax on the table. His mouth opened and closed a couple of times, as if it were unsure whether to let out what followed.

'I have a moment,' Lars went on. 'Or rather a *brief period of time.* It's Thomas's ninth birthday. Marianne and I are standing outside his bedroom door with his cake, candles lit, and his presents. We can't wait to see what Thomas will think of his great big Lego castle. We kiss. The candles on the cake make my wife's eyes sparkle. We open the door. We sing. Thomas leaps out of bed, his whole being shining with anticipation. He forces himself to open the biggest present slowly, although it's obvious that he just wants to *rip* off the paper. He is ecstatic about the castle. He pulls me and Marianne close, and the three of us hug. He smells of sleeping child, and he is so happy. We decide we'll build the castle together, all of us.'

As Lars talked, his eyes fixed on the patch of wax, silent tears had begun to flow down his cheeks. He wiped them away and said, 'That was my special time. The time I've chosen. The thing in the bathtub lets me go back to it. I'm there. Completely. I can relive it, over and over again. I get a little closer each time. I'm almost there.'

Suddenly Lars sat up straight and looked at me. Something like madness burned in his eyes as he gazed right into me and said it again, with even greater emphasis: 'I'm almost there.'

We sat staring at one another and I didn't know what to say. Then he slumped down again, grabbed his glass and had a drink. He turned his attention back to me, his eyes hazy now as he asked, 'And you? What's missing from your life?'

I was pleasantly tipsy as I made my way back to my house after another beer, which Lars had paid for. The rosebush had lost a lot of leaves. *What's missing from my life?* I gathered up the leaves and threw them in the bin, thinking that both Lars and I were tormented by the same thing. A lack, something fundamental missing from our lives.

It was just that in his case, it was a lot more concrete.

I switched on the TV; the same show was still playing relentlessly, and I sat there for a while with my mouth hanging open, as if I were watching the absurd customs of some alien race, until the colourful images began to flicker before my eyes. I turned off the TV, laid out my mattress and allowed the stream of lava inside my head to carry me towards Christmas Eve, which I would be spending with my mother.

*

I see no reason to describe the apartment on Ibsengatan in Blackeberg where I grew up. For one thing I have already done so in detail in *Let the Right One In*, and for another it has no relevance to this narrative. My account of my life might make me seem heartless, a bad son, but I have left out three or four visits to my mother, because they don't bring anything to the story, and I can't include everything.

We did the best we could in our loneliness, watching *Donald Duck and his Friends,* even though it felt a bit desolate. As usual tears sprang to my eyes when the mice helped Cinderella with her dress. We ate our Christmas dinner and my mother asked how things were going and I said fine. Everything was fine. Then we sat next to her little Christmas tree and exchanged presents. Mum was suitably pleased with the expensive slippers I had stolen, and I received a chunky blue jumper that was really lovely, plus a pair of thick socks that she'd knitted herself. At about seven o'clock we hugged each other and said goodbye, and I caught the subway back to the city centre.

By quarter to eight I was sitting on my chair once more. It was the evening of 24 December, and I felt dreadful. I tried crying, but that didn't help. I put on my new socks and jumper, which improved things a little. At least I felt warm and cared for.

Christmas Eve has a tendency to bring things to a head. A summary of who we are and where we have got to in our lives. What we have. It's no coincidence that Christmas Eve is the number one occasion for suicide, if it turns out that the final total is zero or minus.

I looked out and saw that the light was on in the laundry block. Someone was celebrating Christmas with the slime. Good for them. Or not. Whichever might be the case, I longed to go back there with a physical pull that reminded me of abstinence. The thing in the bathtub was what I had, for the moment.

*Shit!*

I gave a start, sitting there on my chair. I had forgotten to return Elsa's key, which I had promised I would do as soon as I'd had a copy made. Elsa took the issue of access to the shower room very seriously, and I was so shaken that I immediately put on my boots and ran up the fire escape, my heart in my mouth, clutching the red ribbon.

A second after I'd rung the doorbell I regretted it, because I could hear the hum of voices from inside. I was about to slink away when the door was opened by a middle-aged man with ruddy cheeks. I held the key behind my back and a wave of warmth flooded over me from the apartment. The man frowned. 'Yes?' he said. 'Hello?'

I waved my hand vaguely. 'I was just going to...I'm a neighbour, but obviously you're...'

The man stepped aside. The scene that met my eyes verged on the ridiculous. Elsa's words a couple of days earlier had been an exact prediction. She was holding court in one of the armchairs, with children sitting at her feet playing with their presents. The boy I recognised as Dennis tugged at her skirt and held up something made of Lego. Judging by the noise there were more people I couldn't see. A real family Christmas.

'Did you want something?' the red-faced man asked. Elsa looked up and saw me. I can't say that her expression was tortured, but it certainly didn't convey the grandmotherly contentment that the situation called for. She seemed more or less indifferent. Something was going on around her and she was there, but that was it. I nodded to her and she nodded back. *It's okay.* I apologised for having disturbed them, and turned away. The door closed behind me and the voices were reduced to a murmur.

To what extent can a person make demands? The scene I had just witnessed ought to be the dream for many people, and is reproduced in endless variations in ads, songs and stories. That scene was what those who put the noose around their neck to the sound of 'Jingle Bells' didn't have. To what extent can a person make demands?

I suppose the answer is that only the individual knows. If there is no God to set the boundaries and exhort us to embrace humility, then we are free to demand whatever we want. In which case there is only one question: does God exist?

I shook my head at myself as I clattered down the fire escape with Elsa's key dangling from my hand. Theological speculation was not my thing, but I suppose I could call myself an agnostic. Ever since I had been able to think in those terms I had had a sense that *something else* exists, something that lies outside and beyond our everyday existence...

I stopped at the bottom of the steps and looked at the laundry block door. The thing in the bathtub fitted that description to perfection. Did that mean the slime should be regarded as some kind of God? It was a long way from the kindly old man with the beard I remembered learning about in junior school, but I had never believed in that image either. Maybe God was actually a black, formless mass, a vague and ambiguous possibility.

The pull as I stood there was almost irresistible. I knew the booking schedule for the shower room was set in stone, and that it was unacceptable to go crashing in during someone else's time. Something was tugging and dragging at my arteries, and I might have broken the rules if I hadn't seen another way out. It was only a substitute, but it was enough to stop me from doing something I would regret.

*

While the rest of the city was festooned with Christmas decorations and coloured lanterns, the Brunkeberg Tunnel stretched before me as dark and silent as ever. The floor was wet with melting snow that had been brought in on people's shoes; it was relatively warm inside, and condensation dripped from the walls as I squelched along to the point where the busker had stood and played, and where I had sat with a skinhead on my knee. The rock face was just as rough and solid there as in the rest of the tunnel.

My palms grew wet when I placed them against the rock and lowered my head. I closed my eyes and erased all thoughts, allowed my mind to embrace the darkness.

This time the first thing that came towards me out of the emptiness wasn't an image, but a sound. My mental eardrums, located somewhere inside the physical, began to vibrate with the sound of a scream. No, more than a scream. A roar. A person roaring in pain. I reached further in, trying to sharpen my receptors so that I could see what was going on.

I don't know if it was because of a weakness in the thoughts of the sender, fluctuations in the rock itself or something else, but the image that emerged was diffuse, the outlines blurred like a photograph developed in fluid that is too diluted.

It was a person, a person running—that much I could make out. The body was in the process of disintegrating, the skin bubbling and pitted like that of someone who has been badly burned, and my internal nostrils picked up a sulphurous odour. As the burned figure ran, it roared with pain. Apart from that: nothing. It seemed to be moving through emptiness.

I concentrated as hard as I could, but my only reward was the perception of grass beneath the feet of the running figure. Grass cut very short, with no distinguishing features. The person was in the field; I couldn't say any more than that. I tried to make out facial features, but the severity of the burns made it impossible.

The image was sucked away and the rock closed around me. The next moment I was back in the Brunkeberg Tunnel, standing in slush with a wall in front of me. If someone was in the shower room right now, deep inside his or her desires, then how could these desires take the form of a badly burned person roaring with pain? Was it a revenge fantasy, something they wanted to inflict on someone else? No—the dreamer and the burned figure were the same person.

I heard the sound of footsteps splashing through the slush and looked up. A woman was coming towards me. She was in her fifties, and life hadn't been kind to her. Dark shadows beneath weary eyes; coarse, dry hair peppered with grey. She was wearing a short skirt and tights with holes in them, and she was clutching a thin fake fur jacket around her upper body. She didn't look at me, but kept her eyes fixed on the other end of the tunnel, as if there was a vision of hope shimmering there that she didn't really believe in. As she passed me I said, 'Excuse me?'

She stopped, slowly turned and stared at me as if I were an hour's sleep she was about to lose. She shook her head and said, 'Not working now. I can do you a quick blow job if you're desperate.'

'No, it's not that. I just wondered…could you do me a favour?'

The look on her face said *I've heard* that *before.* 'I don't do favours. Everything has a price.'

Since I was more or less bankrupt and it didn't really matter, I fished out my wallet and offered her a fifty-kronor note. She snorted and was about to say something cutting, but I got in first. 'I just want you to come and stand here, put your hand on the rock and close your eyes.'

Her eyes narrowed. 'What kind of sick crap is that?'

I held both hands up in the air with the note firmly clasped between the index and middle fingers of my right hand as I backed away from her. I pointed with my left hand. 'There. Stand there and close your eyes. Tell me if you feel anything.'

The woman took a couple of steps towards the spot, suspicion written all over her face. I moved further back until I was a good five metres away from her. She shrugged with such indifference that my heart turned over.

'Okay.'

Her eyes were cloudy. I thought maybe she was under the influence of something or other and had already forgotten what I said, so

I repeated my request: 'Put your hand on the wall. And close your eyes.'

'Why?'

'I just want to know if you feel anything.'

She grinned, exposing a set of yellowish-brown teeth. 'It's been a long time since I felt anything, son.' She leaned heavily against the wall and closed her eyes. I held my breath as the seconds ticked by. My lungs tensed as her body language changed; she became alert, wary of an approaching danger.

Suddenly she pushed herself away from the wall with unexpected strength, almost as if the wall had hurled her away from itself. Her mouth opened and closed and she stared at me. I lowered my hands, held out the fifty-kronor note and asked, 'What did you...?'

Before I could finish the question she turned and ran towards Birger Jarlsgatan. She tottered on her high heels, and after a few steps she slipped and fell in the slush. I went to help her up, but she pulled a Mora knife out of her pocket and pointed it at me.

'Fuck off!' she yelled. 'I'm not afraid to use this—get away from me!'

I stopped and raised my hands once more. As the woman scrambled to her feet, I said as calmly as possible, 'Can't you just tell me what you saw?'

She backed away, waving the knife around in front of her. Was she fighting the ghosts? 'I know people, so you'd better fucking watch out!'

When she was about ten metres away from me she turned and broke into a run again. She glanced over her shoulder a couple of times. I stayed where I was. It didn't really matter; I had got the answer I'd been looking for. She had seen, she had felt. But I would have liked to have known *what*.

*

I went home and flopped down on the chair. *Christmas Eve. It's Christmas Eve.* Inside the shower room there was someone who had chosen to spend this special night running across a field, badly burned and in terrible pain.

I relaxed, forgot my conventional ideas about what was right and wrong, good and bad, and I understood. *When in trouble, when in doubt, run in circles, scream and shout.* I was no different. Under slightly different circumstances my own field-longing might have been exactly the same. Being able to run with my body on fire, run and run and scream to feel numb and escape something else. Instead of fear, I felt a spontaneous tenderness towards the person who was so like me, deep down inside. On some level we all want to fall or burn. I picked up the piece of paper with Thomas's phone number on it and stared at it. The deadline for accepting his offer was fast approaching.

Perhaps I can explain my actions by saying that the experience in the tunnel had softened my moral code and created a longing to drop out of what I thought I was. Thomas answered on the fifth ring, obviously drunk. I could hear music in the background, but no voices.

'Yes?'

I was about to hang up, mostly as a reaction to Thomas's pathetic Christmas celebration, but I hesitated for a few seconds, which gave him time to ask, 'Is that John?'

'Yes.'

'Okay, cool. So you're in?'

I saw the picture Lars had painted: Thomas in his bed, hugging his mummy and daddy when they gave him his much longed-for Lego set.

'I'm in. On condition that...'

Thomas interrupted me. 'No one gets hurt, et cetera, et cetera. You don't need to worry—it's not that kind of job.'

'So what kind of job is it?'

'A house on Lidingö. Owners away over Christmas.'

'How do you know they're away?'

A long, drunken sigh, then: 'Friends of my dad's. I know them. Know where they keep stuff.'

'Is this some kind of...revenge?'

'What are you talking about? Where's that come from?'

'Forget it. Just something that came into my head.'

'For fuck's sake...I'll pick you up tomorrow at six.'

By the time I put down the phone I was regretting my decision, cursing my impulse-driven behaviour. I pulled the jumper my mother had given me down over my knees and tucked my feet underneath me. I sat in my chair curled up into a ball. It wouldn't have come to this if the shopkeepers had been a little more generous. It was their fault.

I wanted to run, roar, burn. Instead I sat there apathetically, glaring at the dying rosebush and imagining a Cruise missile taking down Santa's sleigh. All those children's presents turned to ash, and the reindeers' entrails raining down over the snow-covered earth, while Santa himself was impaled on the spire of the City Hall.

The following day I had booked a slot in the shower room at twelve. Without that knowledge I would have fallen apart. Again. I listened to 'Somebody' eight or nine times, sitting right next to the turntable, mechanically lifting and moving the needle. I tried 'Blasphemous Rumours', but as soon as I heard the introductory sound of the respirator I felt so uncomfortable that I went back to 'Somebody' and listened to it several more times.

*

At twelve o'clock precisely I opened the door of the laundry block and discovered that both machines were hard at work. There were two separate booking systems for the laundry and the inner room. The new key was a little bit stiff, but it worked. I went in, switched on the light and closed the door behind me.

There was something hypnotic about the smooth surface in the bathtub. I moved the knife and the towel and sat down on the stool with my elbows resting on my knees, keeping my eyes fixed on the black mass.

After a while I was convinced that something was moving beneath that mirror-glazed surface. I was also aware, in a way that couldn't be defined by normal perception, that it was much bigger than the bathtub. A blue whale swimming in a kitchen sink. It is possible to write the words but impossible to imagine, and I felt dizzy as the three dimensions of the room collapsed. The bath no longer seemed like a physical object within the room, but simply an opening.

My right hand was still sore, so instead I clumsily cut my left hand. The gash was deeper than I'd intended, and blood poured into the bathtub. Without further hesitation I thrust my hand into the blackness and closed my eyes.

When I got back to my house just under an hour later, I stood in the middle of the floor for a long time, trying to return to what we call reality. My skin was a porous borderline and parts of me evaporated into another world, infinitely distant yet only the blink of an eye away. I took off my clothes, got out a plastic jug and went into the toilet, where I poured cold water over my body, ignoring the fact that it splashed onto the floor. When I had rubbed myself dry and was beginning to drift back to my place in life, I sat down at the desk and opened my notepad at the page headed *The Other Place.*

*

*Maybe it's because of the larger amount of blood, but my body is different this time. Red smoke rises from my skin. Hooks protrude from my fingertips. I am a monster, a sexless creature with the ability to shapeshift. The magic has become physical. I think my arms long and they shoot out from my torso like tentacles, the hooks flashing through the air. It's amazing. This is my real body, not the sack of innards I drag around in my everyday life. This is me.*

*The place is different too, or else I'm in another area. On the horizon a wall of darkness extends from the ground to the sky. The shadows of my neighbours are here, but their heads are at the same height as the darkness and blend into it.*

*A difference in the colour of the grass ten metres away catches my eye. I focus my energy in that direction, lift the object lying there and bring it towards me, allow it to hover a metre in front of my eyes.*

*If I had any doubts that this was the place I visited when I was twelve years old, those doubts disappear in an instant. In the air before me is Rebus, the toy dog. He is completely unchanged. He has been waiting for me for seven years.*

*In the ordinary world I might have experienced a sense of nostalgia, but here I am the monster, and all I feel is rage. Rebus is a reminder of my weakness. I lash out with a tentacle, ready to tear him to shreds.*

*The hooks pierce Rebus's body and the shock of his* scream *makes me let go. It is not the howl of a dog but the scream of a child. That child, exactly the way he sounded when his bones broke. Rebus lies on the grass, staring at me with black eyes.*

*I turn away from him, drift away across the field, breathe in the red smoke from my skin and enjoy the moment to the full before I return.*

*

It might seem peculiar that I simply accepted the life form that the field allocated to me. But you who are reading this—you are not me, and you don't know me. You don't know what images I carry within me. The entity that I came to refer to as my 'field body' corresponded to an unattainable self-image that I didn't know I had. In later years I transformed various aspects of this self-image into characters in my stories: Eli, Teres, the Fisherman, Simon. Dilutions and echoes of the body I inhabited when I was on the field. The field showed me as I really was.

*Know thyself* has resounded as the battle cry of the thinking individual from ancient Greece through to Freud and beyond. It is every bit as unattainable as the exhortation *listen to your heart*. The heart is a muscle; its job is to pump blood around the body. It doesn't say anything. Listening out for its advice is something you can do only metaphorically.

The same applies to self-knowledge. People are as incapable of knowing themselves as the heart is of speaking. At best we can say that we have certain gifts or talents, certain weaknesses and fears. This doesn't mean that we know ourselves, or who we are, any more than could be expressed in a post on a dating website. We also have a tendency to lie, even to ourselves.

Back to the field.

The satisfaction of inhabiting a body and a state that felt utterly *true* is beyond description. To be able to transcend inwards and really be myself, regardless of my bodily form, was a presence and a pleasure I never thought possible, a happiness greater than anything I had previously regarded as happiness.

*

In spite of what I have written above, there was one thing that bothered me: the child's voice. It came from a different place than the rest of my experience in the field, just like when someone speaks in the cinema and breaks the illusion on the screen. The same space, but a different reality. I didn't want it there.

Elsa's key was lying on the table. I put it in my pocket and went to return it at long last, and perhaps to get answers to some of my questions.

She looked worn out when she opened the door. All she said was 'Oh, it's you,' then she shuffled back indoors without checking to see if I was following her. The formerly unified smell in the hallway had now splintered into traces of ginger biscuits, mulled wine, candles and perfume.

On my first visit Elsa had sat straight-backed like a queen; now she slumped so far down in her armchair that she appeared to be disappearing into the stuffing. I placed the key on the glass table and asked her how she was.

'Christmas,' she said. 'That's what's wrong with me.'

'Hard work?'

'That doesn't even begin to cover it.'

'It looked wonderful.'

Elsa glared at me as if I had just described a torture scene as 'tiptop', and to be fair, I knew what she meant. If you have started to associate with the truth, then it becomes difficult to lie, and Christmas is, among many other things, the number one occasion for lying.

'There's a child,' I said. 'In the other place.'

'Is that what you call it? *The other place?*'

'Yes. What do you call it?'

'Nothing. But I think of it as *the refuge*.'

'Okay. There's a child there. Do you know anything about that?'

With a huge sigh Elsa heaved herself up out of the chair and went over to the bay window, where the tarpaulin outside hid the view towards Tunnelgatan. She pointed towards Sveavägen.

'I was standing here,' she began. 'One night just under a year ago. I couldn't sleep. I'd been lying in bed worrying about my children.' She snorted and pulled a face, as if she were recalling a transgression in the past. 'The time was maybe one-thirty when an...equipage drove along Luntmakargatan and stopped by the tunnel.'

'An equipage?'

'I don't know what else to call it. There was a silver-coloured Volkswagen. A bubble. And hooked onto the back of it was a caravan, also silver-coloured. "The egg"—are you familiar with it?'

I nodded. When I was little I'd had quite a few toy cars and caravans. One of them was the egg-shaped model that had been popular in the 1950s.

'It was one of those,' Elsa went on. 'It stopped down below, by the entrance to the tunnel. The car door opened and a man unfolded himself. He was too big for that little car—almost two metres tall. He looked around, but I knew he couldn't see me because I was standing in the shadows.'

I sat there holding my breath; my face must have given something away, because Elsa said, 'Are you all right?'

'I'm fine. Go on.'

She looked searchingly at me, then once again adopted her stance from almost a year ago, perhaps to jog her memory.

'The man opened the door of the caravan and stepped in. My window was open a fraction, so I could hear music playing in the darkness.'

A cold hand reached up from my belly and nails scratched the inside of my throat when she told me she had recognised Jan Sparring's voice singing 'The Man Up There Must Like Me'. I didn't bother correcting her, and she continued.

'After a while he reappeared with a bundle in his arms. He walked quickly towards the tunnel, and I lost sight of him. After maybe thirty seconds he came back without the bundle, got in the car and drove off. I went down to the street and had a look, but there was nothing there. He must have left it in the tunnel.'

My throat felt sore from the scrabbling, tearing nails and I croaked, 'Isn't it locked at night?'

'He might have had a key. Why do you sound so weird? Do you know something about this?'

'Maybe. That bundle...what was it?'

Elsa flopped back into the armchair and pinched the bridge of her nose between her thumb and forefinger.

'I didn't call anyone,' she said. 'I didn't report it. I didn't want to get involved.'

'What kind of bundle was it? Could it have been a child?'

'I don't know. Not a small child, anyway. But there was something about the way he carried it...I should have reported it, I know that. When the tunnel opened in the morning I went down and looked, but all I found were a few rags.'

'Where?'

Elsa frowned. 'I told you—in the tunnel.'

'Where *exactly* in the tunnel?'

'Twenty metres in, perhaps? Why do you ask?'

I didn't want to go over the events with which I was familiar and my own role in them, so I dodged Elsa's questions and made my excuses. I said I had a lot to do and wished her Merry Christmas, then hurried back to my house.

*

*It must have been the child.*

*A year ago the child, who would then have been eleven years old, was left in the tunnel by the policeman. Was the child dead at that point, or was he still alive?*

*He was left where the busker played, and where I had made contact with the rock. Was that place already special beforehand, or did it become special because the child was left there?*

*Seven years ago the child said that he might have created the other place. The blackness in the child, the pull from the child, reminds me of whatever is in the shower room, and the thing in the shower room leads to the other place.*

*Where's the connection? Is the child part of the rock? Is the rock part of the child? Oh my God.*

*And what about me?*

*If it really was the child, then our paths have crossed twice now. Is it a coincidence? X, marked.*

*I don't understand.*

*And the 'equipage'? The car, the caravan and 'Somebody Up There Must Like Me'? The song the child crooned, the song the busker played.*

*I have to*

*

I put down my pen and sat staring at the last three words as I stroked the cross etched into my right arm. What did I have to do?

If I had previously been detached from everything and everyone, I now felt more like a crossroads or a meeting place for people, events, and *equipages*. A rail yard where incomprehensible freight was unloaded from abstract carriages, and fresh cargo crammed in for transportation. What was it and where was it going? What did I know? I was only the place where it occurred.

Maybe I was exaggerating my own role in the proceedings, as I so often did. Maybe it was just a coincidence that I happened to be in Blackeberg and on Luntmakargatan when the child's terrible story unfolded. To be precise, I hadn't even been living on Luntmakargatan at the time; I had moved in later. When the pressure began to get stronger.

I remembered how I had felt when I saw this house for the first time. In spite of the cramped proportions and the seedy atmosphere, the betting slips and the smell of smoke, something had clicked. *This is where I'm going to be.* The memory reminded me of something I had written earlier, and I flicked back through my notepad.

*Perhaps the most important decisions in our lives are made without the assistance of our intelligence. There is good reason to suspect that this is the case. So is it possible to talk about something that resembles the concept of* fate? *Maybe it is.*

It was well expressed, and I felt like Rabbit in *Winnie the Pooh.* He is praised by Pooh for his cleverness and fantastic brain. It is probably thanks to these very qualities that Rabbit never understands anything.

I knew so much, but understood nothing.

*

There was a knock on the door at quarter to six, and I shot up from my chair where I had been dozing. *Fucking hell!* For a few seconds I was completely disorientated. I knew who was knocking and why, but I didn't know how I felt about that. I took an internal sounding and discovered that the decision had already been made, with or without the assistance of my intelligence, so I went and opened the door.

'Nice jumper,' Thomas said, and walked in without waiting for an invitation.

I was still wearing the blue jumper my mother had given me for Christmas, but didn't want to share that particular piece of information. Thomas was carrying a black rucksack, and he was dressed in black jeans and a black jacket. He pushed his hands deep in his pockets as he looked around and said, 'So this is where you hide yourself away like a little Jew. Is that what you're wearing?'

'I'm not used to this kind of thing. Are you?'

'You mean have I done it before?'

'Yes.'

'Do you think I'd tell you if I had?'

'I thought you said you knew me?'

'Exactly. Put on something dark.'

My heart sank as I rummaged around in the wardrobe, searching for the navy blue duffel coat I'd stopped wearing because it was too small and too shabby. What did it say about me if I was upset because a skinhead thought I was unreliable? Besides which, he was probably right. I didn't even trust myself.

Thomas grinned when I pulled on the duffel. 'You look like a boarding-school boy who's fallen on hard times.'

'Thanks.'

'Here.'

He handed me a plastic object about the size of a cassette case, with a picture of Donald Duck on it. It was only when I saw the hole in one end that I realised it was a walkie-talkie. Thomas waved an identical one, except that his was adorned with Mickey Mouse, and said, 'Communication.'

'With *these*?'

'Yes. Have you got a better suggestion?'

'No, I just...'

'You'd just rather have some kind of commando model, which means that anybody and everybody would know exactly what they're for.'

'So do they work?'

Thomas backed away to the desk, pressed a button and spoke into the handset: 'The Nazi to the Jew, over.'

His voice emerged from Donald's beak, tinny but clear. I pressed my button; the best I could come up with was: 'Donald to Mickey. Over and out.'

*

We took the subway to Ropsten and changed to the Lidingö line. We didn't exchange more than a handful of words during the entire journey. I was conscious of the way people were looking at us, and wondered what conclusions they were drawing about me. Baby skinhead, hanger-on, secret Nazi sympathiser? It was a relief to disembark in the darkness at the deserted station in Kottla.

I was surprised at my lack of nerves or pangs of conscience now things were under way. I followed Thomas along Kottlavägen and up onto Pilvägen as if I was simply travelling along a track and completing the action that had been allocated to me.

The two-storey house was illuminated only by an outdoor Christmas tree. It was on a hill, which should ensure that I had a good view while I was standing guard. We got in through a hole in the hedge at the back, which Thomas clearly knew about already. While I kept an eye on the street, Thomas attacked the lock on the French doors with a hammer and a steel bar until it gave way and the door slid open. He nodded to me and then disappeared inside. I took out my Donald Duck walkie-talkie and checked that it was switched on.

Nothing was moving apart from the falling snow, as fine as icing sugar; I could see it in the glow of the street lamps, covering the odd parked car in a layer of powder. An Audi, a BMW. After I while I got bored and took a walk around the outside of the house, staying in the shadows. Thomas hadn't seemed bothered about leaving footprints, so I didn't either.

I crouched down so that I could make my way over to the Christmas tree without being visible over the hedge. It was beautifully, in fact lovingly, decorated with masses of expensive baubles, tinsel and hundreds of tiny lights strung through its branches. It was the finest tree I'd ever seen, something very different from the cheap, straggly objects my mother and I usually put up in Blackeberg. Best of all, it wasn't in a stand—it was actually growing there. It was perfect in its isolation.

I scurried back to the house. I had noticed a little shed by the garage; I opened the door and found that it was full of garden equipment. A lawnmower, a hedge cutter, spades, all barely distinguishable in the darkness. I groped around until I found a saw, then went back to the tree. The blade was far from sharp, and it took me a good five minutes to saw through the base until only a few millimetres of the trunk remained. When I straightened up, Thomas was standing there.

'What the hell are you doing?'

I pointed at the tree. 'If you just nudge it, it'll fall over. It's dead.'

'Okay. The question still stands: What the hell are you doing?'

'Don't know. It seemed appropriate.' I couldn't stop myself—the words just came flying out of my mouth. 'I'm a monster.'

Thomas looked from me to the tree and back again. He shook his head slowly. 'You do know that I can't trust you?'

'Absolutely. How did it go?'

'As expected.'

Before we left, I put the saw away in the shed.

I didn't want to tell Thomas, but I knew exactly why I had destroyed the tree. I had felt nothing as I stood there outside the house with the snow gently falling. Nothing. I had crossed a definite line and entered the world of real crime by aiding and abetting in a break-in, yet I didn't feel the least quiver of excitement, shame or fear. I was standing in a garden in the evening, observing an idyllic scene as the snow fell on beautiful homes.

I had imagined that some kind of dark satisfaction would well up and feed the monster. When that didn't happen, I was forced to take another step. And it worked, to a certain extent. Sawing through the trunk of the tree that would take many years to replace was an unmotivated, malicious act. I knew that the owner of the house would be extremely upset, and feel violated. Every pull of the saw hurt me, while at the same time it was *appropriate*, and that was what I wanted.

When I was finished I felt terrible, which in turn felt good.

As we waited for the train Thomas opened his rucksack and pulled out a piece of white material. He held it up in front of his chest, and I could see that it was a T-shirt.

'I found this in the boy's room. There was a pile of Moderate Youth League stuff, flyers and a load of other crap. And this.'

I had read about the T-shirt, but never seen it in reality. *Palmebusters.* A paraphrase of the Ghostbusters logo, with a long-nosed, evil-looking Olof Palme inside the red 'Stop' sign instead of a ghost.

'Terrible,' I said.

'Isn't it?' Thomas shook the T-shirt, making Palme's nose waggle. 'They've made him just like one of those caricatures of the Jews. Stolen our idea. I hate the bastards. Do you want it?'

He threw the T-shirt at me before I had the chance to answer, and I stuffed it into my pocket. Thomas unzipped one of the side compartments of his rucksack and took out a thick bundle of hundred-kronor notes. He counted off fifteen and handed them to me. 'They had cash. I'll give you the rest later.'

The train was approaching the platform and there was no one else around, so I folded the notes and tucked them in my inside pocket. I couldn't quite work out how I'd earned the money.

'Why did you want me to come along?' I asked as the train pulled in.

Thomas shrugged. 'What was it you said? *It seemed appropriate.* Although I could have done without that business with the tree. Then again...Maybe those fuckers deserve the odd setback.'

The doors opened and we stepped on board. During the journey to Ropsten I wanted to ask some of the many questions I had, but was prevented by Thomas's inaccessibility as he sat there staring out at the snow. We crossed Lidingö Bridge and I remembered my birthday, how Sofia and I had sat in exactly the same way. A train, a bridge, falling snow. It felt like a very long time ago.

Thomas got off at the central terminal, and I decided to keep him company and walk the last part of the way home. When we emerged into Sergels torg the snow was falling more heavily, flakes whirling all around us as we climbed the broad steps up to Drottninggatan. Thomas raised a hand in farewell, turned his back on me and headed towards the Old Town.

It felt pretty abrupt, but what had I expected? A big hug and the promise of eternal friendship? I shoved my hands in my pockets and set off in the opposite direction. Suddenly my fingers touched something: the walkie-talkie. I took it out and stared at Donald's cheerful face, spattered with snowflakes. Then I pressed the button and said, 'Thomas?'

After a couple of seconds he replied, 'Yes?'

'I've still got the walkie-talkie.'

'No shit, Sherlock.'

I pulled a face. I'd never met anyone with such a talent for making me feel stupid, but in spite of that, or possibly because of it, I said, 'Shall we have a beer? Celebrate?'

Thomas said something I couldn't make out, so I stayed where I was. After a little while his dark figure materialised against a backdrop of falling snow. I gave him the walkie-talkie; he slipped it into his pocket and said, 'Where to?'

*

We ended up in Monte Carlo. I went to the bar while Thomas sat down at the same table I'd shared with Lars two nights ago. When I put down the glasses and saw Thomas in the same light and from the same angle, the resemblance was clear. The slightly crooked mouth, the shape of the chin, the way the bridge of the nose curved into the eyebrows.

'I was sitting here with your dad the day before yesterday.'

'Okay.'

'He told me a few things.'

Thomas took a swig of his beer and ran his hand roughly across his mouth. 'He usually does.'

He didn't say any more, and we sat opposite each other in silence, gazing out at the falling snow. I had drunk half my beer when Thomas spoke again. 'He was my best friend—the Moderate Youth League idiot. When we were kids. Magnus. I could have been walking around in one of those T-shirts now.'

'I don't understand.'

'Do you need to? You say you're a monster. In which case you don't need to understand. Anything. That's the advantage.'

Something large and black loomed in my peripheral vision. An enormous man of Slavic appearance positioned himself at the end of our table and pointed at Thomas.

'You,' he said. 'Out. We don't want your sort here.'

Thomas blinked as if he suddenly felt weary. He only got out 'I could say the same—' before the man grabbed hold of him and yanked him to his feet. For a moment I thought he was going to headbutt Thomas, but he settled for half-dragging, half-carrying him to the door. I picked up Thomas's jacket and my rucksack and duffel coat and followed them. The rucksack was heavy; there was something metallic clanking inside it.

I reached the exit just in time to see the man slam Thomas down, spin him around and give him a kick in the small of the back, sending him flying headfirst into the street. He landed with his face in the snow, to the sound of laughter and applause from the bar. The man pointed a threatening finger at me before returning to his friends.

'Are you okay?' I asked Thomas.

He scrambled to his feet, brushing the snow off his jumper. 'That guy is a dead man,' he said, taking the jacket I was holding out to him. He spoke without conviction.

He shrugged on his rucksack and we ambled down Kungsgatan. There weren't many people around, and the Christmas lights swayed in the wind that was driving the snow into our faces. We were passing Café Mon Chéri when Thomas asked, 'So what did my dad say to you?'

I couldn't tell him what Lars had said without revealing what was in the shower room, and I didn't think I had the authority to do that. I also didn't want Thomas to know, so I said, 'That he misses you.'

Thomas snorted and shook his head. We reached Stureplan and walked underneath the Mushroom, where several people moved aside when they saw Thomas striding along with a murderous look on his face. When we had gone about a hundred metres along Birger Jarlsgatan, he stopped in front of the Riche bar's huge window and glared at the yuppies who were babbling away and stuffing their faces beneath the crystal chandeliers.

His face was inches away from the glass, and within less than a minute the atmosphere inside the restaurant had changed. People glanced furtively at Thomas, and their movements became smaller, more subdued, as they suddenly felt the need to concentrate on their food. They tried to avoid attracting attention, as if the Angel of Death was standing there weighing them up. The laughter and the hum of conversation died away, and the party atmosphere was ruined. Thomas gave a nasty smile and turned away.

We walked up towards Kungsträdgården in silence. When we had crossed Hamngatan, Thomas stopped, folded down the hem of his jeans and pulled on his woolly hat, so that he looked perfectly normal. It was hardly likely that any of the gangs who owned Kungsträdgården during the summer would be hanging out there on a cold and snowy Christmas Day, but it wasn't completely out of the question, and a skinhead on his own would be a real treat.

There was hardly anyone around and our footsteps squeaked through the empty space as we passed frozen fountains and elm trees; the wind had forced them to shake off the snow as soon as it landed on their bare branches. I began to suspect that I knew where we were going.

With his hands buried deep in his pockets, Thomas gazed up at the statue of Karl XII, the patina on its bronze surface shining faintly in the glow of a street lamp. Skinheads and National Socialists staged an annual march starting from this spot. Maybe Thomas usually took part. A cloud of vapour emerged from his mouth as he sighed and said, 'Why Karl the Twelfth? Such a useless fucking king. He messed everything up. Sometimes I'm so tired of all the crap.'

'What crap?'

Thomas didn't answer. Instead he dug into the pocket of his jeans and brought out a gold ring, which I assumed was the one I'd seen in the laundry room. He handed it to me and said, 'Give that to my dad,' then he left me standing under the statue and cut across Kungsträdgården, heading back towards Sergels torg. I stayed there for a little while, looking up at the king as he pointed into the falling snow, his expression blank. Then I went home.

*You say you're a monster. In which case you don't need to understand. Anything. That's the advantage.*

When I got back I could see that the light was on in Lars's window. I thought about going up to give him the ring, but decided to wait until the following day. I was chock-full of confused impressions, and I needed to rest.

*

Something happened on 26 December which at the time seemed unimportant, but came to have a crucial significance. It will probably lead to my being contacted by the police once this book is published, provided they believe what is written here. On reflection I'm thinking the risk isn't that great.

The sales began that day, and with money in my pocket I went out to buy or steal a new winter coat. After checking out a couple of stores I finally found what I was looking for.

It was more like an overcoat than a duffel, but it did have a hood. It was reduced from 2500 kronor to 990, and was a perfect fit. The lining was warm without feeling or looking bulky, and I don't think I've ever found a garment I was so certain that I wanted.

All that was irrelevant really; the key element was the colour. No one has heard of *the man in the duffel coat* or *the man in the overcoat* in connection with the assassination of Olof Palme. However, anyone who followed the story has heard of *the man in beige*—the only eyewitness who was never identified.

So the coat was a dark shade of beige. I should add that it had a magnetic tag, so I paid cash (albeit stolen money) for the item that would have the police searching for me in vain for months. Years, in fact. Here I am. You can call me if you like, but everything I know will be set out on these pages, little by little.

*

As I walked up the marble staircase in my lovely new coat, for the first time I felt as if I had the right to be there. I was no longer a scabby slum rat with matted fur, but a well-dressed young man on a mission. I rang Lars's doorbell, and as I listened to his approaching footsteps I tried to find a way of standing that matched the coat. Lars took no notice of my changed appearance, but when I said I had something for him, he hesitated briefly and then invited me in.

The apartment was spotless. The rugs looked freshly washed, and anything that could shine was shining. The draining board, which I could just see from the hallway, was so clinically clean that a surgeon could have operated on it.

Lars looked unhappy as I took off my coat and hung it on a hook. In spite of the fact that it was so clean, the hallway was quite cluttered, with clothes piled on every hook and heaps of shoes on the stand. Most of these items belonged to a woman and a child, and it wasn't hard to draw certain conclusions. As I draped my coat over a little denim jacket, I was sabotaging a carefully planned display in a museum. I pulled off my boots and placed them next to a pair of Sami boots before following Lars into the kitchen.

The window faced west, so there was no tarpaulin to stop the sun from flooding in, making the metal and lacquered surfaces shine with such intensity that I had to narrow my eyes when I sat down on the chair Lars pulled out. I unbuttoned my shirt pocket, took out the ring and gave it to him. His eyes widened, and he read the inscription on the inside.

'How did you get hold of this?'

'From Thomas. He told me to give it to you.'

Lars sank into contemplation of the ring, twisting and turning it in his fingers. I noticed a copy of *Dagens Nyheter* lying on the table; there was something odd about it. The headline referred to Watergate, which I didn't understand until I saw the date: 18 April 1973.

With a ceremonial air and an acquisitive glow worthy of Gollum, Lars slipped the ring onto the third finger of his left hand, and I said, 'So tell me about the ring.'

In a voice thick with emotion, Lars replied, 'It's my grandfather's wedding ring. Marianne had her grandmother's. We wanted time to...' He didn't get any further before a sob prevented him from continuing, and once again silent tears coursed down his cheeks as he gazed down at the ring on his finger.

I felt uncomfortable. 'Could I use your bathroom, please?'

He waved in the direction of the hallway and I got to my feet. As I passed a room with the door standing open, I peeped inside.

The walls were adorned with posters of Chip 'n' Dale, Baloo and Mowgli, plus, rather unexpectedly, a large picture of the entertainer Povel Ramel in a brightly coloured cap. On the floor were finished or half-finished Lego constructions, and from the ceiling plastic model planes were suspended on fishing line. A boy's room, Thomas's room, also preserved like a museum.

It didn't make sense. Thomas's mother had died when he was eleven, and he had continued to live with his father while Lars began to hate life, and everything fell apart. But this was not a teenager's room, or even that of an eleven-year-old. If I had to guess, I'd go for eight. Lars was not preserving, he was *re-creating.*

I went to the toilet, and now I was aware of the situation I recognised the rhomboid pattern on the bathroom mat from my childhood. The Pepsodent toothpaste tube on the side of the washbasin had a different design from the current one. I flushed the toilet and headed back to the kitchen.

Lars was still sitting at the table, totally absorbed in his own hand.

'When's Thomas's birthday?' I asked.

'The eighteenth of April.'

Lars looked at me, his expression telling me that he knew I understood. I nodded towards the newspaper. 'How long have you been working on this?'

'A couple of months.'

The same length of time as Lars had been associating with whatever was in the shower room, I assumed. When he was in there he returned to that special moment in his life, and he was simultaneously trying to re-create it in the real world.

'What's the goal?' I asked.

Once again that flickering veil of insanity passed over his eyes as he replied, 'I'm almost there.'

'What do you mean?'

'I know what I mean.'

He obviously had no intention of passing on this information, but continued to stare at the ring. I couldn't help feeling a little irritated as I said, 'Thomas cares about you.'

Without looking up, Lars said, 'I think you should go now. Thank you for your trouble.'

*

Later that evening I would come to understand more clearly the significance of Lars's project, but before I write about that I must say something about my magic.

I had a performance to deliver on New Year's Eve. Buying the overcoat had severely depleted my resources, and I couldn't be sure I would receive more money from Thomas, so the 1500 kronor was not to be sniffed at.

When I came back from visiting Lars, I got out my equipment to practise. It was a long time since I'd had a corporate gig, and the eight minutes my street routine lasted wouldn't do. I needed at least fifteen, and preferably something adapted to fit the context.

*The Boilermakers' Association*—what the hell was that? Stupidly I hadn't asked the person who called and booked me, but pretended I was fully up to speed. I assumed they didn't sell boilers, so what did they do? Were they some kind of freemasons' group? Dedicated boiler enthusiasts? I decided to ignore that aspect and focus on the concept of *New Year* instead. A presentation based on the idea of something old disappearing, only to be magically replaced by something new. Something to do with time.

*We wanted time to...*

What was the word that Lars had swallowed? Stop? Stretch? Was he trying to create a kind of magic, to draw a particular moment to him by staging that moment, just as the huntsman sets out a decoy?

Concentrate.

The Chinese Rings? One year linked to another? Maybe. It's just such a dull trick. The Cigarette in the Jacket always worked, especially if you used one of the bosses. Something about the fact that the company was going to do so well in 1986 that the boss would be able to afford a new suit, so it wouldn't matter if we burned the old one. If it was a company, of course.

I tried out different tricks, varied my presentation. This was the part I had always really enjoyed—the opportunity to be creative, to dress the old tricks in new clothes—but as the hours passed I realised that my thoughts were elsewhere, and soon I was so bored that I was sitting yawning at my desk.

In the field I had tasted what real magic can look and feel like; I had made things disappear, metamorphose and hover in the air; I had manipulated the hidden mechanisms of physical reality. Which is why sitting there saying *Look, there's smoke coming from the jacket, but hey presto—no burn!* felt dry and pointless.

I gritted my teeth and carried on. I couldn't afford the luxury of living only through the times when I was in the field, just as a relationship cannot be built on the limited time a couple spends having sex.

But I longed for the field, longed for the orgasm of being present in my monster's body.

I don't know the reason for what happened next. Perhaps I had become more receptive through *associating* with the others, or perhaps it was because I was thinking about the field. I could hear the distant roaring of the burned, running creature. I opened the blind and looked out. The light was on in the laundry block, and I knew the roaring man was in there now. I moved my chair over to the window and waited. The noise came and went in waves, and after ten minutes it stopped completely. A shadow passed across the floor, then the light went out and the door opened.

A man with a bottle in his hand emerged into the courtyard, and I recognised him. The circlet of grey hair framing the bald pate. It was the man who had gathered up the dead birds, but he had changed. The beer belly and the puffy cheeks were gone, and he was virtually emaciated. His clothes hung loosely on him, because they belonged to his former body.

I assumed he was about to take a swig from the bottle, and that alcoholism was to blame for his new appearance. So I didn't understand why he scraped away a patch of snow with his foot, then poured some of the contents of the bottle onto the ground.

He glanced up at the facades surrounding the courtyard, then crouched down and took out a box of matches. He struck one, and the flame that flared up made the shadowy hollows of his cheeks stand out. I slid off the chair and knelt by the window with my nose pressed against the glass, trying to see what he was doing.

His shoulders slumped, as if he had let out a long sigh. Then he dropped the match into the pool of liquid. Flames shot up, casting a circle of yellow light across the snow. The bottle probably contained petrol rather than alcohol, I concluded. The man's face contorted in a silent grimace of pain, his lips forming a black ellipse.

I looked down and saw that he had placed both hands in the fire and was holding them there. Though there was a pane of glass between us, I would have heard him if he had screamed. But he didn't scream. There was only that expression of silently endured pain. The flames licked his skin and I could smell burning hair and seared flesh. I couldn't, of course, but those silent screams had such power of suggestion that it seemed as if I could, and my own hands clenched into fists as if to protect themselves.

In less than ten seconds it was over. The flames died away and the man sat there examining his burned hands for a while, before burying them in the snow with a look of deep concentration.

*

*The experiences in the field create an urge to transfer them to this life. A desire to bring the two worlds into one accord.*

*In the field Lars can live in what he calls his special moment, but on Luntmakargatan he can only re-create the details and simulate the occasion. Is that what he means when he says he's almost there? Does he mean he's on the way to bringing those two worlds together?*

*It is not possible to live and to be as burned as the man in the field is, as he wants to be. In this world he can inflict only minor injuries on himself to retain the feeling, at least in part.*

*And me?*

*What about me?*

*

During the weeks that followed I would find the answer to that question. The others had been associating with the slime for longer than me, and had got further in their striving to achieve harmony between the worlds.

So wasn't I put off when I realised this association could lead to incidents like the man voluntarily burning his own hands? Yes, a little. But nowhere near enough to consider giving up the field.

I presume someone has already thought, *It's like a drug*, and to a certain extent it is comparable. The rush from a narcotic can evoke visions, insights and a perception of truth. It is rare, though, that the individual concerned can give a coherent description of those visions and what the truth actually means. Literature written under the influence of drugs is usually overblown, dozy and downright bad, regardless of what the author thinks.

I'm not claiming that what I am setting out here is anything particularly eminent, but at least I am trying to be clear, however strange some of the images I have described and am going to describe might be. If you find it impossible to accept this, then I hope that's because of the nature of the images rather than any obscurity in my style.

To return to the comparison with drugs, there is another reason why I wasn't put off, and here the analogy is more relevant. It's the usual mantra cited by anyone who's tempted by the rush: *It won't happen to me. I won't get hooked. I'm in control.*

*

I had booked a laundry slot for the following day, and I tossed the Palmebusters T-shirt in with everything else. When I stepped outside I saw the overweight woman who had wept and told me how unhappy she was waddling in through the door of the laundry block. She had put on several kilos, and was now morbidly obese. Her body listed and billowed, and her backside was nearly as wide as the doorway. I waited a couple of minutes before I followed her.

There was no sign of her in the laundry room, but the padlock on the shower room was hanging open. I loaded two machines, one with whites and one with coloureds. Before I started them up I stood still and listened, hoping to get a clue about the woman's experiences in the field. I couldn't hear a sound. Just like me, she was undertaking her journey in silence. Maybe it was only the Dead Couple who were different. I switched on the machines, went back home to pick up my notepad, then went out for lunch.

Talk of the devil...In the stairwell I met the couple I hadn't seen for months. If there was anyone who could have scared me off, they were standing in front of me right now.

Both of them were as pale as corpses, and I mean that literally. The epithet I had given them as a result of their manner now also applied to their appearance. The woman's blonde hair, which wouldn't have looked out of place in a Timotei shampoo ad a few weeks ago, now hung in lank, greasy strands over her face as she leaned against the wall, gasping for breath. The man's action-hero air was gone, replaced by what I will simply refer to as *decay*. Everything about him was drooping, sagging, and he was supporting himself on a huge cardboard box that was on the floor between them.

In spite of the alarming way they looked, I couldn't help bursting out laughing. According to the writing and the picture on the box, it contained a Grundig colour TV. The man peered at me from beneath a greasy fringe and said, 'Something amusing you?'

'No, I just thought you said you'd decided to stop watching TV.'

'We've changed our minds.'

He must have chosen to disregard my eavesdropping from a couple of months earlier, because he nodded at the box and said, 'Give me a hand.'

Carrying the television had obviously been too much for the woman. She didn't react as I tucked my notepad into the waistband of my trousers and lifted what had been her end; she just stood there leaning against the wall, wheezing away.

The TV was quite heavy, and we probably wouldn't have made it up the two flights of stairs if I hadn't taken most of the weight. When we reached the landing, the man grabbed his doorhandle to stop himself from collapsing. He just had enough air to croak, 'Thanks.' No beer or small talk this time. I nodded in response and went back down.

The woman had managed to get up a few steps, clutching the banister as if she were a hundred years old. When I reached the main door I turned around and looked at her, and I couldn't help gasping.

She was wearing a thin, light coat with a polo-neck jumper

underneath. Even so, such a large quantity of blood had soaked through the layers of clothing that the back of the coat showed a stain about the size of a rugby ball. I hurried back to her and asked, 'Is there anything I can...'

The hand that wasn't gripping the banister flew out in a jerky, dismissive gesture, and a hoarse 'Shoo, shoo!' emerged from her throat, as if she were chasing away a stray cat begging for food at a pavement cafe. I watched as she laboriously dragged herself up a couple more steps; I felt a strong urge to stick my foot out and trip her up, but instead I turned and walked away.

While I was having lunch at Kungstornet I jotted down some speculative ideas about what might have happened to the Dead Couple, but I won't bother recounting them here, because they were so far off the mark. Their project was far beyond my imagination. I will have to write about it eventually, but until then I will simply note that it was also about bringing the world of the field and our world together. You could say that the field was *leaking*, and that this leak was very difficult to stop once it had started.

*

It wasn't until I went down to the laundry block the following day for my slot in the shower room that I realised I'd left the Palmebusters T-shirt behind when I emptied the tumble dryer. Someone had slipped it onto a hanger and hung it on a hook, so the caricature was now dangling there for all to see.

I thought the T-shirt was incredibly ugly and I didn't want anything to do with it, so I left it where it was. Plus that was a weird thing to do, hanging up a crap T-shirt as if it were an expensive dress shirt. Maybe the person who had found it sympathised with the message? In which case they were welcome to adopt it. I went into the shower room.

What happened in the field on this occasion would play a crucial role in my life, but just as with the beige duffel coat, I didn't realise it at the time. I will quote from *The Other Place*, and after that the tone of this narrative will change, because my way of thinking, or rather *not* thinking, changed.

*

*I love my monster's body—it is everything I have wished for and missed. I am made of and held together by magic, running like nectar through my veins, and I project a representation of myself that I chop up, set fire to and reassemble before I allow it to dissolve in a shower of sparks, with my neighbours' shadows as a silent audience.*

*It's not enough. I construct Carola Häggkvist, everyone's sweetheart, and I have her stretched on a rack made of gold until the skin on the crook of her arm splits and I am able to see quivering, bleeding sinews at breaking point and I turn her howls of pain into songs before I put her back together again.*

*I can't get there. One last thing is missing. I catch sight of Rebus lying on the grass and draw him towards me. As I sink the hooks on my tentacles into his body I hear the scream of the child. I ignore it and tear him to pieces. The scream falls silent and something I wanted to kill within myself actually dies.*

*I look around with burning eyes. There is nothing in the field, apart from the neighbours' shadows and the shredded remains of Rebus. I can do exactly what I want. And yet.*

*'What?' I yell up into the empty blue sky. 'What?'*

*I create more magic, more illusions; I give the performance of the millennium in a state of ecstasy which lacks only that last thing, that one last thing.*

*What?*

*

When I got back to my house my entire body was itching; the sensation was worst over the X-shaped scar on my right arm. I scratched both arms until they were covered in red marks, then managed to stop myself. The memory of the bloodstain on the Dead Woman's back made me clench my fists and lower my hands. I remained motionless for several minutes, as if I were standing to attention, then took out the subway ticket with Thomas's phone number on it and called him. After seven rings he answered, sounding distinctly irritated.

'Yes?'

'It's John.'

'Wait.'

In the background I could hear music and several voices, all male. I picked out the words 'Like, old men in caps', then the phone was carried away from the noise, presumably using an extension cord. A door closed and the voices were gone. Thomas got straight to the point.

'You get four thousand.'

'Why so little?'

'That's just how it worked out.'

I sensed that it would be pointless to push the matter, so instead I came out with the real reason for my call: 'Anything else on the horizon?'

Thomas laughed. 'Keen, are you?'

'Very keen.'

'Well, since you ask...Tomorrow. Have you got a torch?'

'I can get one.'

'You do that. I'll be there at nine.'

The urge to scratch had subsided. With a sigh I took out my magic paraphernalia and practised without any real commitment for a couple of hours. Just after eight I heard a dry rustling sound. The last leaf had dropped off the rosebush. Appropriately enough, Sofia called half an hour later.

She wanted to know what had become of me, which was not a question I could answer. Her voice reached me from a time so distant that I couldn't be sure whether it was something that had really happened, or just a dream. I couldn't remember what she looked like—not the slightest detail. Only when I recalled that she resembled

Anna Lindh was I able to put a face to the voice on the other end of the line, but that face definitely belonged to the chair of the Social Democratic Youth League.

'This is pointless,' I said. 'I don't remember you.'

'What do you mean? It's only a week since...'

'I mean exactly what I say: I don't remember you. I don't know who you are.'

There was a brief silence, and when Sofia spoke again it was clear that she was fighting back the tears. 'You forgot your backgammon set.'

I had a vague memory of board games, of sitting with Anna Lindh playing board games, but it had nothing to do with me now, so I said, 'Keep it.'

A sob. 'John, what's happened to you?'

I didn't like her saying my name in that way. Hesitantly, pleading with a version of me that was no longer relevant. I said, 'Don't call me again,' and hung up.

I sat with my hands resting on my knees, and realised I was smiling. Did Sofia think I was a monster now?

*

*If we cannot gather around the light then we gather around the darkness*

*If we cannot gather around the light then we gather around the darkness.*

*If we cannot gather around the light then we gather around the darkness.*

*If we cannot gather around the light then we gather around the darkness.*

*If we cannot around the light gather then around the darkness we gather*

*If we cannot around the light gather then around the darkness we gather*

*If the light cannot gather us then we allow the darkness to gather us*
*We grate the light and around the darkness gather*
*Shreds of light and shreds of darkness we gather*
*Around every house a light around every door a darkness*
*Etc, etc.*

*

The next day I was slightly horrified when I looked at what I had written on my notepad during the night. After repeating the first sentence a number of times, the various permutations went on for four pages.

Yes, I had seen *The Shining* and I knew what it meant. *All work and no play makes Jack a dull boy.* But I hadn't been in an unconscious trance state as I filled those pages, oh no—I had been focused and resolute like someone with a problem to solve, a mystery to unravel. What horrified me was the time I had spent on something that now appeared utterly meaningless. The only insight I gained was the realisation that I must have been a little bit crazy the previous evening.

Too much sitting indoors and silent brooding. I decided to spend the day outside. Away from the house. I felt quite energised as I dressed warmly in my gloves, woolly hat and scarf, and my lovely duffel coat.

I walked for hours, and perhaps a description of our capital city in her winter garb might be appropriate here, but that kind of thing is never going to be one of my skills. I'm not sufficiently interested in buildings, light, atmosphere. I hardly ever notice them.

An old man was sitting fishing through a hole in the ice in front of the City Hall, and from the St Eriksbron Bridge I saw a group of cross-country skiers swishing away towards Karlberg. Some children were building a snowman by the palace, and had amusingly placed a crown on his head. I stopped by Slussen and watched a woman with her dog. They both stood motionless, gazing up at the Katarina Lift. On Götgatan I saw a policeman eating a kebab in a very deliberate, almost *coquettish* manner.

People in their kaleidoscopic incomprehensibility, the city as a silent stage set. I walked with my hands deep in the roomy pockets of my duffel coat, looking at people and trying not to understand what they were doing and why.

*I am a monster. I don't need to understand.*

I walked, I was a monster and at the same time I was one among many, and at that moment it was a much-needed feeling. The itching was lying in wait, but I was holding my own against it. I had lunch at Pizza Hut on Klarabergsvägen. A perfectly normal day as a prelude to an anything but normal evening. I finished it off by stealing a head torch from Åhlén's sports department.

*

When Thomas knocked on my door just before nine, I was already dressed. The beige duffel coat wasn't right for the night's activities, but I had thrown the old navy one away, so I had opted for two jumpers. The top one was a mossy green, with a woolly hat of the same colour. Of course the first thing Thomas said when he saw me was: 'Hello, Kermit.'

'Shut your mouth.'

'What did you say?'

'Shut your mouth.'

Thomas looked down at the floor, and seemed to be considering whether to cooperate or come up with an even worse insult. Instead he took a step forward and shoved me with both hands, so hard that I fell backwards onto the rosebush, which crashed to the floor. Dried-up thorns found their way through the wool, and the pain brought tears to my eyes. A couple of branches got stuck under my back as I lay there.

'We don't use that *tone of voice*,' Thomas said. 'We don't speak *in that way*. Do you understand?'

'But you were the one who...'

'No, you're the one who doesn't understand. Who thinks you're something you're not. Can we agree on that?'

I wriggled my right hand to try and extract the thorns from my jumper, and said: 'No'.

'What do you mean, no?'

I scratched the palm of my hand and probably pulled a few threads, but I managed to extricate myself and got to my feet. 'No, we cannot agree that you can say whatever the fuck you like to me and I'm not allowed to respond. We definitely cannot agree on that.'

Thomas gazed at me with his eyelids half-closed and I tensed, ready for another shove or a flying fist. I knew I couldn't match him, but maybe I could avoid falling over again. As if he'd never even considered such an option, Thomas pushed one hand into the back pocket of his jeans, nodded towards the dead rosebush and said, 'I see you have green fingers.'

It was quite funny, and I let out a snort of laughter. Thomas shook his head. 'Okay, so are we ready? Can we go?'

'Absolutely.'

He took a thick envelope out of his jacket pocket and tossed it on the desk. I pretended I didn't care, which wasn't difficult, because I really didn't. We left.

*

The house we were visiting that night was also on Lidingö, by the headland at Talludden, four stations further on than last time. I was given my walkie-talkie and we set off into a forest, where the wide treetops hid the clear, starlit sky to such an extent that it was pitch dark. We switched on our flashlights; I sensed that Thomas wanted to make a disparaging comment about my head torch, but he refrained. I regarded that as a victory.

After trudging through deep snow for five minutes, we reached a wall. Thomas must have done a recce in advance, or else he was familiar with this place too, because he immediately went over to a pine tree and clambered up onto the wall. I followed him, and we perched there shining the beam of our torches at a considerably more opulent home than the previous one.

'Okay,' Thomas said. 'This is more of a risk. I don't know this house as well.'

'No convenient childhood friends?'

The question was meant to be ironic. The property looked as if it was in the twenty million kronor bracket, with a large covered swimming pool. I'd never even been close to a place like this. Either Thomas didn't pick up on the irony or he chose to ignore it. 'I've been here a couple of times, but that was years ago.'

We lowered ourselves from the wall, dropping the last couple of metres and rolling over in the snow. Thomas plodded along the edge of the pool while I went to look for a ladder to secure our escape route. There was a separate garage, big enough to house two tractors. A snow shovel was propped against the wall, with a ladder hanging above it. The street below was in darkness, and I could see lights in only one or two houses. No doubt everyone was in Hawaii.

The ladder had frozen onto its hooks; I freed it with some difficulty and carried it on my shoulder up to the house, where Thomas was fiddling with the lock on the French doors. I put down the ladder, leaned it against my body and waited.

Thomas swore quietly as he tried to force the lock with a screwdriver, but he couldn't do it. I got the impression that he wasn't all that skilful, and had just been lucky or had prior knowledge last time. After a couple of minutes he angrily shoved the screwdriver in his pocket, turned to me and shook his head. I nodded, grabbed hold of the ladder

*Monster*

lowered it like a lance and took a couple of rapid steps towards Thomas. When he realised what I was about to do, he half-screamed, half-whispered, 'No, for fuck's...' But even if I'd wanted to, I couldn't have stopped the impetus. The end of the ladder crashed into the French doors, which shattered into hundreds of shards. The noise was so brutal in the silence that it sounded as if something had smashed inside my head. Then nothing.

'There you go,' I said.

Thomas stared at me with a mixture of anger, disbelief, and...was there a spark of fear too?

'What the fuck...What if they'd had an alarm?'

'Apparently they don't,' I said.

We listened. We couldn't hear anything, but what did I know about alarm systems? Maybe a silent signal was passed to a security firm. Anyway, my action felt absolutely right, and I wanted to keep on destroying things, so I said, 'I can go inside.'

As if Thomas sensed my intentions he held up his hand. 'You stay here, you fucking lunatic, and keep watch.' He kicked away a few pieces of glass from the bottom of the door and went in. I considered going after him, but instead I followed our footprints back to the wall and propped the ladder against it. Then I went over to the garage and gazed down the drive, where a solitary light illuminated a pair of closed iron gates. Inside the house I could see the beam of Thomas's torch flickering over the walls.

I wasn't thinking about anything. My hands were itching.

After a few minutes a car drove along the street, but as far as I could tell it didn't have a security logo. Maybe it was just a neighbour who'd heard the sound of breaking glass, or seen the light of Thomas's torch. The car stopped by the gates and the driver's door opened. I took out the walkie-talkie: 'Someone's coming. Can you hear me?' Thomas answered, 'Okay. Let's get out of here.'

By this stage the man who had got out of the car had opened the gates. He was middle-aged, wearing a suede jacket and a checked cap with ear flaps. He still hadn't noticed me, because his attention was focused on the house. Thomas had switched off his torch.

The snow had been cleared from the drive, so the man was able to make rapid progress. I knew what I was going to do. I clicked my head torch onto full beam, grabbed the snow shovel and went towards him. As I had expected he held up his hands to shield his eyes from the dazzling light; there was no way he could see my face.

I had originally intended to use the shovel as a threat. After a few steps I had decided to hit the man with it, but when I saw him standing there blinded and defenceless, I changed my mind yet again. As the distance between us diminished I ran the palm of my hand along the aluminium edge. It was sharp, and if I struck hard it should be enough to separate the man's head from his body. Possibly. I gripped the handle more firmly and moved the shovel to the side so that I could swing it in an arc.

However, the man must have been able to see enough to perceive the threat. I had just tensed my muscles to begin the movement that would end his life when he spun around and ran back to the gate. I started to follow him, then stopped because a *no* had flashed inside my head.

A month earlier I would have been devastated, terrified at what I had been about to do, an act that would have changed who I was beyond repair. As I stood on the drive and watched the man leap into his car, I simply thought something along the lines of: *Oh dear, I got a little bit carried away there.* No big deal.

I walked back to the house and found Thomas standing with his arms folded. Presumably he had seen everything, because he slowly shook his head when I put down the shovel and switched off the torch.

'What the fuck is wrong with you?' he said. I interpreted this as an expression of admiration rather than a question, so I didn't answer. What could I possibly say?

*

The balance of power between Thomas and me shifted that night. The way he looked at me and spoke to me changed. Maybe it was because he thought I was crazy, and the respect he showed me was the respect with which you treat a mad dog. Whatever—it was still respect, and there was a certain wariness in the way he addressed me.

I should have been pleased. Ever since I first met Thomas I had felt that same respect for him, regardless of his political views, and without admitting it to myself I had striven to win his admiration. Now that I had it, to some extent, I felt nothing; and maybe that was a prerequisite. The train clattered along on the Lidingö line, and my strongest feeling was a sense of dissatisfaction, gnawing at my gut like hunger. We had passed through several stations when Thomas asked, 'Could you do me a favour?'

'No problem.'

'Could you stop smiling like that?'

I hadn't even been aware that I was smiling, but when Thomas pointed it out I realised my cheeks were hurting. Perhaps it was an involuntary reaction, like when a hyena laughs after missing its prey. I relaxed my cheek muscles and said, 'I'll smile however I fucking like.'

Thomas shrugged and lifted his rucksack onto his knee. 'Aren't you even going to ask what we got?'

'What did we get?'

'Nice of you to ask. Next to nothing. If they had any good stuff, it was locked away. Some small change. Here.'

He glanced around, then held out a hundred-kronor note and a fifty-kronor note, which I waved away. 'Keep it.'

Thomas looked almost hurt. 'What the fuck is wrong with you?'

'You've already asked me that.'

'And?'

'Stop asking.'

Thomas glared at me and I could see that he wanted to punch me, shake me, throw me down on the floor. That was okay. No problem. But he resisted, and peered into his rucksack instead.

'I picked up a few bits and pieces that might make a few thousand. But I presume you're not interested?'

'Wrong.'

When I didn't say anything else he closed the rucksack and put it back on the floor. We spent the rest of the journey into town staring out of the window. The hunger barked and screamed.

*

There was no suggestion of going for a drink that night. We parted company at the central terminal after Thomas had looked closely at me and actually said, 'John? Take care of yourself.' I said I would, and chose the Åhlén's exit so that I could walk home via Drottninggatan and Hötorget. The hunger was there all the time—or maybe that's not the right word. Maybe *lust* is better. A growing bubble of lust that would have to burst at some point.

I cut across the square, kicking a lump of ice in front of me. It was gone midnight, and there were very few people out and about on this bitterly cold night. I shivered and flapped my arms around my body to try to get warm. I was missing my duffel coat. I put on my head torch and dazzled the driver of a cab coming towards me on Kungsgatan. He swore at me, but drove on.

As I approached the window of Dekorima, I could see that Santa had finished his task. A completed *Still Life with Oranges and Carnations* now filled his canvas, and he was facing the street with a satisfied grin, as if to say *Look what I can do.* I stared at him and the bubble grew much bigger.

I turned down Tunnelgatan and rummaged around among the building materials until I found a piece of iron piping about three metres long. I picked it up and went back to the shop window. I opted for the double grip like a pole vaulter and aimed at Santa's head as I hurled the pipe at the display. For the second time that evening my head was filled with shattered glass, and the bubble burst. Pieces of the broken window rained down on the pavement, and though I hadn't managed to decapitate Santa, the pipe hit him smack bang in the middle of his face, and he fell onto his easel, sending carnations and brushes and tubes of paint and all the other crap crashing to the floor.

As I let go of the pipe and ran towards the Brunkeberg Tunnel, a siren began to scream. Dekorima had an alarm system. Far behind me I could hear someone yelling, 'Hey! What the hell are you doing?', but I kept on running, past the builders' huts, without looking back.

It wasn't until I tugged at the handle of the door leading into the tunnel that I remembered it was locked at this time of night. I was about to turn and run up the steps when I caught a glimpse of movement in the darkness inside.

I switched on my head torch and shone the beam through the reinforced glass, but after a couple of seconds I heard running footsteps behind me. I threw myself over the railing and dashed up the steps to Malmskillnadsgatan. When I reached the top I glanced over my shoulder and saw that my pursuer had stopped halfway up and was leaning against the railing. A shudder ran right through me when I thought about the fact that what I had seen in the tunnel was now directly under my feet, and I jogged off towards St Johannes Church. It rose up from the ground like a mountain, blocking out the sparkling, starlit sky. My heart was pounding, hot and red inside my cold skin. I sat down on a step that lay in deep shadow, out of the moonlight, and gazed out across the snow-covered gravestones, shining pale blue beneath bare chestnut trees.

Human beings are *layered* and we are capable of harbouring contradictory emotions, but on different levels. I was at peace and in uproar. I was calm and my pulse was racing. The sight of the churchyard was a balm and a source of anxiety. What had happened at Dekorima gave me tranquillity; what I had seen in the tunnel worried me.

Before I draw any conclusions, I will tell you what I saw during those few seconds when the beam of my torch lit up the dark interior of the tunnel. I saw a slim person slowly walking in the direction of Birger Jarlsgatan. The figure was wearing a grey jacket with the hood pulled up. Next to the person was what I first thought was a dog, but when I saw the long, swishing tail, the shape of the body and the way it moved, it seemed to me that it resembled a tiger. A black tiger, hard to make out in the faint light.

That is what I saw. I immediately dismissed the idea of a tiger, because it was hardly possible, but I was convinced that the figure I had seen walking away from me was the child. Judging from the build and height it could easily have been a twelve-year-old, and the figure was also *limping* in a way that was painful to watch, as if the legs had broken

*been broken*

then healed and broken again until all that remained were these shattered crutches that just about provided enough support. When the child and the animal saw the light of my torch, they stopped and turned around. That was when I jumped over the railing, but I did have time to see the shape of the animal's face, its nose, its eyes. It *was* a tiger. I also saw that the child's hood was drawn up so tightly that it completely covered the face. Then I fled.

I sat by the church door, shivering. Over by the steps someone came up onto Döbelnsgatan and looked around, presumably searching for me, but I was safe in the knowledge that he couldn't see me, and after a little while he gave up and disappeared back down the steps.

I took off both jumpers and swapped them over so that the pale red one was on the outside. I would get sick if I sat on the cold stone any longer, so I got up and took a detour via David Bagares gata. My teeth were chattering when I finally turned into Luntmakargatan via Apelbergsgatan. Even though I'd changed my jumpers around I didn't dare risk checking out what was happening at Dekorima; I went straight home.

Once indoors I put on my dressing-gown over the top of my clothes and wrapped myself up in a blanket. It was five minutes before my fingers loosened up enough to hold a pen.

*

*The policeman left the child dying in the tunnel. He survived against all the odds, his bones healed to a certain extent and now he walks in there at night. And the tiger? The tiger? Did it spring from the child? From the rock? Is the tiger...Sigge? That sounds like a children's book, for fuck's sake. Sigge Tiger. I sensed that it was old, more than old. Ancient.*

*What do they do together, the tiger and the child? Where do they go when morning comes?*

*Did the child actually survive?*

*Did the child survive?*

*

I had set the alarm for the following morning so that I could be there when the tunnel opened at seven. It was still dark when I went out, dressed in my duffel coat. I glanced over at Dekorima and saw that the window had been boarded up with a sheet of plywood.

At two minutes to seven a man in blue thermal overalls arrived and unlocked the tunnel doors. He stared at me for quite some time as I stood there bobbing up and down. I had the feeling that he recognised me from the night before, and I turned my face away. As soon as he opened the door and set off to unlock the other end, I followed him in.

*Did the child survive?*

There was no sign of either the child or the tiger inside the tunnel, which had been locked all night. The man in the blue thermal overalls was moving away from me; he was exactly where I had seen the child. He had switched on the light, and I had a clear view all the way to the door leading to Birger Jarlsgatan. There was nowhere to hide.

I walked slowly, carefully examining the walls, but there were no doors or openings, no possible way out. When I reached the far end I turned back, this time staring up at the ceiling.

Every thirty metres there was a grille covering an opening that presumably led to ventilation shafts. I reached up as high as I could with my right hand, and when my outspread fingers were about five centimetres below the grille I could feel a stream of warm air coming through the grubby, sticky iron bars.

*How does he get up there?*

If I really thought the child was hiding in the ventilation shafts, it wasn't hard to come up with a solution. A stool or a ladder that was lowered down, then pulled back up again. I walked the length of the tunnel and counted eight grilles. The last one was close to the spot where I'd had contact with the rock. If I wasn't mistaken, it was cleaner than the others. As if it had been *handled.*

And the tiger, the ancient tiger? Was it some kind of field-creature, something that had come out of the rock, or an aspect of the child? When I tried to think about it, my thoughts slid away like an object going out of focus. For the moment I consigned it to the scrap heap and concentrated on the child.

I wrapped my arms around my body and let out a hissing sound, 'psst', which made the hairs on the back of my neck stand on end when I remembered standing below the tree house in the woods and making exactly the same sound. I clenched my jaws tight shut to prevent myself from screaming if an answer should come out of the darkness, if a pair of eyes should appear behind the grille. But there was no answer, and I didn't repeat my call; I left the tunnel.

The air must have been drawn into the ventilation shaft somewhere before being warmed by the rock and flowing out into the tunnel. As the faint glow of dawn crept across the sky and the stars began to fade, I wandered around looking for the opening. Much to my relief, I didn't find it.

*

'You didn't actually answer the question. You didn't say whether you've seen or heard a child in the other place.'

Elsa had just lifted the pot of coffee off the hotplate and was pouring us each a cup. I noticed that she had to hold it with both hands, because they were shaking.

'Ginger biscuits,' she said, nodding towards a basket on the table. They were standard shop-bought heart-shaped biscuits, so Elsa clearly wasn't the kind of granny who did lots of baking. Or she was *no longer* that kind of granny. I picked up a heart, placed it on the palm of my hand and pressed with my index finger. It snapped into three pieces. I couldn't remember why you were supposed to do that, what it meant.

'It's hard for me to know,' Elsa went on eventually.

'Either you noticed the child or you didn't. Yes or no.'

'What's with the tone of voice?'

Despite her trembling hands, the frailty I had seen in Elsa on my last visit had disappeared, and the regal manner had returned. I backed off.

'Sorry. Recently I've...'

'Yes?'

'Changed.'

'Everyone changes,' Elsa assured me. 'When they begin to associate. Have you changed for the worse?'

'I don't know. It *feels* good, but when I look at what I'm doing, I'm not so sure.'

I picked up the smallest of the three pieces of biscuit, popped it in my mouth and chewed. It tasted of nothing.

'You're the only one who can decide,' Elsa said. 'If you're going to carry on or not. And to go back to your question...' She blew on her coffee and took a tiny sip. '...as I said, I'm not the right person to ask.'

'Why not?'

'Because my experience is such that it's hard to make out a child.'

'I don't understand.'

'No, how could you? You don't know what I look like when I'm there, what I do.'

'And you don't want to tell me.'

'The fact is, I was thinking of contacting you today anyway. Most of us are meeting up tomorrow night.'

'On New Year's Eve?'

'Yes, it felt right, somehow.'

'And what are you...or rather we...going to do?'

Elsa didn't give me a direct answer; instead she took another sip of coffee while staring blankly into space, as if she were recalling an image in her mind. She put down the cup and said, 'Have you noticed that there's a frustration? A...dissatisfaction?'

'Yes.'

Elsa nodded. 'That feeling has become increasingly painful for those of us who've been involved for longer than you, and something has to be done. So we thought we'd show ourselves to one another.'

'In the field?'

'Yes. I'm sure you've seen the shadows. We thought we'd try turning them into flesh, so to speak, by travelling together.'

I remembered the *What?* that I had yelled out in the field, that sense of dissatisfaction that had given rise to the destructive urges I felt in this world, and I asked, 'What time?'

*

The meeting in the laundry block was due to start at ten o'clock on New Year's Eve, so when I arrived at the Boilermaker's Association HQ on Sankt Eriksgatan half an hour before I was due to appear at eight, I assumed I had plenty of time.

The party was in full swing, with drinking songs and speeches. As I waited in a storeroom with piles of stacking chairs, I left the door ajar so that I could listen. I still wasn't sure what these people actually did.

At eight-thirty the person who had booked me and who had also met me when I arrived came in to say things were running a little late, there were more speeches than expected, but people were pretty merry, which was bound to be an advantage as far as I was concerned, wasn't it? Without waiting for a response the man tottered back to the party, leaving me grinding my teeth.

As I mentioned before, there is no advantage whatsoever if my audience is *pretty merry*, quite the reverse in fact, and at a party like this it's even worse. The merriment could easily lead to a desire to show off, to shout comments or actually clamber up on stage to tell a joke or demonstrate some magic trick of their own during my performance. It had happened before.

I decided to walk. The man hadn't even apologised for leaving me stuck in this fucking storeroom—he probably thought there was no need because I was there to *serve* and would wait politely until I was told to perform my *services*. I got to my feet, picked up my bag and was on my way out of the door when I came up with a better solution. Revenge. I sat down again, crossed my legs and smiled.

The man reappeared just before nine, his eyes watery and unfocused. He informed me that the atmosphere was absolutely brilliant—yes yes yes, showtime! I stood up with dignity, gave him a little bow, grabbed my bag and my stool and followed him into the room.

There is no need for me to describe the party or the room in any detail; they're all the same. The long tables, the red faces, jackets off, blouses unbuttoned maybe just a little too far. There were around sixty people in the smoky room, where the temperature was approaching thirty degrees and most of the partygoers had reached the stage of intoxication where they had started stubbing out their cigarettes in the potato gratin.

The man who had booked me stepped onto the stage and executed a few clumsy dance steps before waving his arms in an attempt to silence the crowd. He was aged about fifty, and I assumed he was the company's Minister of Fun. A garish tie adorned with fireworks and shot glasses dangled over an impressive belly, which bumped into the microphone stand and meant he had to lean forward to get his mouth anywhere near the mic.

'Comrades!' he bellowed. 'Fellow delegates!'

Loud whistling and cheering. I didn't think the Boilermakers' Association had anything to do with the Socialists—the man was just being *ironic*, and it worked. He went on: 'I now have the honour of introducing a young man from Blackeberg. I lived there for a few years in the sixties and I knew his mother, so you never know who I'm actually introducing! Thank you very much!'

Laughter and applause. If there had been a sharp object within reach, a fork or a steak knife, I might well have picked it up and stabbed him. What right did he have to talk about my mother? Every right, in his opinion. Hatred flared up inside me, and only the thought of revenge enabled me to climb up onto the stage and say, 'Good evening! So you're the Boilermakers' Association? Is that why it's so warm in here?'

Strangely enough, the performance went well. The venom I felt towards every single person in the room emanated from me in the form of an intensity that was able to cut through to their booze-addled minds. The Cigarette in the Jacket was a success, and the poisonous jokes I aimed at an under-manager provoked bursts of laughter, even though the manager himself was clearly upset. Fine by me. The applause at the end of my act was loud and heartfelt. I smiled, bowed and waved. *Bye bye, everyone—I'm just a clown without the slightest trace of resentment.*

The man with the festive tie accompanied me to the cloakroom and then down to the foyer, where he gave me an envelope containing my fee and said, 'Er...I hope you didn't mind...that comment about your mother...it might have been a bit...'

'No problem,' I said, patting him on the shoulder. 'I thought it was funny.'

He looked at me with a certain amount of scepticism, then seemed to decide that I meant it. He shook my hand and said, 'Great show. I might call you again.'

'Do that,' I said. I opened the door, walked out into the street and set off slowly, listening hard. My revenge depended on what the man did next. When I arrived the door had been locked. I had rung the bell, and he had come down with a key, but when we went up to the party room, he had forgotten to lock it behind us. He was even more drunk now, and I hoped he would make the same mistake again.

I went about twenty steps without hearing a key turn, then headed straight back. I was right: the door wasn't locked. I slipped inside and up the stairs.

A set of closed double doors separated the cloakroom from the party. Originally I had only intended to take money from the wallets and purses that would probably be in various coat pockets, but there was no reason to be so circumspect. The outside door was open, which meant anyone could walk in off the street. Besides which it was quarter to ten, and I didn't have time to mess around. And possibly the most important reason of all: most people can cope with losing the odd hundred-kronor note, but to lose the whole wallet and everything in it? That hurts.

Methodically I moved along the rows, dropping whatever I found into my doctor's bag. I ended up with around twenty wallets, several pairs of very nice gloves, a couple of empty hip flasks and a few other things, including a Bricanyl inhaler. With a bit of luck someone would have an asthma attack and find they couldn't get it under control. That should put a bit of a dampener on the party atmosphere.

No one came out of the party as I went about my business, and I ran down the stairs and out into the street with my bag stuffed full of stolen property. I hadn't done any serious shoplifting since the incident in Åhlén's, and I had almost forgotten the fizzing sensation in the blood when I stepped across the line and into freedom—I hadn't felt the same at the two houses on Lidingö—and my footsteps were light as I hurried up to Fleminggatan and hailed a cab. Home to the meeting.

*

Before I go on I want to deal with the aftermath of the raid at the Boilermakers' Association party so that it doesn't drag through the rest of the narrative like a tail—so *what happened next*?

The man who had booked me called the next day, wondering if I'd seen anything; quite a lot of wallets had gone missing. In his voice I could hear both nervousness and suspicion, or maybe it was just a hangover.

Of course I said *Oh dear, that's terrible*, I was really sorry to hear that, but no, I hadn't seen a thing. Had he locked the door behind me when I left? Silence as he tried to disentangle what were no doubt confused memories of the previous evening. Eventually he said, 'I'm sure I did—didn't I?'

'I don't know, but I don't think you locked it behind us when you let me in. Presumably the same thing could have happened again.'

I suspected that a clear memory had suddenly come into his mind, because he whimpered, 'Why didn't you say anything?'

'Well, I don't know what your routines are, do I?'

He must have realised the battle was lost. If he still suspected me he had nothing to go on, and best of all, *he* was responsible, and he would have to face the consequences.

We said goodbye and I had to bite my tongue to stop myself from adding, 'Mum sends her best.'

My haul came to 6200 kronor, more than four times what I earned for the actual performance. Plus a really good pair of gloves.

*

It was five past ten when the cab driver dropped me off on Luntmakargatan. I hurried in through the main door with my bag, which was now quite heavy. The light was on in the laundry block, the door was ajar and I could hear voices from inside. The last time I had witnessed that same scene, I had taken to my heels. Now I was looking forward to going in. I ran up to my house, dropped off the stool and the bag, then slowly walked back to the laundry block, savouring the evening. The smell of snow, the plume of light from the door, the approaching new year. I could hear the odd rocket going off in the distance.

Six people had gathered together: Elsa, Lars and the man who had burned his hands. His name was Gunnar. I also recognised the overweight woman—Petronella. The Dead Couple weren't there, and I had never seen the other two before.

One introduced himself as Åke; he was a man in his fifties with such a staggeringly boring appearance that he would have fitted perfectly in a farce. Light brown trousers and an equally light brown pullover with a dark and light brown checked shirt underneath. A long narrow face and thin brown hair. An accountant with a medium-sized company who only poked his nose out when the annual audit came around, the guy whose name nobody could remember. That gives a better picture than saying he was a pharmacist, which is what he actually was.

The last person was a woman in her early thirties, spiky hair stiff with hairspray, zebra-striped tights and suit jacket with enormous shoulder pads. Both the hairstyle and the clothes would have been better suited to someone ten years younger. She was wearing so much make-up it was impossible to tell what she really looked like. Her name was Susanne, she worked for Swedish Television, and there was something about her that made me feel uncomfortable.

On the table provided for folding clean laundry there were cups, a thermos of coffee and the basket of biscuits from Elsa's apartment. Plus two bottles of champagne and plastic glasses. The requisites for a normal if slightly substandard gathering, if it hadn't been for the seven knives of different shapes and sizes laid out beside them. The table was directly beneath the Palmebusters T-shirt, dangling there like an altarpiece over some perverted sacrament.

'I think you're the last, John,' Elsa said. 'Could you close the door—it's cold.'

I did as she asked, and when I turned back to the group it struck me that it would have been impossible to guess what these people, myself included, might have in common. To be fair, we didn't have anything in common, at least on the surface. Only the longing for that chaotic opportunity.

Which immediately raises the question: why only us? There were other people who lived in the apartments surrounding the courtyard, other people who used the laundry block. The booking system for the shower room had been adjusted so that no one came or went at the same time as those who were only using the laundry, but that's not enough of an explanation. It should have aroused our suspicions.

I can only speculate. Maybe they didn't feel the pull, but rather the opposite. If they didn't have an inclination towards *the other*, then it seemed repellent. Some are drawn to dark rooms and want to investigate what's in there; others refuse and *don't even want to think* about going inside. Are there strange noises coming from the darkness? Hurry away and forget about it. Do your laundry, stay in the light.

That's one possible explanation. Another is that this is Sweden. If someone puts up an official-looking piece of paper that says this facility is closed for maintenance until further notice, then that's the way it is. No point in asking questions, particularly if it feels a little… dark. Look after yourself and ignore everybody else.

'Okay,' Elsa said. 'We all know why we're here. Some have declined to take part in the experiment, and if anyone wants to drop out, then now is the time. After all, we have no idea what we're going to see. And more importantly, perhaps, what we're going to reveal.'

We looked at one another. No one left. The woman from Swedish Television was biting her nails, Lars stared expressionlessly at the floor and Petronella fanned herself with her blouse as Elsa unlocked the door of the shower room. We each picked up a knife and went in, shuffling so that everyone could fit.

Working together we managed to pull the bathtub and its contents half a metre away from the wall, then we knelt down around it. Because of her age Elsa was allowed to sit on the stool, and Petronella's bulk meant she had to go at the short end. We raised our knives and Elsa counted to three. Then we cut our hands or arms, looked at one another, gave our blood to the blackness and were transported.

*

It is not yet time to describe what happened and what we saw in the field. For the moment I will simply say that the journey was considerably longer than usual thanks to the large quantity of blood, and that it was almost midnight when we returned to the shower room.

As the clock struck twelve we were standing out in the courtyard with our arms around one another, as close as we could get, all seven of us with tears of joy pouring down our faces. We were struck dumb by the deepest happiness, stroking each other's hair and cheeks as the sky above us shimmered with flares and explosions in all the colours of the rainbow. A new year. A new life.

# 3. Beyond

The six weeks that followed what I came to refer to as *the gathering* are unclear in my memory, as if someone had taken an Hieronymus Bosch painting—*Hell* or *The Garden of Earthly Delights*, whichever you like—and poured acetone over the myriad figures. Those tortured individuals would dissolve and flow together, so that you couldn't see where one ended and the next began. That's how January and the first half of February 1986 seem to me.

My notepad with its account of *The Other Place* is a great help when it comes to working out the chronology, but not everything is in there, and events in the real world are touched on only occasionally. I will describe them as far as I am able to make them out in the acetone soup, but I can't swear that everything will be in the right order.

Certain events are among the most wonderful things that have happened to me in my whole life, while I am deeply ashamed of others. The first category belongs to the field, the second to the ordinary world, but both changed me and, in the end, an entire nation, because of what took place at the intersection of Tunnelgatan and Sveavägen on the evening of 28 February, two days after my—and my neighbours'—final journey.

So were we to blame for the assassination of Olof Palme? No more than a child playing with a grenade who blows up himself and his friends. However, we were *responsible*. Without our actions it wouldn't have happened. There is a difference, and I am holding on to that difference.

*

*The gathering* is a good description of that New Year's night, because that's what it was: we gathered, we came together. I will shortly include the section from *The Other Place* in which everything is described in more detail, but for it to make sense, I must first say a few words about this business of coming together.

It's hard, not to say impossible, to really know another person. No matter how open-hearted we are when talking about our views and preferences, our history and our fears, however long we spend with the other person, we can't help suspecting that the most important element is not being shared: who that person *is*, beyond the sum of his or her qualities. People much wiser than me have wrestled with that question, and it is equally complex and banal.

I have already talked about the field's ability to reveal my real being, my innermost character. I had no idea what a gripping experience it would be to see others in the same way. When I look back at this narrative so far, I see that the theme of *community* runs through the whole thing. The isolation of human beings behind the barriers of skin and skull, the inability to achieve a genuine sense of belonging on both a personal level and within society.

For anyone who hasn't had the experience, it's difficult to understand what it can mean when these barriers fall, and you get closer to a group of people than you would ever have thought possible. It can't happen in the real world, where we put on our masks and adapt our behaviour, subconsciously or otherwise. Even if we manage to drop all pretence and honestly stand naked before each other, those naked bodies would still not be our true bodies, merely the collection of bones, cartilage and tissue that has been randomly allocated to us. Our field bodies tell the truth about us, and a closeness that is impossible in the real world can arise.

Maybe it's not a coincidence that this happened in the mid-1980s. Ten years earlier the experience wouldn't have been nearly as overwhelming, but now individualism was becoming the norm. It was all about going to the gym and the tanning salon, Susanne Lanefelt bouncing around in pastel colours, time to stop restricting yourself and realise your possibilities. Invest in yourself!

Yuppies had started flashing their Rolex watches around on Stureplan, and the credit market had been deregulated, enabling people to borrow until they went under. Appropriately enough, a change in the law converting rental properties to a right-to-buy option meant that there was something to buy with the borrowed money. The Socialists' membership numbers plummeted.

Song lyrics had changed: they used to be about the transformation of society and what we can build together, and all of a sudden they were about *nothing*. Symbols tossed around without a thought, la-la-la, oh-oh-oh. Meanwhile, literature focused mainly on man's basic isolation in an indifferent world, while the communal experience of sitting in a cinema was in the process of being replaced by loneliness in front of the video-player.

Anyway. Even if I didn't think about all that while it was going on, I can't have avoided being affected by and part of a Zeitgeist that declared the collective no longer valid, and looked to the individual. To be able to experience the direct opposite within this Zeitgeist, to be *together* in the deepest sense, was worth a great deal. Everything, in fact.

I'm not trying to make excuses for myself, and yet this is a speech in my defence and a plea for understanding. If you'd been in my shoes. At the same time I realise it's pointless, because the experience that forms the basis for the whole thing is impossible to convey. It's a waste of time, I'm on a hiding to nothing, but still I keep going.

Here, in an abridged form, are the notes I made during the first day of the year 1986.

*

*We are together in the field, seven people. Only Lars's field body is entirely based on his everyday body, a version of himself that is ten years younger, and so deeply and quietly happy that he is very different. I feel his happiness and share it. Such love for his wife, his child, and for life itself, such fragile, beautiful gratitude.*

*Next to me is Elsa. I know it's her, in spite of the fact that she's virtually unrecognisable. Maybe I should be afraid. I try out the thought: 'This is horrific,' but it means no more than 'This is grass, this is the sky.'*

*Her body is deformed from carrying other bodies, children's bodies. The skin hangs in pouches from her skeleton, and in these pouches are children of different ages. They crawl around, up over her belly and breasts. One arm swells to the thickness of a tree trunk as a child forces its way in beneath the skin. I can see the contours of its face as it slithers down towards the elbow.*

*The children giggle, growl, purr as they move around one another inside Elsa's skin like puppies playing under a blanket, and her body is in a state of constant flux.*

*'Hi Elsa,' I say.*

*'Hi John,' Elsa says, and I catch a glimpse of a blonde fringe as a giggling little head tries to push its way up through her throat, only to sink back down into her chest. Elsa's gaze travels over my monster body and she smiles. 'There you are.'*

*'Yes,' I say. 'Here I am.'*

*Behind her I can see the burned man, Gunnar, running around the field screaming. A whiff of something similar to the smell of a barbecue reaches my nostrils and I inhale deeply, because it brings me into contact with him and who he is.*

*I am so happy.*

*

At this point I am going to leave out the rather verbose descriptions of Åke and Susanne's field bodies. To me they were vitally important, of course, but as a reader you haven't got to know them in the ordinary world. There might be an opportunity to come back to them later on, but for the moment I will just say that Åke was a version of Conan the Barbarian or a Spartan warrior with an enormous sword, while Susanne was a little girl, perhaps six years old, as pretty as a doll and with long blonde hair.

The key point is that I not only *saw* these people and their field bodies, I also *felt* them and instinctively knew what they meant and wanted to communicate, and all this happened simultaneously. My attention didn't shift from one to the other—no, they were all with me at the same time, and it was this sense of community that took my breath away.

In spite of the fact that you have met Petronella only in passing, I would still like to quote from *The Other Place* and describe her field body, because it has a role to play in this narrative.

*

*You might think that Petronella would be a curvaceous film star or something along those lines, in the same way as Åke is a warrior. But the field is all about truths, not wishes. What we think we want is not necessarily what we do want.*

*If Petronella is fat in the ordinary world, here she is a flesh-mountain. It's hard to grasp how she can even stand up, because her belly hangs down and covers her legs all the way to her knees. She is naked, her breasts sagging towards her navel like overstretched sacs filled with lard. Her skin glows with softness and wellbeing. Her face is embedded in layer upon layer of rolls of fat, and somewhere deep down are her eyes, glittering with joy and mischief.*

*In a way that I understand when I am there, but cannot put into words, she has crossed a line and become something else, something attractive and undeniably sensual. Something you want to be with.*

*

The fireworks had died away to a sporadic flicker in the sky when we returned to the laundry block, red-eyed, frozen stiff and sated with stroking. No one said anything, because nothing needed to be said. Åke and I each opened a bottle of champagne and poured everyone a glass. We toasted the new year and drank, then sat around for a while, exhausted by intimacy. Once again Elsa was given the chair.

After a long silence, with everyone lost in thoughts that belonged only to the process of thinking in that moment, Petronella gestured towards the T-shirt and said, 'It's this'—she waved her hand, encompassing everyone in the room—'that's missing.'

In our different ways, we were all suffering from the lack of community feeling that was prevalent in society; in spite of his promises, Palme had been unable to fix it. But none of us had suffered more than Petronella. In the field I had got to know her story in so far as my brain was able to process it, as it flowed together with everyone else's.

She worked as a teacher in a school that was steadily getting worse and worse. The atmosphere among the staff was appalling, and for the past year Petronella had been subjected to constant bullying because of her weight. She had signed herself off on the grounds of ill health for a while, but had been forced back to work because the social security office refused to accept her size as a valid reason for absence.

I knew that she was a binge eater. She was capable of buying a Princess cake and consuming the whole thing while flicking through fashion magazines and weeping. I couldn't have condemned her even if I'd wanted to, because I understood her feelings. I knew her story and I knew that was how it had to be. I didn't even feel sorry for her, because pity is a form of judgement.

In the same way I was aware that the others also knew *me*. My lonely childhood, the bullying and my unreasonable fantasies of success. And the shoplifting, the night in the cell, the incident with the snow shovel, the attack on Dekorima's Christmas window display. Yet they regarded me with eyes that were more than kind. If we know and understand everything about another person, it is hard to judge them. Whether this is a good or a bad thing is another matter.

I stood up and stretched my stiff limbs, leaned against the doorjamb and contemplated the thing in the bathtub, our saviour and our means of transport. I thought I could see a change, and I beckoned Gunnar over; he was busy picking flakes of dead skin off his hands.

'Look,' I said. 'Don't you think it's a bit...paler?'

He stepped into the shower room, rested his hands on his thighs and lowered his face towards the surface.

'Yes,' he said. 'Yes, maybe.'

Others came in and looked. The difference was small, but it was definitely there. The blackness had faded almost imperceptibly, and had lost something of its deep, oily lustre. We speculated as to the reason, but couldn't agree on anything. We knew so much about each other and so little about the field.

With one exception: Lars. I had seen his field body and been given access to his feelings, but at the same time there were elements that were unclear. It was like watching a film in a language that you speak only moderately well. You can keep up with what's going on and get involved with the characters, but the reasons behind their actions are slightly fuzzy. They explain themselves, but you don't quite understand what they say.

I didn't know whether Lars's consciousness was hiding parts of himself, or whether something about his character was responsible for the situation. He was the one who had been least moved by the collective experience, and although he had joined in with the group hug, he had been the first one to pull away. His expression was as dour as ever when he stood up, thanked us for a wonderful evening and headed for the door.

I followed him out into the courtyard, touched his arm and asked, 'How are you?' He was the only one I could ask: I knew exactly how everyone else was.

He turned to me and said, 'What you're getting up to with Thomas—don't do it any more, please.' I was about to respond, but he held up his hand and went on: 'I know exactly why you're doing it. Of course. But I'm still asking you to stop.'

Regardless of the fact that there were blank spaces on my map of Lars, he was closer to me than anyone in the world, just like my other neighbours, so there was only one answer I could give: 'Of course. I promise.'

'Good. Thank you.'

He slowly walked across the courtyard to his door, and I went back to the others. It turned into a long night; we finished off the champagne, then carried on talking while we emptied the thermos of coffee too. There was a lot to talk about, because even if the field gave us a great deal of knowledge about one another, that didn't mean that every detail was in place. There were lots of questions, and totally honest answers. Anything else was impossible.

*

It was gone three o'clock in the morning when I got back home, euphoric and exhausted. The last thing we had decided was that from now on, everyone in the group had a free choice when it came to how we would travel. Alone, with someone else, or as part of the whole group. We spent ten minutes compiling a list of phone numbers. I stuck it on my wall, then sat down on the chair and looked at it. My people.

The combination of coffee and euphoria meant that I couldn't sleep, in spite of the tiredness. I sat down cross-legged on the floor, grabbed my doctor's bag and tipped out the contents, then went through the wallets one by one. As I said, my total haul was 6200 kronor. There were also luncheon vouchers worth 800, and forty US dollars. Plus three condoms, so maybe yet another aspect of the company's New Year party had gone wrong for someone. If it was a company.

I put the money, the vouchers and the condoms in my desk drawer, then dropped the wallets into a plastic carrier bag, along with the hip flasks. Much too easy to identify. I added all the gloves, except for one pair, then I went and threw the bag down the rubbish chute.

I laid out my mattress and made up the bed. I lay down and contemplated the list of phone numbers. My people, my nearest and dearest. I could call any of them at any time. Just as I was considering contacting someone, possibly Åke or Petronella, the phone rang. I scrambled out of bed and picked up the receiver.

'Hi, this is John!'

'Goodness me, you sound better.'

I hadn't heard from the busker for over a week, and had assumed he'd forgotten about me or given up on me.

'Yes,' I said. 'I'm fine now.'

'Pleased to hear it. I just wanted to wish you Happy New Year. I'm heading south. Like the birds.'

'I haven't seen you in the tunnel for a long time.'

'Didn't you say Sigge had arrived?'

'Yes.'

'Well, I'm not going to stand there if he's arrived—are you crazy?'

'But I heard you once after…'

'After what?'

'After it happened. You were playing 'Somebody Up There Must…'

'Well, yes—that's Sigge's song. Among others. You get caught up. So now I'm heading south, as I said. All the best to you.'

I didn't have the strength to protest or even ask him to explain—I just sat there with my head against the receiver as the line cut out. I was too tired for any more questions, but if I'd had time to say anything before he disappeared, I would have asked if we could sleep together one last time. Now I had no choice but to cope on my own. Eventually I managed it.

*

New Year's Day began with the phone ringing once more, at ten o'clock in the morning, and the conversation with the Minister of Fun unfolded. After telling him a string of lies I hung up and fell back into bed. Vague, disjointed memories of the previous night passed through my mind. I fell asleep with a smile on my face, and didn't wake until two.

I had taken on a task that was to be carried out at around five o'clock. During the conversation over champagne and coffee, the question of the Dead Couple had come up, among other things, because their project threatened to draw attention to our secret. You can't just wander around town bleeding. They had declined to take part in the gathering, and we knew very little about them.

Elsa had explained something that I didn't know. If you were transported to the field soon enough after another person, then something of that person lingered in the field as more than a shadow, perhaps until the blood had all been used up. The Dead Couple were booked into the shower room at four o'clock on New Year's Day. Because I was the one who brought it up, and because I also had a good view of the laundry block, I had offered to follow in their footsteps and try to work out what they were doing.

I made coffee and ate a couple of cream cheese sandwiches that tasted divine. I hadn't eaten since lunchtime the previous day—the Boilermakers' Association hadn't had the sense to offer me anything. I counted the money once more, and for the first time in ages I felt financially secure.

Just before four I saw the Dead Couple enter the laundry block. No bloodstains on their clothes this time, but they were leaning heavily on each other, dragging themselves along like two condemned prisoners on the way to their execution. I sat by the window and waited.

My head was still woolly after the gathering, my thoughts idly circling around the connection between the busker, the child and 'Somebody Up There Must Like Me'. I might have nodded off for a little while, only to wake up with a start when the door of the laundry block opened and the Dead Couple staggered out. No blood this time either, of course. The slime would have taken everything. The bleeding in the stairwell was connected to their project in the ordinary world. I watched them as they made their way to the door leading out of the courtyard, one step at a time. As it closed behind them, I ran down to the laundry block.

The remains of the previous day's party were still there, and I downed half a glass of flat champagne before I opened the padlock and went into the shower room.

The Dead Couple hadn't tidied up after themselves. The knife hadn't been washed, and there was blood on the floor next to the bath. As I was standing by the basin rinsing the knife, the door opened and Petronella came in. 'Hi,' she said. 'Can I come with you?'

'Of course. But we'd better hurry.'

We knelt down by the bathtub, side by side. I made a cut in her forearm and she made a cut in mine. We looked at one another and smiled, then pushed our arms down into the blackness.

*

*The first thing I see is Petronella's fat lady, standing next to me and swaying. Her arms look short, as they are forced out to the sides of her pear-shaped body. There is a shimmer to her skin, as if it has been strewn with glitter. She is perfect in a way that cannot be carried across to an earthly existence.*

*But there is another figure, and to my surprise it is indeed one figure, not two. The sky is growing darker, in the midst of an unnaturally rapid twilight, falling towards the night. Soon there will be only shadow.*

*My first impression was wrong. The figure is both two and one, a symbiosis in the making. It is not possible to recognise the Dead Couple's features, because their faces have blended. One of the woman's nipples has melted into one of the man's. The other has pushed its way through the hand the man has laid over her breast, and now sits on the back of his hand like a dark red abscess. She has one arm thrust so far down his throat that his lips, half of which are her lips, are sucking her elbow. Their legs are entwined, sharing so much skin that it is impossible to say which leg belongs to which person. The man's penis has disappeared somewhere among the layers of flesh.*

*They are constantly moving. Tiny, tiny movements, twitches and spasms, as muffled sounds emerge from their throats. It is erotic in a way that is beyond what we think of as erotic. Petronella and I stand side by side, watching the creature as the scene fades to black and becomes a shadow.*

*We turn to face each other. Petronella lies down and I conjure up an abnormally long sexual organ, which allows me to find my way under the rolls of fat and into her body. I writhe around over her star-strewn skin, create tentacles and lift myself above her like a spider, swaying.*

*It is not intercourse in that sense and does not bring the pleasure associated with sex—it is a union that must be sealed. Beauty and the Beast, Esmeralda and Quasimodo. Or the other way around.*

*

When Petronella and I returned to the shower room, we sat with our arms resting on the side of the bath as the other-worldly pleasure slowly left our bodies.

'John?' she said.

'Yes?'

'Could you touch me, just…touch me?'

I shuffled closer and embraced her, gently stroked her back where the strap of her bra was buried in the subcutaneous fat. She shut her eyes as I ran my fingers over the back of her neck and her throat, and she was as close to me as my own skin; the sweat in the creases beneath her chin was my sweat too.

'You can take off your blouse,' I said. 'If you want to.'

'Are you sure?'

'Of course.'

She wriggled out of her blouse, which had a bold floral pattern, and I folded it and laid it on the edge of the bath. I caressed her face, let my hands move down over her shapely shoulders.

'Thank you,' she whispered. 'It's been such a long time.'

'I know. I know.'

There was nothing aesthetically pleasing, no sensual beauty in the way the pale, billowing rolls of belly fat spilled over, not in this world and not for me. I don't think I would have been able to manage to make love to her, but after all this was Petronella, one of my nearest and dearest. I could give her comfort with my hands, so I stroked her distended skin, allowed my fingers to slip into moist folds, to flutter as gently as a butterfly's wings over the voluptuous curve of her hips, until eventually I kissed her on the cheek, and we remained sitting there for a long time, our foreheads touching.

*

*You say you're a monster. In which case you don't need to understand. Anything.*

As I said at the beginning of this section, things flow together, and maybe the absence of thoughts is part of the reason. By brooding about things we anchor them in time and in ourselves. Consider a painting. If you don't *think* about what you're seeing, you will neither remember the painting nor when and where you saw it. To continue the metaphor: my life after the gathering became like rollerskating through the Louvre. Everything flickers past and flows into one. I know that I had sex with Petronella's fat lady, turned on by the Dead Couple's symbiotic figure, but it might have been on a different day and under different circumstances.

I will do my best to reconstruct that period, but what I can't provide are thoughts, because hardly any existed. For the same reason, I am unable to give any explanation for my behaviour. Everything I and the others did seemed perfectly self-evident at the time, so there was no point in pondering over it. It just happened. It felt right.

*

A few days into the new year I got a call from the police. The night in the cells at Kronoberg and what preceded that night belonged to a different life, but the justice system was unlikely to take that into account. In the eyes of the law I was still the same person, and a week later I found myself outside the enormous doors of the city courthouse.

Something I'd read by Kafka flashed through my mind as I opened a smaller door inset into the larger ones. I made my way to room E5, which was a disappointment. I wasn't doing much thinking, but I had imagined something similar to a scene from an American movie. A courtroom, a judge sitting behind a bench, banging his gavel. Room E5 was an ordinary office in which a little man with narrow lips whose skin seemed too tight for his face was sitting at a desk.

He rocked back and forth on a large upholstered chair as he went through my case and established that all the details were in order. I had admitted the offence and signed my statement. Because my declared income for the previous year was so minimal, he had issued the lowest level of fine, twenty payments of forty kronor each, and he hoped that my current income...

I had stopped listening. On his wall hung a picture of—believe it or not—a weeping child, which took me back to a journey I had made with Elsa and Susanne a couple of days earlier.

The significance of Elsa's field body wasn't hard to understand. Proximity to her children and grandchildren wasn't enough: she wanted to *enclose* them within herself, carry them and own them, and consequently the best times of her life had been during her pregnancies. As soon as they left her body, her children had begun to move away from her.

During the journey Elsa had allowed the children to emerge from her skin, and Susanne's little girl had played with them, turning somersaults on the field while I tried out a different aspect of my monster-body. I made my jaws enormous so that I could seize the screaming, sobbing children with my tentacles and swallow them, feel them kicking and fighting all the way down into my belly before regurgitating them and starting all over again. It had been fun.

'Did you hear what I said?' The man leaned forward and tapped on the desk. I tore my eyes away from the picture and said no, I hadn't heard what he said.

'I said: What do you actually live on?'

I met his gaze and smiled. 'Love and dreams.'

A look I couldn't interpret passed across his taut face, and he lowered his voice: 'Are you...for sale?'

I shrugged. That was one way of looking at my magic; I hadn't even given it a thought since the Boilermakers' Association party. The man got up and went over to the door. He locked it and took a couple of hundred-kronor notes out of his wallet. He placed them on a shelf filled with legal tomes, and said, 'Maybe I can give you a nice time.'

'Couldn't you just knock it off the fine?'

He gave a nervous laugh. 'I'm afraid that's not how it works.'

He wanted me to sit in his big, comfortable chair while he knelt down in front of me and sucked me off. He made little noises as if he was in pain, and he wanted me to pull his hair and force him. His hair was quite thin, but I wound my fingers through the strands as best I could. I tore out a tuft along with a piece of his scalp and he let out a yell, but he didn't stop even though blood was trickling down his cheek. So I picked up a hole punch from the desk and hit him over the head a couple of times, but even that didn't put him off. I spotted a letter-opener and considered driving it into his ear, but decided to let him carry on. We all have our fantasies, our journeys. And besides, it was very pleasant.

When it was over and he had wiped his lips, which had swollen and now looked much better, I picked up the hundred-kronor notes and left the same way as I came in.

*

Despite what I said earlier about prudishness, I have noticed that sexuality is given a certain amount of space in this narrative. I think it's to do with the *physicality* created by my association with the field. When thoughts disappeared, the physical gained greater significance, and it also expressed itself in different ways.

For example, maybe a week or so after the incident at the courthouse, Åke and I went on a journey. As I've already said, his field body was a barbaric warrior, Conan or something along those lines, a murderous machine with bulging muscles and cheekbones like bolt cutters.

If there is an archetype that's all about Beauty and the Beast, then there's another called the Warrior and the Monster, and that was the one we were going to experience. As we weren't sure how injuries or death transferred between worlds, Åke put aside his sword and I promised to exercise a certain level of caution.

Even so, it was a battle worthy of the sagas when we clashed. Åke rained down blows as heavy as lead on my thick skin before I locked his arms with my tentacles, threw him to the ground, thought 'teeth' and inflicted a deep bite on his shoulder. No blood appeared, and we intensified our conflict until we lay exhausted side by side, gazing up at the blue sky. Then we left the field.

After agreeing that the black substance in the bathtub had now faded so much that it could no longer be called black, we went out into the laundry room and carried on fighting. We didn't feel the least vestige of hatred or ill-will towards each other, quite the reverse, but we were completing the movement we had brought with us from the field. We punched each other's bodies and hurled ourselves against walls and washing machines with love flowing between us and we didn't stop until both our mouths were bleeding, at which point we embraced and went our separate ways.

It is still not time to talk about the Dead Couple, but they had gone further than any of us in transposing the physical aspects from the field into our world. Maybe it was because they had travelled together right from the start, and had had more time to reach the stage they were now at. More of that later.

*

These journeys to the field-world, which I increasingly came to regard as the real, true world, were turning into the central element of my life, but even on this side of the field a great deal was changed by being part of a group that was genuinely *close*.

I started going to the shops with Elsa, helping her to carry her bags, then we would have coffee in her kitchen while she talked about what life in Stockholm used to be like, filling out the memories of which I picked up only fragments when we travelled. Dancing at Nalen, the smugglers' boats that sometimes sold their wares direct from Strömkajen, the problems during the war years. I liked listening to her.

Just as I had suspected the first time I saw Gunnar's burned body running across the field there was a spiritual connection between us, though we had lived very different lives. He was a caretaker and general handyman for several properties in the area, and while ambling around carrying out his daily tasks he had developed an attitude to life that had led him to embrace Beckett wholeheartedly. The stubborn chipping away, searching for an emptiness and lack of lustre so great that it acquires a different kind of lustre. The silent panic.

Everything I know about Beckett I learned from Gunnar. I borrowed books from him and together we went to see a performance of *Endgame* in a basement theatre. We agreed that it was very poor, because it was deadly serious. We also went bowling a couple of times.

The wariness I had felt when I first met Susanne had more or less gone when I got to know her, and it disappeared completely when she called me one night and asked me to come and sleep over. As a result of certain experiences in her childhood she was asexual, and had kitted out her apartment with cuddly toys, cushions and brightly coloured posters. She fell asleep with my arms around her as I lay behind her, looking at a picture of Pegasus soaring up into the sky. A week or so later I was suddenly overwhelmed by a sense of emptiness. I called her and she came down and lay behind me on the mattress.

Petronella, Åke and I were all prone to sentimentality, and we would meet up in Åke's apartment every Saturday night to eat Princess cake and watch *This Is Your Life*. We had tears in our eyes when Björn and Benny made their entrance on Stikkan Anderson's program to the sounds of 'Waterloo'.

Regardless of who I was spending time with and what we were doing, the hours we spent together were characterised by a simple sincerity. We knew each other so well that we instinctively steered away from topics of conversation that might be difficult for someone, and we never hurt one another. Being with them was like putting on a favourite old jumper, and the monster who leaked out into the world through me never showed its teeth to the neighbours. It was a good time.

*

As the attentive reader will have noticed, there was one person who took part in the gathering, but didn't hang out with the rest of the group or accompany anyone on a journey afterwards. Lars. Days and weeks went by; he wouldn't go to the laundry block if someone else was there. I tried phoning him a couple of times but he didn't answer, so one day at the beginning of February I went up to see him.

By this stage my arms were covered in so many cuts that I had started to use my calves instead now and again, and occasionally the loss of blood took its toll and everything would start to spin around. Walking up the stairs to Lars's apartment made me so dizzy that I had to lean on the wall after I'd rung the doorbell. I decided to take a few days off from travelling to the field to regain my strength.

The door opened slowly and Lars peered out at me as I stood there with my head down, trying to steady my breathing.

'Yes?'

'Hi Lars.'

'Hi?'

His expression was blank, and there was nothing to indicate that he recognised me. 'It's John. From downstairs.' His eyes narrowed as if he were trying to work out whether I was telling the truth. 'We had a late night at the Monte Carlo restaurant, you and I. The day before Christmas Eve.' I searched my memory for something that might make that particular evening stand out. 'There was an elf dancing. On TV.'

It seemed as if that detail made the penny drop. Lars's eyes widened and he said, 'John'.

'That's right. How are you?'

'Fine, thanks.'

'Can I come in for a little while?'

He glanced over his shoulder as if checking with someone inside the apartment before he opened the door. 'Just for a little while. I've got things to do.'

The hall looked exactly the same as when I had been there the last time. Exactly. Coats and jackets were hung up in the same places and as far as I could remember the shoes were in the same order. The odd thing might have been added, but I'm no memory man.

We went and sat down in the kitchen, and it didn't take an expert to see that there was something new on the table: four boxes, a pair of scissors, Sellotape, ribbon, and a roll of wrapping paper covered in stars.

'Boxes,' I said.

'Mmm. There's just one missing—Marianne's gone out to get it.'

'Your wife Marianne?'

Lars nodded and gave a big smile. If I'd had the capacity to feel sorrow, I would probably have done so then. As it was I just got a bit of a lump in my throat that made it harder to swallow.

'Lars,' I said. 'You never join us. Down in the shower room.'

'I do go down there.'

'Yes. But never with us.'

Lars leaned closer and whispered, as if he were revealing a secret. 'There's a way to make the journey...on a permanent basis.'

'To the field, you mean?'

'The field?'

I didn't know what Lars saw when he was transported. His body had been more or less unchanged in the field. Perhaps it was the surroundings that looked different in his eyes, so I said, 'The other place.'

'Yes. That's right.'

'Okay. So how does that work?'

Lars had clearly lost his mind and almost managed to convince himself that he was thirteen years back in time, on Thomas's ninth birthday. Which didn't necessarily exclude the prospect that he'd come across something worth knowing. Children and fools tell the truth, as the saying goes, so I followed him when he stood up and went into the hallway.

If Lars had found a way of staying in the field, was that a step I was ready to take? I wasn't sure, but it was certainly possible. He went over to a small chest of drawers and beckoned to me. He glanced at the closed door of Thomas's room and opened one of the drawers. Inside lay a revolver, a Smith & Wesson. The sight of the large gun in the little drawer was so striking that all I could say was: 'Where... Where did you get that?'

'Monte Carlo.' Lars lowered his voice to a whisper as he added, 'It was *expensive*,' and closed the drawer.

'So you mean...' I pointed at my temple with my index and middle fingers, and Lars nodded enthusiastically. This wasn't the solution I'd been hoping for, nor was it a step I was willing to take, in spite of everything.

'What makes you think you're right?'

'I just am. If you do it...' Lars jerked his head towards the laundry block. '...there.'

'Are you sure?'

'Depends what you mean by sure...'

I grabbed him by the shoulders, looked him in the eye and said, 'Lars, you mustn't do this. I'm going to take the gun and—'

I moved my hand towards the drawer, but Lars knocked it aside and said in a voice that suddenly sounded wide awake and fully compos mentis, 'No fucking way. This has nothing to do with you. Get out.'

The blissful look in his eyes was gone, replaced by a seething rage. If we started fighting he wouldn't hold back as Åke had done, and things could go badly wrong. Plus he was right: what did any of this have to do with me? Just like the rest of us he would do what he had to do; it was only the thought of Thomas that had led me to try to intervene. I left him and went home.

*

It might come as a surprise to learn that I cared about Thomas, but there's something I haven't told you about. Apart from the neighbours, there was another group I could tolerate in the ordinary world—Thomas and his gang.

I had kept my promise to Lars and not got involved in any more housebreaking with his son, but as we wound up our business affairs we had gone for a beer at Thomas's regular haunt in the Old Town. A couple of his fellow skinheads came and joined us, then we went on to an apartment where there was a party going on, and that's how it happened.

It is clear from this narrative that I harboured a kind of latent violence during this period, a projection of my monster-creature into this world. At the beginning of February I stopped using the subway, because the urge to push people onto the track was so strong that I no longer trusted my ability to resist it. Like everything else it was simply a fact of my world, but I still didn't want to end up in jail for murder.

I enjoyed hanging out with Thomas and his friends. They had the same tendency as I did, and our association had a thread of brutality that suited me. There were plenty of hard shoves and crude jokes that sometimes turned into fights, especially if booze was involved—and it often was. I both took and gave plenty of punches, then it was *Cheers, for fuck's sake*, and that was the end of the matter.

The music they listened to was harsh and bombastic with lyrics full of rage, and their conversations often contained hate-fuelled diatribes against all those bastards who were destroying our wonderful country. I didn't agree with much of what they said, but the tone made me feel at home. There was also a vein of sentimentality when they talked about things that were gone, from the death penalty to the little cottage where someone's family used to spend every summer holiday.

As a skinhead gang they had one particular quirk that must have come from Thomas. Those who called themselves boneheads listened to White Power bands such as Skrewdriver and Ultima Thule, while the less extreme among them preferred classic ska bands like Madness and the Specials. Plus Povel Ramel.

A sparsely furnished apartment with mattresses on the floor among beer cans and bottles of Explorer vodka, and in the haze of cigarette smoke sits a gang of young men with shaven heads, stamping their booted feet and singing along with 'Look, It's Snowing', booming out from the record-player. Their real favourite was 'Daddy, I Can't Crack My Coconut', and no party was complete unless it had been played at least once, and preferably several times.

I occasionally went into town with them because I enjoyed the sense of danger that pulsated from the group as they shoved their way through the crowds, yelling about that stubborn coconut that just wouldn't break open.

Maybe they were less aggressive than many other gangs, because their squabbles and provocations—even minor fights in town—never crossed over into actual violence, at least not when I was with them.

A couple of days after my conversation with Lars, Thomas and I met on Gullmarsplan because a mutual friend, Palle, had got a basement flat as a sublet, and was having a party to celebrate moving in. I couldn't travel by subway, as I've explained, and Thomas grinned when I got out of a cab carrying a bag from the state-owned liquor store containing a bottle of schnapps and a bottle of Fanta.

'Jeez, have you come straight from Café Opera or what?'

We trudged along towards Grafikvägen side by side, me in my beige duffel coat with my long, unkempt hair, Thomas in his skins' uniform with his shaven head. Once or twice someone in the gang had offered to shave my head and called me chicken when I declined. That had kicked off one of the fights, in fact, but although I enjoyed their company, I didn't want to be part of the group to that extent. I was keeping my hair.

'By the way,' I said, 'I met your dad the other day.'

'And?'

'And...I know you don't care, but...' I stopped so that I could look

Thomas in the eye when I went on. 'I'd say there's a risk he might take his own life.'

Thomas was good at maintaining his stony-faced expression, but I could see that my words had hit home. Something about the mouth, something in the eyes, a sudden *softness* that passed through him before he gritted his teeth and set off again. 'And what the fuck do you expect me to do about it?' he snapped.

'Nothing. I just thought you'd want to know.'

'I don't want to know.'

'Okay. Forget it.'

We carried on towards Palle's flat, where the sound of another Povel Ramel song came pouring out of the windows.

*

In the middle of February, a couple of days before we found out the truth about the Dead Couple, I went on a journey with Susanne. Until then Petronella had been my usual travelling companion, but she had now lost her job and spent her days almost exclusively arguing with the social security office and eating. She had put on so much weight that she was becoming more and more like her field body, and she rarely went down to the laundry block.

As soon as I got to know Susanne, the wariness I had felt when I first met her had gone, as I have already said, and had been replaced by a sense of dread. The essence of Susanne's being was in fact emptiness. Because emptiness cannot have a physical manifestation, the sweet, innocent little girl she showed us in the field was no more than a provisional measure. Of us all, she was the one whose journeys caused her the least damage. On the other hand, the intensive association with the emptiness of both life in general and her own life in particular had made her frail and hesitant, as if she were gradually fading away from the world.

Before we went into the shower room, we spent a little while standing in front of the T-shirt that was still hanging on the wall.

By this time I knew it was Susanne who'd put it there. She had been involved in the reporting around the Harvard affair, and believed that Palme had abused his power, like so many others. She pointed to the caricature and said, 'He was the one we could believe in. He was going to do what he promised to do. See you again, comrades! We were going to fix things together—we were going to be together. That was the dream he sold us.'

'We *are* together.'

'Yes, but only you and I. Only at this moment. No one else. I think that's why people hate Palme. He was elected on a dream of community and togetherness that not even he believed in.'

'Come on.'

We went into the shower room. We travelled. Without any real desire we moved across the field. I created a rainbow and Susanne lay on the grass and gazed at it. Then she sat up and fiddled with the remains of Rebus as I stood there motionless, staring at the black wall. We returned.

The pleasures of the field had lost something of their lustre. There is always a tipping point where we become sated. By this stage the substance in the bathtub was pale grey, with wisps of white floating around in the greyness so that it increasingly resembled sperm. It was impossible to say whether this was the cause or the effect of the diminished joys of the field.

Being there was still better than the ordinary world where our false bodies chafed, but the frustration had begun to grow once more. It was as if there were something missing, as if there were one more step to take.

*

It was Åke who found the blood two or three days after Susanne and I had been on our journey. Because I lived the closest and I was usually at home, he ran up the stairs and knocked on my door. Åke had also changed since the gathering. He now went to the gym five days a week and took anabolic steroids, which had made him bulk up so much that he'd had to buy a complete new wardrobe. On that occasion he was wearing sweatpants and a checked shirt with the sleeves rolled up, exposing the veins on his forearms.

I went down with him, and along the well-trodden path leading from the laundry block to the main door I could see a trail of fluid that had flowed out into the snow; it could have been anything. Coffee, oil. I was about to say that to Åke, but when he opened the door and pointed to the floor, I changed my mind.

Over the past few months I had seen enough blood in various stages of coagulation on skin, tiles and concrete to know exactly what the trail across the marble floor was. Fresh splashes and pools continued up the stairs to the Dead Couple's door.

It says something about us that we didn't rush straight up there, or call an ambulance. No, the first thing we did was go to the laundry block to fetch a mop, a bucket and a cloth. We spent ten minutes meticulously removing every trace of blood.

When the stairs and landing were clean, we mopped the laundry room floor, rinsed out the bucket and put everything away, then we went to see Elsa. There was an informal hierarchy; she was *number one* and must be kept informed.

She was almost always at home these days. The movement that had begun with her taking the photographs down from the walls had continued, and no one came to visit any more. In the middle of January Dennis had been sitting on her lap, and in a moment of weakness she had bitten him hard on the shoulder. There had been screams and tears, and as a consequence Elsa herself had told her nearest and dearest to leave her in peace, simply to protect them.

She had put on several kilos, having switched to a diet consisting almost entirely of meat. There was an element of cannibalism in her desire to envelop, and the mastication and swallowing of half-raw steak provided at least some compensation when human flesh was not available.

Åke and I told her what we'd seen, and she accompanied us to the Dead Couple's door. We rang the bell, but no one came. We didn't really want to call anyone from outside until we knew what we were dealing with. Just to exclude the possibility that the door was unlocked, I pushed down the handle. It opened. We glanced around the stairwell, then went inside and closed the door behind us.

If the Dead Couple had travelled with the rest of us, I would have understood them and would therefore have been unable to have an opinion about the sight that met us in their apartment, but as it was the whole thing seemed beyond sick, and I would like to warn sensitive readers at this point.

I have already described their field creature, the figure in a state of increasing symbiosis. Trying to achieve the same thing in our world with our tough skin, our dense flesh and our bleeding veins is another matter, and the pain must have been beyond belief.

There was blood everywhere. Old, congealed blood spattered across the white wallpaper, clumps and spots on the skirting boards and in corners, drops that had even reached the ceiling. The floor where we were standing was covered in fresher blood, and the apartment smelled like a butchery counter after a power cut.

We moved cautiously through the hallway, taking care not to step in the blood, and continued into the living room, where we found our neighbours on the white rug, which was no longer white.

Our legs and arms were covered in cuts at various stages of healing. What we saw on the bodies of the naked couple on the floor cannot be described as cuts. They were deep lacerations, wounds, gouges, cavities where shining flesh lay exposed, the skin hanging off.

A gash several centimetres long ran down the woman's back, presumably the cause of the bleeding when I met her in the stairwell that day. The man had inserted his hand so far into this gash that his knuckles were visible beneath the skin covering her shoulder blade. He, meanwhile, had an open wound in his inner thigh, and the woman had managed to get her foot into this incision. Shreds of flesh that had been cut away to make room hung down over his knee, and his own foot was pushed into a hole in her hip.

On top of this was something that might be regarded as normal in certain circles. Her right arm had been forced as far as the elbow into his anus, while his arm was almost equally far up her vagina. To achieve their embrace, they had broken a number of bones. One of her arms was twisted in a way that isn't possible with the skeleton intact, and one of his knees was facing in the wrong direction. They were covered in blood, and lying there on the sodden rug they looked like a pile of human slaughterhouse waste, extremities and lumps of flesh randomly tossed onto a heap.

Åke, Elsa and I stood there in silence for a long time, contemplating the conjoined creature in front of us. I haven't mentioned this, but it was dead. The Dead Couple were dead, and what they had done would not have been possible without the syringes and phials that lay scattered around them. Morphine and fentanyl. They had drugged themselves into a state of physical numbness to bring home their project, and the drugs might well have contributed to their deaths.

I looked up at the big television that I had helped them carry up the stairs. The blank screen was splattered with blood, and from the back a cable ran to a video camera on a stand. A red light indicated that it was recording. On the shelf below the TV was a row of videotapes with handwritten, dated labels.

*

I will spare the reader a detailed description of the contents of the tapes, but I have to give a certain amount of information so that the Dead Couple's project will make sense.

We took the camera and tapes because they might contain things that would give away our secret. No one had seen us enter the apartment, and we decided not to call the police. Hopefully it would be a few days before the stairwell started to stink, by which time any trace of us might have been destroyed by micro-organisms. We hoped.

Elsa didn't want to see what was on the tapes; she was happy for Åke and me to report back. We went to my house and connected the video camera to the television I'd bought from the couple we were now going to observe. We were both very uncomfortable. Åke shuffled on the chair, and my fingers were sweaty as I ran them over the spines of the tapes.

'What shall we do?' I said. 'Start from the beginning?'

'Mmm. We can always fast-forward. If need be.'

Regardless of how hardened we had become by the scenes played out before our eyes in the field, looking at bodies being destroyed in this world was something quite different. I inserted the tape marked 28/9–18/10/1985.

*We can always fast-forward. If need be.*

The first sequence was filmed in the shower room, possibly on the night when I came home from Mona Lisa and heard the sound of fucking in there. I don't need to go into too much detail. Violent sex with the woman leaning over the bathtub while the man frenetically thrust into her from behind. I felt myself getting slightly hard, and avoided looking at Åke. The woman was bleeding from a couple of fingertips; she dipped them in the tub from time to time and her body went limp in the man's hands.

This went on in the same way for several days, but only very occasionally in the laundry block. He started penetrating her anally, and she stuck her fingers in his anus and his mouth. It was so monotonous that I fast-forwarded through long sections, with no complaints from Åke. I changed tapes and it was only when we reached the middle of December that things started to go seriously downhill.

By that stage their intercourse had acquired an air of desperation, and their whimpers conveyed frustration more than pleasure. Then they started cutting. First it was only small incisions, wounds that could be picked at, kept open. Distorted faces, blood trickling over their limbs. Then bigger cuts into which fingers could be inserted—and even though they gasped with pain, it was as if a transfiguring light had come over their faces.

That might have been when they realised what they were actually doing, what the *aim* of their project was. Until then they had simply been driven forward by the same unarticulated feeling that made me want to push people onto the subway line, for example. Now they knew *what it was all about*.

It only became nauseatingly hard to watch when they began to use the painkilling injections that allowed them to go significantly further. By the time we reached the tape marked 18/12/1985–10/01/1986 I had to whizz through certain parts, after a quick glance at Åke, who had curled up on the chair. Flesh was now visible in gashes several centimetres wide; skin was being peeled off to leave the nerves naked and exposed.

In a thick voice Åke said, 'Maybe that's enough now?'

I switched off the video-player and we sat staring at the blank TV screen for a long time, until I said the only thing I could come up with: 'That's what can happen.'

'Yes, for fuck's sake. And then they sat there *watching* all this.'

'On their big TV. Yes.'

Silence once more. I ran my hand over the tapes, which would have to be destroyed or disappear, the documentation of the Dead Couple's truest urge and longing, hidden beneath their ice-cold attitude. Beyond the field, people are very difficult to understand.

*

That evening I watched the last tape, the one that ended with an hour of stillness before Åke, Elsa and I arrived on the scene and the camera was switched off.

Does it make sense if I say that the badly assembled creature on the floor had a kind of beauty in its dead slumber? The process leading up to that final rest most definitely did not, and I had to go into the toilet and throw up before I'd finished watching. Paradoxically, the whole thing became more real when it was filmed on a neutral, static camera than when I had actually been in the room. I had to close my eyes more than once as they fought to achieve something that is not for man to create.

It seemed most likely that an overdose of morphine had led to their deaths. They injected more and more to endure what they had already done, and to keep going. They didn't say a single word throughout, but as the final torpor approached, they looked each other in the eye and exchanged a loving smile. They had done what they had to do, or at least they had tried their best. Now their toil was at an end, so goodnight, my friend. If it hadn't been so revolting I might have got quite carried away.

This might sound absurd, bearing in mind what I've already written, but it wasn't until I had finished watching the tapes that I was struck by a thought: *The field is dangerous.* Then Lars came into my mind. Parts of him had already been obscured on New Year's Eve, which was why the revolver had come as a surprise to me. The fate of the Dead Couple made it clear how far the field was capable of driving us.

It was after midnight when I picked up the phone, but I knew Thomas kept late hours like me, and often had difficulty sleeping. He answered almost right away. After greeting him briefly, I said, 'Listen, I'm pretty sure your dad's going to kill himself.'

'And what the fuck do you expect me to do about it?'

I hadn't told Thomas about Lars's project, because it involved our secret—I had just spoken in general terms about a sense of loss. Now I took a step into more dangerous terrain: 'Everything he does is about you. He's trying to recapture a special moment you shared. Your ninth birthday.'

There was a brief silence. Maybe Thomas was trying to remember the occasion, or to get his head around what I'd just said. I sensed a gentler tone in his voice when he said, 'What are you talking about? How could he possibly do that?'

I came up with a neutral response. 'He believes he can. He thinks it's possible. He's bought all the things you had on the day. Your presents. The cake. Everything. And he intends to kill himself when it's all in place.'

'What sort of a crazy fucking idea is that? How's he come up with such a stupid plan?'

'I don't know. He really misses you.'

'He doesn't want anything to do with me.'

'I think you're wrong, and I also think you ought to go and see him. I'll come with you if you want.'

'Why do you care about any of this?'

The answer I gave would have surprised me a few months earlier, to say the least. 'Because I care about you.'

Thomas wasn't someone who explained himself or his decisions, so it was equally unexpected and natural when he said, 'I'll be there tomorrow at seven.'

'Good. See you then.'

'Goodnight, you fucking pansy.'

*

I slept well that night. I no longer had problems sleeping since I'd started travelling. If you don't have a physiological problem, then it's usually thoughts that keep you awake. Since I'd stopped thinking about myself and my shortcomings, sleep usually came quickly.

I started the day by going up to see Elsa and briefly reporting on what I'd seen on the tapes. We agreed that they must be destroyed, and I offered to deal with the matter.

When I got back to my house, I sat down on the floor in front of the TV. I picked up one of the tapes, lifted the flap at the front and started pulling out the plastic tape with its magnetic strip. It was longer than I'd expected, and by the time I got to the end there was a big tangled heap on the floor. I moved on to the next one. And the next.

I paused when I reached the very first tape, remembering how I'd got the stirrings of a hard-on when I watched the scene in the shower room. I looked at the tape, then at my desk drawer. But no, it was too dangerous. I ripped it out and the pile grew even bigger.

Finally I pressed the eject button on the video-player and took out the last tape. I sat and weighed that one in my hand for a moment too. It wasn't that I wanted to watch it again, absolutely not; what made me pause was a certain level of respect for the Dead Couple's efforts. They had suffered to achieve their goal and the tape was the evidence they had left for posterity.

I pulled myself together. Posterity couldn't possibly see this film, precisely because it was *evidence*, and Åke, Elsa and I were all on it. The spools made a whining sound as I ripped out the tape and let it spiral down onto the pile, then I stuffed the whole lot into a supermarket carrier bag.

There wasn't a soul in sight when I reached St Johannes churchyard, and I tipped out the contents of the bag in a corner between the steps and the wall. I crumpled up a couple of sheets of newspaper I'd brought with me, tucked them underneath and lit them. I waited until I was sure the plastic had caught, then I walked away. As I turned into Döbelnsgatan I glanced over my shoulder and saw a pillar of black smoke rising in front of the stained-glass windows like a sacrificial fire.

*

*Why do you care?*

I knew exactly why I had poked my nose in, got involved in the relationship between Thomas and Lars. What I had said to Thomas was true: I did care about him. But not *that* much. After the conversation with Lars I cared about him too, but there were others in the group who were more important to me because I had travelled with them, spent time with them.

Perhaps it was to do with my own father. He and my mother had split up when I was one year old, and we'd had only sporadic contact since then. I went to see him in Södersvik once or twice a year, and occasionally he came to Blackeberg. The visits grew more infrequent as I got older, and since I'd moved into the city centre I hadn't seen or spoken to him at all. He always used to come to Blackeberg on my birthday, and I had pretty clear memories of my ninth or tenth birthday, when he gave me a typewriter, which I used to write a diary for two years.

Maybe there was a connection, maybe not. At any rate it was a waste for Thomas and his father to be so distant when there was a desire for something else on both sides. That was how I saw it, at least.

When Thomas hammered on my door at ten to seven, he was clutching a bag from the liquor store. 'The old man likes whisky.'

'I know. So does mine.'

The fact that Thomas had made the effort to buy a bottle of Scotch suggested that he was in a more conciliatory frame of mind than I'd expected; was it possible that something good might come out of this? That would be nice, after the experiences of the past twenty-four hours. We went over to the main door of Lars's block, which was a different one from the Dead Couple's, fortunately. I would probably have picked up the stench even if it wasn't there.

Thomas had perked himself up with a couple of swigs from the bottle, and was in a good mood. As we walked up the stairs he asked, 'So your dad was an alkie?'

'What makes you think that?'

'The way you said, "So does mine." Maybe that's why you're sick in the head. And gay.'

'You could be right.'

Thomas glanced at me.

'You're not gay, are you? For real?'

'Do you think I'd tell you if I was?'

'You might be in love with me.'

We were standing outside Lars's door. I gazed deep into Thomas's eyes. He couldn't hold my gaze, and I said slowly, 'Thomas. I am *not* in love with you.'

He let out a belly laugh and punched me on the shoulder before ringing the bell. The sound that must have been so familiar since childhood seemed to make him realise how odd the situation was. He looked at me. 'So what are *you* doing here? Really?'

I shrugged. As I said, I wasn't sure myself. Ever since New Year's Eve, when I had made my promise to Lars, I had felt somehow *responsible*, and that could have been part of the equation.

The door opened a fraction and Lars peered out. Just like the last time there was nothing in his expression to suggest that he recognised me, and what was worse, he didn't appear to recognise Thomas either. 'Yes?' he said.

Thomas grabbed the door so that it flew open, waved the carrier bag and said, 'Evening, Dad. Fancy a drink?'

Lars backed into the hallway, obviously terrified. Thomas dealt with his uncertainty in the way that people often do, by becoming even pushier. He grabbed hold of a lined denim jacket that must once have been his and said, 'So I hear you're turning this place into a museum!'

'Leave that alone!' Lars snapped.

'What the fuck is wrong with you? It's *my* jacket! I used to wear it when we went walking in the forest, you and me. You remember that, don't you?'

'I've no idea what you're talking about.'

I glanced into the kitchen, where five presents were now piled up on the table, the last much bigger than the others, and I suspected it was the Lego fortress Lars had mentioned. The one they were going to build together.

Thomas's smile was strained as he took a step towards Lars, opened his arms wide and said, 'It's me, Thomas. Your prodigal son.'

Lars backed away even further, shaking his head as he pointed to the closed bedroom door. 'My son is fast asleep in there. You'll wake him up, making all this noise!'

Thomas blinked, and his face took on an expression I had never seen before, and which I was sure he really didn't want anyone to see. Sorrow. Pleading, helpless sorrow. His arms dropped and any sign of joviality disappeared as he said, 'Dad, stop this now. I'm here. Your boy. I'm here now.'

Lars shook his head even more frenetically. 'Today is my son's ninth birthday and we're about to go in and give him his presents. I don't know who you think you are, pushing your way into my home and disturbing us, but I'd like you to leave right now.'

Thomas's moment of weakness had passed. His jaws tensed beneath the skin and his fists clenched as he moved towards his father, but Lars went to the chest of drawers and took out the revolver. He pointed it at Thomas and said, 'Get out of here! Now! Nobody is going to ruin my son's birthday!'

Thomas stopped dead. There was no mistaking the insanity and fury in Lars's eyes. I was ready for the shot, but fortunately Thomas decided not to push his luck, in spite of his despair. He raised his hands and stepped back.

'Okay. Okay, Dad, that's fine.'

Lars lurched forward, the barrel of the gun shaking as he threatened us: 'Out! Get out!'

We edged backwards until we reached the landing. Before Lars closed and locked the door, he glanced in the direction of the bedroom as if to make sure that all the noise hadn't woken his darling boy.

*

I nipped back to my house and pulled on an old padded jacket before joining Thomas out on the street. It was bitterly cold, and we kept our heads down as we walked along Tunnelgatan to Norra Bantorget, where we sat down on the loading bay of a grocery store, passing the whisky bottle to and fro between us.

'I'm sorry,' I said. 'I really thought that if he saw you...'

'Shut up and drink,' Thomas said, passing me the bottle. I made no further attempt to broach the subject. As we sat there in silence, that moment outside Lars's door came back to me. *You might be in love with me.* Wasn't that a strange thing to say, and hadn't the punch he delivered to my shoulder seemed a bit...unnatural?

I had no such feelings for Thomas, but if he felt that way about me, then on top of everything else it must grieve him deeply that he had exposed himself, albeit ambiguously and only for a second.

There was a dark cloud surrounding Thomas as he determinedly knocked back the whisky. I kept up as best I could, hoping that the booze would enable us to have a conversation. Fucking hell, it had gone badly. Lars had finally withdrawn into his memory, and it appeared that nothing could entice him back out. Was this when he was going to die? Maybe, but there was nothing more I could do.

As the level in the bottle dropped without our exchanging a word, my mood became increasingly gloomy. Fucking Lars fucking Dead Couple fucking field fucking life. My thoughts were spinning in ever-decreasing circles, being inexorably sucked towards a black hole.

When the bottle was empty Thomas suddenly hurled it away. It smashed to pieces as he leapt down from the loading bay and ran off towards Barnhusgatan. I could see a lone figure silhouetted against the lights of a shop window. That was where Thomas was heading, and I followed him.

I soon realised that the man Thomas was approaching had curly black hair. He had his back to us; he turned around when he heard us coming, but it was too late. Thomas kicked his legs out from under him with his steel-capped boots, and the man crashed to the ground.

'Get back to the fucking jungle!' Thomas yelled, kicking the man in the stomach. 'Fucking black bastard!' The next kick split the man's forehead open, and blood spurted out over the dirty snow.

My thoughts disappeared into the black hole and darkness billowed up before my eyes. I kicked out and struck the back of the man's head. He raised his arms to protect himself, and we carried on kicking.

After a while we started singing the song about the stubborn coconut that wouldn't crack, repeatedly kicking the man's arms to force him to lower them so we could crack that fucking coconut.

*

A cab came along Barnhusgatan and the sight of its lights brought me to my senses before Thomas and I succeeded. The man's arms were still clamped rigidly over his head when I pulled Thomas away. We ran through a dark car park and across Tunnelgatan. I turned around and saw that the cab driver had stopped and got out next to the man on the ground. Then I kept on running.

We didn't slow down until we came out onto Kungsgatan. We walked through Hötorget and paused behind the Orpheus fountain to catch our breath. The cab driver had a radio, and the police could be looking for us any second now. Thomas bent over, his hands resting on his thighs, and gasped, 'Fucking hell.'

'Yes. Fucking hell.'

At that moment everything came crashing down. It might have had something to do with the fact that I hadn't travelled for four days, so the field's influence on me was unusually weak, but during that minute behind the fountain I saw what had become of me.

Just a few months ago I had met Sofia there. A sweet, lovely girl with whom I could have had a really good relationship, if only I'd made the effort. I had been working at Mona Lisa, loving my magic and looking forward to the future with confidence. I had left it all for *the other*, and now I was standing here with a skinhead, hiding after almost kicking another human being to death. The field wasn't just dangerous—it was utterly destructive.

I pulled off my jacket and threw it into the sculpture beneath Orpheus's feet, said, 'Goodbye, Thomas,' and set off without turning around.

I barely knew what I was doing, and was acting in accordance with the instincts of a creature being pursued as I turned down a passageway and into a cinema where a showing of *Rocky IV* had just started. I bought a ticket and sat down in the back row of the large, dark cinema. I saw nothing of the film: I was merely aware that people were hitting one another. I definitely didn't want to see that, so I kept my eyes fixed on the floor while time passed and my trail went cold.

Everything was growing clearer by the minute, and I was appalled by what I had become. A monster. A banal, everyday monster, nothing more than a bad person. I saw the black man's head jerking back and forth in the snow as we kicked him, his defenceless body curled into the foetal position. I remembered how I had wanted to smash his head, see it crack. Monster.

When the film was over I wandered home without bothering to keep an eye out for the police. Even if I had no intention of handing myself in, it would have been nice to be arrested. Locked in a cell, away from the field.

I passed the Orpheus fountain and saw the sleeve of my jacket sticking up next to one of the Sylphides' plinths. I pushed my hands deep in my trouser pockets, hunched my shoulders and kept moving. I don't think I've ever hated myself as much as I did during that short walk.

Dekorima had replaced the broken window, and the new display was all about painting a self-portrait. A mirror had been placed on the easel so that you could look at your reflection. As I stood there with my arms wrapped around my body, I couldn't think of anyone less worth painting.

The thoughts from which I had been liberated for a couple of months kept on going round and round in my head, and by the time I got home I was suffused with such self-loathing that I could hardly breathe. If I'd had a revolver I would probably have used it to remove myself from the earth. Instead I sought refuge in music, as I so often did.

Depeche Mode's latest single, 'Stripped', had come out a week earlier, and it had barely hit the shelves before I was there stealing it. Since then I had listened to it over and over again. It was already on the turntable, so I switched on the record-player and moved the needle across.

Something of whatever was ripping and tearing at me eased a little as I sat on the floor in front of the speakers, swaying in time to the heartbeat rhythm which I knew was the sound of a slowed-down motorbike engine. Dave Gahan sang, and I listened. The heavy, sombre atmosphere of the song encapsulated some of my own darkness, making it seem possible to live, at least for the moment.

In extreme emotional states, whether joy or despair, we have a tendency to interpret song lyrics as if they applied to us. 'Stripped' was about me. Me and my neighbours.

Dave Gahan sang about taking his hand and coming back to the land, to the place where everything was ours for just a few hours. It was the field he was referring to, and even though I knew I was reading too much into it, I listened to the song as if I could find the answers I needed within it. Over and over again I listened, curled up on the floor with my hands clenched over my belly.

No matter how horrified I was at my actions and the person I had become, the thought of never seeing the field again was unbearable. Never to stand beneath that sky again, feeling the magic and the joyous truth in my body. Instead of being an enchanted creature in a supernatural world, I would be reduced to a lost young man in a dark, cramped house. Abstinence was already taking its toll; it was a burning lump in my belly that brought tears to my eyes.

*It's impossible. I can't do it. I have to do it.*

*

It was after midnight and 'Stripped' was still playing when I caught sight of a movement through the slats of the blind. I dragged myself to my feet and swayed, still intoxicated from the whisky, and staggered over to the window just in time to see the door of the laundry block close. The light came on, and I blinked a couple of times. It took me a few panic-stricken seconds to find the key before I rushed to the door and down the steps. I didn't even put my boots on.

In spite of my intention to abandon everything to do with the shower room, I couldn't just sit and wait while Lars took his own life. He had been naked, with the revolver in his hand.

Maybe my shame over what I had done earlier that evening made me feel compelled to intervene. If I could save Lars's life, it would constitute a kind of atonement. I ran across the courtyard in my stocking feet, the densely packed snow grabbing hold of my warm soles as if it were trying to stop me. I reached the door and fumbled with the keys before managing to unlock it.

The shower room door was open. Lars had climbed into the bathtub and sat down, so that the grey-white slime reached the bottom of his rib cage. It was moving of its own volition, thin runners feeling their way over his skin like fingers.

'Lars,' I said, walking towards him. 'Lars, wait. This isn't going to work.'

'How would you know?' he said, raising the barrel of the gun to his temple.

'It's not *real*,' I said, reaching out to take the gun away from him.

'It's all there is,' he said, and pressed the trigger.

A deafening report echoed around the room as a flame shot out of the barrel. Lars's head jerked to the side, blood and brain matter splattered across the tiles and his body sank backwards and disappeared. At the same time I felt a burning pain in my right hand.

The bullet had gone through Lars's head, ricocheted off the wall and torn open the soft skin between my thumb and forefinger. The shock of the bang and the unexpected pain made me stagger and stumble forward. I saw the revolver fall from Lars's hand into the bathtub, and at that moment my own bleeding hand went down into the sperm-coloured slime, which resisted like skin before it broke, and I was transported.

*

*The first thing I see is Lars, lying at my feet. The skin on his right temple is burned from the flame, and the entry wound shows as a darker patch. He is on his side, so I can't see the exit wound.*

*The naked body is motionless. His arms are covered in cuts and scratches. His grandfather's wedding ring gleams on the third finger of his left hand. His mouth is hanging open, and I can just see a few gold fillings. The revolver isn't here—it must still be in the bathtub.*

*The sight of Lars's ordinary naked body on the field feels like a distortion, and yet it is wonderful to be in my true body once more. I reach out a tentacle and make Lars hover half a metre above the ground. Blood pours from his head and is absorbed with unnatural speed. The grass and the earth are drinking.*

*The sense of distortion grows: it is like being on a boat that is beginning to list. The atmosphere of the field is changing and I know why. Lars isn't supposed to be here. Death isn't supposed to be here.*

*The dense darkness on the horizon has acquired a shimmer that reflects the monochrome light of the sky, and I see a movement in the grass far away, a movement that is coming closer as the wall of darkness grows.*

*Only when it is about a hundred metres away from me am I able to work out what it is. The wall is not growing: a cloud is billowing out from it. Rain is falling from the cloud, racing towards me. I run, and have managed to get about fifty metres away from Lars by the time the rain reaches him. The drops land on his body, burning holes all over his skin. He is dissolving, disappearing.*

*I spin around. The black wall looms up from the horizon in all directions. The field is shrinking, being sucked into itself. Then the rain is upon me.*

*I just have time to feel the first drops burning through my thick skin, to see the red smoke mingling with the black before I am jerked back and I am on my knees at the end of the bathtub.*

*

An odour of burnt flesh found its way into my nostrils, and my body felt as if I had been rolling in a bed of nettles. The substance in the bathtub had now become solid, and looked like lard. When I pressed the surface with my uninjured hand, there was no give. Lars was gone, sucked down into the whiteness, no longer in this world. I slumped on the floor and rested my forehead on the side of the bath.

*It is ending.*

I had no idea how the field had come into existence, but I knew that it was in the process of coming to an end. The chaotic possibility would become an impossibility as the slime hardened and the door closed. The wall of darkness was growing, the horizon was contracting. Soon neither would exist. The place had once again got me in its clutches, and the knowledge that it would no longer be there evoked a paralysing sense of grief. All I could do was to sit there with my head on the enamel, weeping.

*It is ending.*

Looking back it seems utterly grotesque, but my grief was as deep as if I had watched a much-loved person fade away and slip into death, taking the future with them. There was nothing left. I looked at the wall, spattered with the blood and brain matter from inside Lars's head, I looked at my empty hands crisscrossed with scars and I carried on weeping.

I dragged myself home across the courtyard and sank down on my chair. Once again I felt a powerful urge to kill myself. The revolver had fallen out of Lars's hand before he was taken, and presumably it was still in the bathtub. That was a possibility. Anything rather than live through the night.

*Take me away.*

It all came down to the fact that I didn't have the energy. I sat and stared at the wall for half an hour. Then I got up and cleaned the wound with washing-up liquid over the sink before curling up on the floor. I didn't bother laying out the mattress. My body was wracked by convulsions, then I fell asleep.

I can't swear that what happened next wasn't a dream. My state of mind was so confused and agitated that Raskolnikov comes across as a clear-headed individual by comparison. When I turned over in my sleep, the pain of my burned skin shot through me, waking me up. I didn't know if it was day or night, or which world I was in. The only indication that I was awake and real was the pain in my hand and the heat of my skin. I sat up and stared into the darkness.

I don't know how it came about, but a little while later I was standing in the street. Was I wearing my outdoor clothes? Boots? I can't say: I see the images as if I were a stranger peering out through my own eyes. It has started snowing again. It is dark. My head is aching, and when I press my fingertips to my temples, I notice that I have put on the head torch.

Only then do I understand what I'm doing. One step at a time I make my way along Luntmakargatan and turn right into Tunnelgatan. The Bohemia restaurant is empty and the lights are out. I don't feel the cold against the soles of my feet, so presumably I do have my boots on. I am moving towards the Brunkeberg Tunnel.

The snow muffles every sound, or else there are no sounds to hear. The city has fallen silent; all movement has ceased. There is not a footprint to be seen in the blanket of snow on the steps leading to Döbelnsgatan. I blink as the flakes fall into my eyes, and switch on the head torch. A cone of light slices through the snow and illuminates the glass doors of the tunnel.

The child is standing there with the tiger beside him, as if they have been waiting for me. The child has his hood pulled up over his bowed head, and only when I reach the door does he look up, narrowing his eyes against the light.

There is no more than half a metre between us, and even though the glass is dirty, I can see the child's face with absolute clarity. I stagger and reach out to the brick wall for support. The face is less of a face and more of a badly healed wound. A deep X-shaped incision runs from the left temple to the right jawbone, from the right temple to the left jawbone, dividing the face into four. Each eye has its own section, the mouth too. The nose is crushed at the bridge where the lines meet; they must have been inflicted with considerable force and violence. I cannot look any more, and when I glance down at my feet the snow is far too close and I realise that I have dropped to my knees.

Through the glass I can hear the child humming 'Somebody Up There Must Like Me'. The sound fades as he moves away along the tunnel, but I don't look up. I draw an X in the snow with one finger as the dampness soaks through the knees of my trousers.

*

When I woke up in the middle of the day, I found myself lying on the floor of my house. At some point during the night I must have felt cold, because I had pulled my duffel coat over me. The knees of my trousers were damp, so I assumed the events of the night had happened in one of the worlds, or on the borderline between them.

A thin scab had formed over the wound on my right hand, and my left arm was aching because I'd slept with it bent under my head. The dust from the floor tickled my nostrils, and a violent sneeze sent a shock through my skull that made me sit bolt upright.

*It is ending.*

The skin on the nape of my neck and my back stretched tight as I wrapped my arms around my knees and drew them up to my chin. I felt terrible, and the solace the field provided was about to disappear for me, for all of us. Soon there would only be February left. February and flat, grey days to drag myself through.

I shivered as I pulled myself up onto my chair, then spent half an hour calling the neighbours at home or at work. I told them what had happened to Lars, and what was happening to the field: the portal was closing, or had already closed. After a series of conversations it was decided that we would meet at seven for one last journey, if that were still possible.

I sat there with my duffel coat wrapped around me, feeling heavy and empty. My heart was beating slowly, like the pulse in 'Stripped'. Everything in my house was infected by the approaching farewell, and I decided to seek refuge in the streets. I swallowed a couple of painkillers and put on two jumpers underneath my duffel. When I reached the stairwell I sniffed, checking for the smell of decaying corpses, but I was getting a cold, and my nose was also blocked by dust. I couldn't detect anything, and went on my way.

It was 26 February, but winter still had Stockholm firmly in its grip. However, the air was damp and a low-lying cloud of exhaust fumes hovered over Sveavägen when I came out of Tunnelgatan.

I walked along with my hands in my pockets, inhaling the petrol fumes as I glanced at the displays in the shops. I resisted the temptation of the mirror in Dekorima's window but then stopped for a while outside Casablanca, where they were offering a video-player and two films for two hundred kronor. I wasn't interested; I had already seen enough, and felt a sudden urge to rub dirty snow in my face. Instead I moved on.

A hundred metres further along I stopped again at a second-hand record shop. An LP I recognised from my childhood was in the window, and my stomach contracted when I looked into Jan Sparring's pious eyes. A black shirt with the top buttons undone and a jacket in exactly the same colour as my duffel coat. *Jan Sparring Sings Country.* My mother had played it often enough for me to remember that 'Somebody Up There Must Like Me' was one of the tracks.

It was like finding a carelessly thrown together arrow made of branches in the forest. Is it there by chance, or has it been deliberately placed there? What is it pointing to? For most people it doesn't matter—there's an arrow, so you go where it's pointing. I went into the shop and paid ten kronor for the album, then hurried home.

Listening to the song made me feel neither happier nor sadder. I grasped nothing that I hadn't grasped before, but as I sat on the floor in front of the turntable at least I experienced a tenuous sense of context and connection as Jan Sparring sang about how good life had been to him, how he had lacked nothing. There was an air of summing up, of departure about the lyrics, sitting on a moving train and waving goodbye to something that has been good and is now over.

Jan assured me that somebody up there must like him, somebody who had given him everything. He wondered why he had been so fortunate, and finally pointed out how little we understood.

I could definitely identify with the last line. As usual I listened to the song over and over again as the afternoon turned to evening.

The wound in my hand started to hurt, and when I squeezed it pus oozed out. I washed it and applied a dressing. I cooked a pan of rice, tipped in a tin of black beans and ate sitting on the floor with my back leaning against the desk. I counted my money. I cried a couple of times. When I had finished crying, I put the song on again. At quarter to seven I put on my best white shirt and the trousers from my suit, then went down to the laundry block.

*

The only person who had arrived was Petronella. She was sitting on the chair fanning herself with a magazine. It must have taken a huge effort for her to get down there, because she weighed at least thirty kilos more than when I first saw her, and rolls of fat spilled over the arms of the chair. When I came in she turned to me with sadness in her eyes and said, 'It's impossible.'

'What's impossible?'

'Living. Living is impossible. Without it.'

'I know. It's hard.'

Petronella shook her head and the smooth, puffy sacs of fat beneath her chin rolled to the sides as she said, 'Not hard. Impossible. It can't be done.'

'Surely it can.'

'Why?'

I had asked myself that question without coming up with an answer. Why should we live? In the end it's a matter of how appealing we find the alternative. Maybe something else too. I said, 'If there's an arrow in the forest. You follow it. Just because it's there.'

'What do you mean?'

'I don't know. We're here.'

'I don't want to be here.'

One by one the others turned up, until we were all gathered. Several expressed feelings similar to Petronella's, but it was only Gunnar who displayed the same degree of despair. His left hand was bandaged. He hadn't doubted the truth of my message on the phone, and after our conversation he had gone into the staff kitchen at work, turned the electric hotplate up high and placed his hand on it. He was now signed off sick for an indefinite period.

Susanne, Åke and Elsa were more like me. Their voices and body language would have been appropriate at a loved one's funeral, but at least it was a loved one's funeral and not their own. This life was over, but unlike Petronella and Gunnar they were able to consider the possibility that there was another life, even if it was hard to see right now.

We opened the door of the shower room, where the white substance in the bathtub was moving all on its own, like a creature trapped inside a thick layer of rubber, its limbs groping beneath the covering, searching for a way out.

'What's happening?' Elsa asked.

'I've no idea,' I replied. 'It's changing. Everything's changing. It's coming to an end.'

We turned off the light in the laundry room, barricaded the door by pushing a broom through the handle, then gathered around the bathtub. We had to help Petronella to get down on her knees. We looked at one another, and there was so much sorrow in the room that it was a seventh, invisible presence, hovering above our heads. We cut our hands and pressed our palms on the white surface.

The blood flowed in thin trickles, forming pools that were absorbed as if by osmosis. But nothing happened. We weren't transported. Gunnar slapped down his hand so that a shudder ran through the white mass and yelled, 'Come on! Come on! Just *once* more!' As if his plea had had an effect, the field flickered before our eyes, only to disappear again. We slumped to the floor.

'More blood,' I said. 'It wants more blood.'

'How do you know?' Susanne asked.

'I don't know anything—I'm just guessing. If anyone has a better idea, then please say.'

No one had a better idea. I leaned over the edge again and placed the blade of the knife in the crook of my right arm where one branch of the X-shaped scar began. In spite of all the times I had harmed myself in order to travel, this went against the grain. For one thing it would be a much bigger wound and would really hurt, and for another I would be tearing apart something that my body had knitted together.

I gritted my teeth and began to cut. The first few centimetres were easy. The knife was sharp and I didn't have to press too hard to pierce the skin. Then came the reaction. In the past I had simply made an incision, pushed my hand into the bathtub and off I went. Now I had time to feel the nerves protesting, sending pain and revulsion throbbing up through my arm and into my brain, a message that said: *Stop, don't do it!*

I didn't stop. When I reached my wrist I narrowed my eyes, pretending that I was looking at nothing more than a piece of pale meat.

My other senses weren't having any of it. The taste of rusty iron filled my mouth, and I could hear the blood dripping into the bath. My left hand stiffened, unwilling to complete its task, so I gripped the handle more firmly and dragged the knife back up towards the crook of my arm, following the line of the X and making a deep gash. Air was forced in and out through my nose in short gasps as the lines met and I carried on upwards. My entire arm was now covered in so much blood that I could no longer see the scar, and I was working blind as I completed the last couple of centimetres.

I dropped the knife, lowered my throbbing, burning arm onto the surface and felt it stick fast as if it were being held by a faint magnetic force or a sucking reflex. Through half-closed eyelids I saw that my neighbours had also begun to make longer and deeper cuts, and that the white substance was now covered in streams of red. Only when the light changed did I open my eyes. We were in the field.

*

*Gunnar is running, lifting his arms to the sky. His screams express triumph as much as pain. The black wall on the horizon is closer than ever, and it feels as if we are in the bottom of a sack that is slowly being drawn up. At my feet lie the ring that Lars was wearing and his gold fillings. Everything else has been eaten away and disappeared. I leave them where they are.*

*We do everything we can, everything we love in the field, but with greater intensity and for longer. We wander around in our true bodies, we fight, we embrace, we dance and we enjoy, as if these were the final moments before the bomb drops and it's all over.*

*We have never stayed in the field for so long, and we reach a point where even our field bodies are exhausted. Åke, Susanne, Elsa and I lie on our backs on the grass. Only the children inside Elsa's body keep moving, their giggles rising up to the sky.*

*I turn my head and see Petronella's fat lady moving off towards the darkness. She manages only a few steps before her body collapses under its own weight. She tries to get back on her feet, but without anything to hold on to she is like a beached whale, rocking helplessly from side to side.*

*We know what she is trying to do and why, so we get up and help her. Åke is the strongest, so he grabs both her wrists while Susanne and I take a leg each. Elsa's field body, like Petronella's, is incapable of doing very much apart from being there. She stumbles after us as we drag Petronella towards the darkness.*

*The closer we get, the stronger the attraction. The darkness is pulling at our bodies, but only Petronella has answered its call. We don't know what is in there, but Petronella refuses to return to the ordinary world. Anything is better than that.*

*The fat lady weighs several hundred kilos, and we only just manage. I send magic to levitate her, which helps a little, but I can't lift her. My powers are fading. We haul her across the grass, the fat billowing beneath her overstretched skin.*

*The darkness is sharply delineated. It really does rise from the ground like a wall, hiding part of the sky. When we are a few metres away, we have neither the strength nor the courage to go on. We sink down on the grass, utterly spent, and watch as the fat lady wriggles and rolls, dragging herself forward by sinking her fingers into the ground. We hear her whisper 'Thank you' before she disappears into the darkness with a deep sigh and a final heave.*

*The last thing I see before we return is Gunnar, running towards us across the field. Then we are back in the shower room.*

*

We didn't know how long we'd been away. The bulb in the ceiling light had gone out, and the room was dark. Our bodies were physically exhausted, and all we could do was crawl into the laundry room. I was the last; I turned back and whispered, 'Petronella? Petronella?', but there was no answer. Nor could I make out the shape of her body in the faint light seeping in through the window facing onto the courtyard. She was gone, just as she had wished. I closed the door and secured the padlock before crawling away and collapsing, leaning against one of the tumble dryers.

I could hear the others breathing, see the contours of their bodies slumped against walls or machines. It was over. We had been on our last journey. Gunnar convulsed with a sob from time to time as he sat there with his head drooping between his knees. He had been on his way to the darkness, but he hadn't made it in time. Now he was doomed to live in this world, and I didn't think he'd be with us for very long.

The gash in my arm had been sucked clean, and the edges of the wound had begun to stick together. We must have been away for a long time. I tried to think *Now what?* or something along those lines, but all that came into my mind was a black wall and that fateful engine noise from 'Stripped'. The only reasonable possibility was that this moment would go on forever. There was no way out of this room, no escape from Gunnar's sobbing.

I might have fallen asleep a few times. At any rate, I had

summoned up enough strength to get to my feet when there was a knock on the door. Someone wanted to come into the laundry room.

'What time is it?' I whispered to Åke, who was the only one who wore a watch.

There was another knock before the answer came. Eleven-thirty. Nobody ever did their washing at that hour; it wasn't even allowed. I went over to the door and fiddled with the broom handle; I didn't know what to do.

It was only when the third knock came that I realised it wasn't coming from the outside door, but from the shower room. Someone was in there, wanting to be let out. I held my breath and looked the others in the eye, one by one. I was absolutely certain that Petronella hadn't been in there when I left the room. The person knocking was a...new arrival.

Up until that moment we'd had control, or at least the element of predictability that even the worst junkie has when it comes to his next fix. He might be lost in the eyes of society, but at least he knows what he's dealing with. This was something new, an unforeseen consequence of our trips. Something had been *created.*

We looked at one another. No one moved. The door was pushed outwards, rattling the padlock. I switched on the light and whispered, 'What shall we do?' Under different circumstances Elsa, Gunnar, Åke and Susanne would have looked quite comical, because all four were sitting in exactly the same pose, eyes wide open with a hand in front of their mouth, like children whose game has gone too far, and who just want to go home to safety and security. Another knock.

Whatever was on the other side of the door, it was a relief that it was knocking. It suggested some kind of human rationality, or even politeness. *Excuse me, could you please let me out?*

'It's the thing that was in the bathtub,' Gunnar said, his voice still thick with tears. 'What else could it be?'

I remembered what the slime had looked like a while ago, the unfinished creature striving to get out. We had nourished it with our blood and our dreams, and now it was complete. I placed the palm of my hand on the shower room door and remembered what I had thought after a conversation with the busker: *There is no evidence that whatever lies beyond means us any harm. It is far more likely that it's indifferent.*

That was pure speculation. As I felt the door vibrate with the impact of another knock, I wasn't quite so sure. I reached for the padlock and glanced at the others for guidance. Only Gunnar nodded. I took a deep breath, turned the key and removed the padlock. I backed away from the door, which slowly opened.

The creature that emerged had a human form, but that was all I could say. At first I had the impression that it was entirely white with no features, then I thought it resembled Martin Gore from Depeche Mode, and the next moment it was that terrible policeman from when I was twelve years old. Before I had time to feel scared it had changed again. This time it looked like Olof Palme, then it was white and shiny once more, with a pair of big eyes and a mouth.

I heard someone gasp, and I didn't know whether it was because of the creature's shapeshifting ability, or the fact that it was holding the revolver that Lars had dropped in the bathtub. I was standing two metres in front of it, and raised my hands to show that I surrendered, if that was what it wanted.

There was nothing to suggest that was the case. The figure, which was in a constant state of metamorphosis, seemed just as bewildered as we were. It looked from one to the other, its features changing depending on whose eyes it met. A whole range of appearances flickered past and disappeared in the place where its face was meant to be, but Olof Palme's recurred with increasing frequency.

I edged cautiously sideways until I was near the others, then slid down onto the floor. The creature was still standing there as we stared at it, its features constantly shifting. Elsa said breathlessly, 'It's trying to decide.'

'Decide what?'

'What we want to see. What we are.'

I gazed at the figure, its face now displaying Olof Palme's

distinctive nose flanked by deep lines that came and went depending on which age it was trying to portray. If the creature was cut from the same cloth as the field, with its origins in our blood and our dreams, then it was now trying to find a form that was not individual but collective, our lowest common denominator and our movement. It was settling on the idea that this *we* was to be represented by Olof Palme.

I have only mentioned the face so far, but the body and clothes were shifting equally rapidly, like a video tape on fast forward; watching it made me feel dizzy. I closed my eyes and pressed the heels of my hands against my eyelids in an attempt to stop a headache that was threatening to explode. My brain felt like a sandbag that had received far too many blows, and was about to burst open and spill out its contents. I heard someone stand up, and just about managed to open my eyes sufficiently to see what was happening.

Gunnar had positioned himself directly in front of the creature, which had almost consolidated into the Olof Palme who was our current prime minister, wearing corduroy trousers and a medium-length overcoat, the hand holding the revolver concealed in a pocket. Only the odd ripple of another appearance passed across its face.

Gunnar stepped forward and spread his arms wide. For a moment it looked as if he intended to wrestle the creature to the ground, but then I saw that he had ripped open his wounds and was bleeding from both arms as he enveloped Olof Palme in a bear hug.

They stood like that for a little while, then Gunnar began to be absorbed by the thing he was embracing. His chest disappeared into Palme's chest, as if he were sinking into some kind of viscous substance. His shoulders were forced back and he loosened his hold at the same moment as his head became part of the creature's head.

Those of us who remained sat on the floor and watched Gunnar slowly being sucked into the other world through the portal that had acquired a human form. The last thing we saw was the fingers of his right hand, fluttering briefly like those of a dreamer, before they slipped into the crook of Palme's arm and were gone.

The figure stretched, now one single entity. It looked at us with black, empty eyes and opened and closed its mouth as if it wanted to say something but had no language in which to say it.

It turned its head from side to side. It was hard to say where its bottomless gaze rested, but there was something pleading about its posture. It almost seemed to be seeking our help, without knowing what that help might consist of. When none of us stirred or spoke, the creature shrugged its shoulders in a jerky gesture before moving over to the outside door, opening it and walking out into the courtyard.

*

I don't think any of my readers will be unaware of where this is going, where it's been going right from the start. With hindsight everything seems so clear. The building blocks were in place and the movement had begun. Unfortunately it is only distance in terms of time that makes such a perspective possible; back then, when everything was close to me, I saw only chaos and understood nothing.

As I write this narrative almost thirty years later, I find it difficult to comprehend my own actions. How could I have been willing to sacrifice so much to be in the field? Regardless of what I have said previously about homecoming, truth and pleasure, those are only words. The feeling escapes me, and while I have been writing I have started each day by listening to Laleh's 'A Little While on the Earth' and have then left it playing in the background, hoping that its joyous sound will help me to capture it on the page.

*I was close, I was close, I was close, I was THERE.*

It is playing now as I write and it helps, but still I only get *close*. I can't get *there* any more, and maybe that's for the best. If I really did manage to describe everything perfectly I would have no need to write in the future, and then what would I do? In the absence of alternatives I must follow Beckett's example—continue to fail, and fail better.

It might seem as if my neighbours and I were strangely passive in the face of what was unfolding before our eyes. Maybe we were, but for one thing we were completely exhausted, and for another there is a line beyond which an event becomes so alien that it is impossible to intervene. The planes that flew into the World Trade Center, or the tsunami. When you have no experiences to help you deal with a particular occurrence, the normal reaction is simply to stand there and stare, if you survive, and afterwards to say, 'It was just like a movie.'

I didn't have the tools to deal with seeing a white creature laboriously take on the appearance of Olof Palme and then absorb one of my neighbours, so like the others I sat there and let it happen. When the creature had left us and we heard the street door slam behind it, we still sat there without saying a word.

Just like the previous night, the sequence of events at this stage had a dreamlike quality. I was so cripplingly tired, and if I stick to the image of my brain as a sandbag, I felt as if it had now split and disgorged its contents beneath my eyelids. I can't remember whether we spoke to one another, can't remember how I got home, but at least I laid out the mattress before I fell asleep.

*

I woke up around dawn. The night before I had felt as if I'd been rolling in a bed of nettles; now it was as if an army of red ants was having a party on my right arm. I blinked at the grey light seeping in through the blinds, and prayed to God to let me go back to sleep. The forthcoming day would be hellish enough without a lack of sleep. I drew my knees up to my stomach, rested my arm on top of the covers so they wouldn't chafe, and managed to embrace the darkness.

It was after two o'clock in the afternoon when I rose to the surface once more. I lay there with the covers pulled up to my nose, and discovered that I didn't feel as bad as I'd expected. Empty and worn out, but the nightmare that I had feared would sink its claws into me as soon as I regained consciousness was keeping its distance, and all that remained of the pain in my arm was an itch. I looked at the wound between my thumb and forefinger and the wound on my arm, and felt something like happiness at the thought that I would never harm myself again—that it was over.

I rolled onto my side, switched on the turntable and dropped the needle onto 'Somebody Up There Must Like Me', then I got up and filled the coffee machine. After I'd listened to the song several times and drunk four cups of coffee, I picked up the record and broke it in half. I dropped the pieces in the bin, then got dressed and went out.

It was a beautiful afternoon with the smell of snow in the air and a high, clear sky. I blinked at the light and the clarity of everything, like someone who has been wearing sunglasses and just taken them off. The colours of the cars parked on the hill nearby shone brightly, and windows covered in rime frost reflected the sunlight in subtle nuances I hadn't noticed for a very long time.

At the risk of droning on, at that moment it felt as if everything that had happened was a feverish dream from which I had now awoken. I walked along Luntmakargatan enjoying the perception that I had legs to walk with and feet to stand on, appreciating the worldly body that had seemed to me so false and contemptible. No doubt it would all catch up with me soon enough, but the mere fact that I wanted to live was more than I had expected.

Sveavägen was bathed in sunlight, and after a couple of hundred metres I needed to rest my eyes, so I went into a cafe I'd never visited before. I had a café au lait and a cinnamon pastry while I read a copy of *Dagens Nyheter* that someone had left behind. I hadn't caught up with the news for a few months, and a lot had happened while I was wrapped up in myself. Ferdinand Marcos had fled the Philippines, and Gorbachev had condemned the Brezhnev era. Things were looking up in several parts of the world. They had even launched the Viking satellite at long last.

I continued my stroll along Sveavägen past the Grand, where they were showing *The Mozart Brothers*, but I decided it probably wasn't my kind of film. I went to McDonald's for a Big Mac before heading home.

As I was passing the builders' huts and the closed entrance to the subway station, I looked up at the steps leading to the Brunkeberg Tunnel. The sky darkened and the easy lightness in my body dissipated. Next to the cast-iron plaque at the bottom of the steps stood *that* policeman. I froze on the spot, clenched my fists in my coat pockets and was about to run to my door when I noticed the barely perceptible flicker in his expression, the indecisiveness in his dark eyes. As soon as I had seen through the figure it became a white creature with no distinguishing features. Its hands were hidden by the plaque, and I couldn't see if it was still holding the revolver.

The face turned in my direction, and a shudder ran through me as I dashed inside and stopped at the foot of the stairs. I didn't know what a rotting corpse smelled like, but the faint odour of strawberry ice-cream mixed with excrement drifting down from the upper floor could hardly be anything else, and I hurried out into the fresh air of the courtyard.

The party was over, and all that remained was the clearing-up and the uninvited guest who refused to go home. When I opened the door of my house and looked at my dark hovel and the mattress lying on the floor, I decided to move. I didn't want to stay in the middle of all this misery now that it was nothing more than misery—I wanted to get away, start afresh, forget.

I spent the evening reading Beckett. *You think you've had enough, but that is rarely the case.*

*

As far as I was concerned, the day that would change Sweden forever began with a phone call to my landlord. I was supposed to give two months' notice on the non-existent contract, but I had an enormous stroke of luck. Someone else wanted my house, and I could move out in two weeks, plus there was a one-room apartment available on Kungsholmen if I was interested. I was definitely interested, and arranged to go and see it later on.

I hung up with hope beginning to grow in my heart. Maybe it would be possible to put all this behind me, place parentheses around this part of my story too. After breakfast I took another step towards freedom by travelling on the subway for the first time in a month.

On the platform I made a point of standing just behind an elderly man who was half a metre from the edge. An arrow of light shot along the rails, a gust of wind made my hair flutter, then the first carriage came thundering out of the tunnel.

A smile crossed my lips, my hands flew up of their own accord and with a shiver of pure lust I saw the little man's startled expression as he fell onto the track and was mashed to a pulp beneath the wheels of the train. For one liberating, horrific moment I thought it had really happened, but I had managed to stop my hands in time and clenched them tightly across my body. The man stepped on board without having noticed anything, and I followed him.

The monster was still living inside my body, and that was something I had to deal with. I would need strategies and discipline to keep it locked away. Even if it took a number of years, that subway journey might have been when the first seed was sown that would eventually lead to what became my job. Writing stories about the monster is *one* way of appeasing it.

I got off at Fridhemsplan and walked over to Svarvargatan, where I was shown a small, shabby apartment that would cost me four thousand a month. I said yes right away. There was a large window with a view of the Karlberg Canal; there was light. I could become someone else in this place.

By the time I got back to the house on Luntmakargatan, in my mind I had already left it. If it had been possible to move the same day, I would have done so. The smell in the stairwell had become even more noticeable now that I was aware of it, or maybe it was getting stronger. However much I would miss my neighbours and what we'd had, I didn't want to be here any longer. It was over.

The infection in my hand had started to recede, and an X-shaped scab had begun to form on my right arm. I had more or less managed to cut along the lines that were already there, but the scar would probably be even uglier than it had been before. I would just have to live with that, like so many other things. I opened both windows and spent the rest of the day cleaning.

*

In the evening I decided to go and see the comedy film *Whiskers and Peas* at the Saga cinema. While doing my housework I had got myself into such a state of enthusiasm and optimism about the future that I didn't give the visitor from the other world a thought until I passed the builders' huts on Tunnelgatan and found it standing right in front of me.

There were plenty of people out and about who could see it moving around on Sveavägen, and no one seemed to find anything strange about the white figure staring into the window of Dekorima, because everyone saw what they wanted to see. An ordinary person interested in the display, nothing more.

The creature's attention was focused on the mirror. I kept very close to the wall of the building opposite so that I could sneak past and avoid those black eyes fastening on me. When I was directly behind it I stole a glance over its shoulder. Reflected in the mirror I saw myself standing a couple of metres behind Olof Palme, and when I looked back at the creature it had taken on the same appearance as its reflection, which I assumed was its self-image. Our eyes met in the mirror, and the impotence in those dark orbs haunted me as I carried on along Kungsgatan.

A sense of foreboding hovered inside my body and stopped me from enjoying the film, which was apparently very funny. Roars of laughter filled the cinema when Gösta Ekman took a rolled-up tartan blanket for a walk as if it were a dog, but instead of laughing I was seized by a fit of shivering, and pulled my duffel coat more tightly around me.

The film ended just after eleven and I went to Mon Chéri to warm myself up with a cup of coffee, but when I sat down at a little table I couldn't stop jiggling my leg up and down. I had a feeling that there was something I ought to do, but I had no idea what it was. I tried to think about the apartment on Svarvargatan, about the future, but nothing helped, and by twenty past eleven the unease had driven me back out into the street.

It was like the poem 'C Major' by Tomas Tranströmer, except the other way round. The city is downhill, everyone smiles behind turned-up collars, everything on the way towards the note C. As I said, the other way round, except for the downhill part. I walked along Kungsgatan feeling as if everyone was glaring accusingly at me while the sound of the engine from 'Stripped' throbbed behind it all, an implacable machine set in motion. I was somehow linked to the creature from the other place, and its impotence and self-loathing in this world found an echo in my brain, which had been part of its creation.

My body was still wracked by shivering as I turned into Sveavägen. I glanced over at Monte Carlo, considered going in and drinking myself into oblivion, but the memory of the man who had pointed at me after he'd thrown Thomas out made me think again. With my hands deep in my pockets I carried on towards Tunnelgatan, hoping the creature would be gone.

I had a moment of relief when I saw that it wasn't standing outside the shop window, but when I looked north along Sveavägen it was coming towards me in the form of Olof Palme. The confusing thing was that it was now accompanied by someone else; it took me a couple of seconds to recognise Lisbet Palme.

The sound of the engine roared through my brain when I realised that the person less than a dozen metres away from me was the real Olof Palme together with his wife, while the Palme who had just stepped out of the shadows from a doorway behind them was the other one, the creature.

There was so much noise inside my head, singing and whining, that I barely heard the crack of Lars's revolver before Olof Palme collapsed in the street and Lisbet screamed and turned to me, desperate for help. I saw the creature, whose face was once more flickering and shifting, bend down and place the palm of its hand on the blood pouring from the prime minister's body, and I silently screamed, 'Run!'

The creature, which by now was blurred, straightened up and ran down Tunnelgatan. Cars screeched to a halt on Sveavägen and people were drawn towards the body slumped on the ground while I backed away in the direction of Kungsgatan. The engine throbbed and throbbed and I wanted to run too, flee, disappear, but I forced myself to walk down to the subway mall below Hötorget and take a stroll around the shops, sweat pouring down my back.

People came and went through the barriers as if it were just an ordinary Friday evening, while Olof Palme lay shot above their heads. When I emerged on Kungsgatan once more a police armed response vehicle hurtled past, but people were chatting and joking with their view of the world still intact.

The question that haunts me to this very day was already in my mind as I went up the steps to Malmskillnadsgatan: Why had the creature fired the gun? It would be liberating if I could answer the question so many people have asked, the *why* that might perhaps go some way to soothing and healing our society, but I didn't know then and I don't know now. All I have is speculation.

An important moment in the creature's origin was Lars's suicide with what has been known ever since that evening as the Palme weapon. It hated itself and didn't want to be in this world. Perhaps the sight of the person it perceived as itself evoked the urge to kill and to get rid of this self. Or maybe it was just after blood. I don't know.

All I wanted to do was get back to my house, lock the door and curl up in the darkness. My hopes of being able to put everything behind me had been shattered, and I knew that I would never really be free again.

The sound of sirens filled the air, and when I reached Luntmakargatan I saw a police officer running past on Tunnelgatan, heading for the steps. Only then was I able to assimilate the unthinkable and formulate the words: *The prime minister of Sweden has been shot.* Whether he survived or not, the place would soon be crawling with police, and I hurried towards the main door.

My heart stopped and I let out a scream when I saw the creature standing in the doorway, still holding the revolver. I wanted to run, but I didn't dare. Where would I go? I had been close by when the shot was fired, and people had seen me. If a police officer got hold of me there would be no end to the interrogation, and what would I say?

The sirens grew louder and there was no time for ifs and buts. I glanced at the gun and gritted my teeth as I turned away from the creature to key in the entry code, ready for the bang, for a burning pain in my back. But there was no bang, no pain. I grabbed the creature's arm and dragged it through the door.

We passed through the stairwell, filled with the stench of dead bodies, and came out into the courtyard. The arm I was clutching was firm to the touch, its soft contents giving under the pressure of my fingers, like a plastic sausage stuffed with baked beans. My head was whirling as I dragged Olof Palme's killer across the courtyard.

*You don't know he's dead.*

No, but there was something about the way he'd gone down after being hit, limp and without any attempt to break his fall, that made me fear the worst.

With trembling hands I found my keys. I unlocked the door and pushed the creature inside the laundry block. I didn't want to touch its jelly-like body any more than necessary, so after opening the door of the shower room I picked up the scraper I'd used to finish off the gull and shoved the creature into the darkness. Before it had time to turn around and look at me, I slammed the door and fastened the padlock.

I caught sight of the Palmebusters T-shirt, still hanging on the wall. A wave of guilt came crashing towards me and sent me back out into the courtyard. At that moment I felt as if I personally had killed Palme, and in a way of course I had. I scuttled across to my hovel and switched on the TV.

Nothing. Not a word about the incident on the radio either. I lay down on the floor and stared up at the ceiling, incapable of doing or thinking anything as P3 played music. Time passed. It was ten past one when I heard a series of pips, followed by a man's voice. Sounding as if he were reading with some difficulty from a piece of paper, he said: 'Sweden's prime minister, Olof Palme, is dead. He was shot this evening in central Stockholm...'

The violent shivering returned, and my whole body was shaking as I grabbed the beige duffel coat, stuffed it into a plastic bag and carried it outside. The atmosphere in the air was different, the night sky was different, as if we were all now below the surface and had to move through water. I tossed the bag down the rubbish chute, went over to the laundry block and into the shower room. If the creature wanted to shoot me, then it could.

It was gone, along with the gun, and thin smoke hovered in the room. Just like the child in the tree house the creature had folded in on itself, a door going out through a door. I took a deep breath and allowed the smoke to seep down into my lungs.

I can hardly even say that I was transported. The smoke was so sparse and widely dispersed that it wasn't enough to give me any more than a glimpse of the field from a bird's-eye perspective. I saw the grass below me, the blue sky above. The white creature was walking across the grass. There was no sign of the revolver; maybe it had been left in the darkness. The last thing I saw before the image faded was Gunnar's burned body running along a track at right angles to the white creature's route.

Then I was back in the shower room, where all that remained of what had gone on was the blood on the enamel of the bathtub, on the walls and the floor. I went and fetched a mop, a bucket and a scrubbing-brush and set to work. When the dawn crept across the rooftops, there was not a trace left behind.

# Epilogue

I followed the news reports obsessively after the murder. One of the guns that Hans Holmér, the chief of the special investigation unit, dangled from his index finger during a press briefing was identical to the gun that had been used. Fighter planes flew over Stockholm, searching the rooftops. I could have saved them the trouble, but I knew it was pointless to try.

Identikit pictures and conflicting witness statements about the perpetrator's appearance came thick and fast. Everyone had their idea of what a killer looks like, and it was this image they had seen when they looked at the white creature. Much later several witnesses, including Lisbet Palme, would agree that it was a man by the name of Christer Pettersson they had seen, which didn't surprise me at all. If I were forced to imagine a murderer, he would have looked a lot like Pettersson.

Twelve of the witnesses to the shooting were eventually identified and questioned; only the thirteenth was missing. A number of the others had noticed him at the scene. The man in beige. The police hadn't even searched the waste bins in the area, let alone the big garbage containers. When they came knocking on my door after quite some time I was just in the process of moving, and they didn't notice my racing heart when I assured them that I had neither seen nor heard anything.

I never spoke to any of my neighbours again. When Åke and I met in the courtyard one day, we didn't even exchange a nod. I could see in his eyes that he knew, that he too had found out what had happened through his connection to the creature, and that he didn't want to say a single word on the subject.

The Dead Couple were discovered a day or so after the murder, but the police must have covered up the circumstances surrounding their deaths to avoid giving rise to pointless speculation, realising they had been dead for far too long to have any link with the murder.

They searched for possible motives, looking at groups in Sweden and around the world who could be behind the shooting, but throughout it all that one question grew stronger and stronger: Why? *Why?*

As I said, I have no simple answer to give. For almost thirty years I have brooded on that same question, gone over and over my motives and those of my neighbours for embarking on the journey and embracing the chaotic possibility that in the end was the cause of the tragedy. The conclusion I have reached is paradoxical, as the answers to impossible questions often are: it was our longing for a sense of community that brought forth Olof Palme, and that was also what killed him.

*Rådmansö, April 2015*